AMBITION!

be careful what you ask for

Johnathan Isom

M2N
PUBLISHING

Johnathan Isom

M2N PUBLISHING

AMBITION!
be careful what you ask for

First published in hardback in 2005 by

PUBLISHING

Suite 104
558 Ridgeway Center Parkway
Memphis, TN 38120-4011

Isom, Johnathan M.
AMBITION! Be careful what you ask for
A Novel/Johnathan M. Isom
p. cm.

MANUFACTURED IN THE UNITED STATES OF AMERICA

ISBN 0-97618797-0-4

This book is printed on acid-free paper.

First Edition

visit www.jisom.com

For Angela, Nigel, Mackenzie and Meredith

ACKNOWLEDGEMENTS

First of all, I acknowledge and give thanks to the Creator for bringing
such wonderful people into my life who helped to make this project a reality.
I sincerely thank Dr. Bess A. Isom for her editorial assistance and
Angela S. Isom for making me pay attention to all the small details.
Kai EL Zabar of Visionary Ink challenged me to write on a higher level
and Judge Shelly Williams-Hayes made possible my "hook up" with Kai.
Lynette Sesler of LY designs completed the Herculean task associated
with text layout and cover design while Paul Mainor of Mainor Media
developed the website, Chris Perry of Perry Associates Marketing and
Photographer Jeff Frazier contributed their exceptional skills.
I am immensely grateful to Rick Durr for his handling of all the legal
aspects of this project and I am blessed to have an unbelievable support
group of family and friends whom I thank for believing in me.
Finally, I thank each reader for allowing me the opportunity
to share this novel with you.

AMBITION!
be careful what you ask for

Ambition (*n*)

A strong desire to succeed in life:
to be recognized by achieving status through
wealth, fame and power

CHAPTER

one

She didn't hear them enter, but they had subdued Stenson and Mickey tying them to wooden chairs. Their feet and chests were bare and their bodies immobilized with rope and wide clear duck tape. They both had dirty, blood-stained towels stuffed in their mouths and had been severely beaten. Open cuts covered their faces and heads. Fleetwood lay motionless at their feet, with a stream of blood running briskly from the back of his head.

The three men in the room looked familiar. Melanie had seen one of them at her home the previous night, the one whose fingers Mickey had cut off. His hand was wrapped in a bloody dressing. The other two men resembled Adam Wellington and Franciose Baptiste. They were all dressed in black, standing at the foot of the small bed where she huddled.

Sunlight from a small window appeared to create a halo around Stenson and Mickey; in one motion, without hesitation or stimulus, Adam turned and placed a gun to Mickey's head and pulled the trigger. Brain matter and body fluid covered the wall as the impact pushed Mickey's head back when his body fell to the floor. He lay motionless but remained in the chair, the towel falling from his mouth, his eyes empty.

Stenson sat upright in his chair, rigid but not shaking, his soft brown eyes connected to hers and closed as he fell backwards, his splattered brain matter created a similar pattern on the wall as Mickey's. Melanie screamed but it was inaudible and her eyes were tightly shut. The persistent barking of Kitty filled her ears, but she could not see him in the room.

Her clothes were drenched with perspiration but the room was cold from the breeze of the window air conditioning unit. She continued to hear the barking dog and a voice calling her, which sounded like Stenson.

Eight Weeks Earlier

The July night was typical for Memphis: hot, humid, and as sultry as the blues songs played on Beale Street. It was close to nine o'clock and Dr. Stenson Hawk stood among a five-member trauma team waiting on the roof of the Tennessee Medical Center for the arrival of a Life Flight helicopter. Stenson thought the trauma patient was certain to be a victim of Memphis' very active Knife and Gun Club, whose members were a collection of common thugs. They settled their disagreements by putting 38mm gunshots into their rival's head. Sometimes they settled arguments by giving their opponent an unmerciful ass-whipping with a blunt object; usually a baseball bat.

As Chief Surgery Resident Stenson felt good about his three-month rotation in trauma surgery. He had great freedom to make independent decisions and enjoyed the challenges that sharpened his clinical skills. He had to admit that, all in all, this trauma stuff was as exciting as an NBA fast break.

The 'copter pilot reported transporting a fifteen-year-old African American girl who had shot herself in the chest. Stenson remembered a conversation with his father about Black-on-Black violence and suicide. His father had said in a smooth, soothing, Southern voice,

"Son, I must tell you, suicide is one of the downsides of integration! Before the advent of Civil Rights there were some things Black folks just didn't do. We didn't drive European cars, we didn't eat Sushi and we didn't kill ourselves!"

Maybe his dad was on to something.

The evening sky held a full moon which some old timers viewed as an indication of a bad night ahead. On such nights, in some folks, all evidence of sound reasoning and common sense became nonexistent. Stenson said to himself, "On hot summer nights like this, some people just flat-out act like damn fools."

He had observed that some youngsters in the 'hood substituted the word "people" with "niggas", and belligerent attitudes ran amuck.

Caroline Lewis, an honor student enrolled in summer courses at Germantown High, was upset because her mother had grounded her as punishment for smoking weed at school with two classmates. After their heated argument about the incident Caroline took her father's 25-caliber pistol, placed it to her chest, called out her mother's name and pulled the trigger.

The initial bright red mist on her blouse didn't alarm her; nor did the dull, aching pain and numbness in her left arm. Instead, Caroline experienced a feeling of euphoria, warmth, and a sense of well-being. She thought, "This must be what it feels like to die." Then she dismissed the thought and was not alarmed, although she understood this sensation to be a result of her injury. Caroline had no real sense of what was to come.

The helicopter approached its landing against the back drop of a full moon and starless night. Stenson along with two trauma nurses, a senior anesthesiology resident, and Mark Bradford, a fourth-year surgery resident prepared to do battle with a familiar foe. The stakes were always high; life or death, all or none. The foe was formidable and unwelcome. It was one to which all living things eventually succumb. The foe was Death.

With a soft thud the six-passenger medical chopper landed and the door was hurriedly opened. As Stenson and Mark approached the 'copter they lowered their heads to avoid the still moving blades. The trauma nurses and anesthesiology resident were trailing them carrying the resuscitation equipment, when Stenson recognized the two flight nurses but couldn't quite remember their names. He looked at their name tags and remembered Mary Kilpatrick and Joan Sawyer. The pictures on the name tags were fair to both.

He had great respect for them because they were battle-tough nurses with good skills and years of experience. They had seen it all.

Caroline appeared much younger than her fifteen years. A quick glance at the monitors showed her heart rate to be extremely fast and her blood pressure disturbingly low. Her dark complexion appeared pale and ashen and her rapid breathing created a mist on the oxygen facemask. There were large IVs running wide open as they pumped fluids into both of Caroline's arms. Her vital signs were consistent with significant blood loss.

The flight nurses had placed mast trousers on Caroline's legs which, when inflated, helped to maintain her blood pressure. But even with the inflated trousers Caroline's blood pressure was ominously low. Joan quickly began to direct her conversation to Stenson, as he was the senior physician.

"Dr. Hawk," she spoke loudly to be heard over the slowly circling helicopter blades, "the patient is Caroline Lewis; she has no known allergies and no significant medical or surgical history. But, she has a self-inflicted small caliber gunshot wound to her left chest. I can't find an exit wound, so the bullet is probably still in there somewhere. I'm also unsure of the degree of internal damage; but I believe her left lung has collapsed because I can't hear any sounds of breathing on that side."

Joan continued, "Oh yes, she has a full stomach. She shot herself right after dinner."

Stenson nodded his head to confirm his understanding of the report. He turned to Caroline and removed his stethoscope from his soiled, once-white, lab coat. He smiled at the frightened teenager and said, "Hello, my name is Dr. Stenson Hawk. I am the trauma surgeon here to help you."

Caroline nodded.

Stenson continued, "I need to listen to your lungs, is that okay?"

She nodded "yes".

Stenson placed the stethoscope to the right side of Caroline's chest and instructed her to take a deep breath. She did. Everything sounded okay. Then he put the stethoscope to her left side and again asked Caroline to take a deep breath. She did, but Stenson heard nothing.

Stenson thought, "As expected the nurse has made the correct call, the left lung has collapsed."

"If this is really the extent of her injury," Stenson commented openly, "Caroline should be okay, assuming her parents won't decide to kill her when she recovers for committing this certifiable act of teenage stupidity!"

Stenson then turned to Mark and said, "She has a pneumo. So let's move her to the transport stretcher, take the elevator down to the emergency trauma holding area and insert a chest tube. That will inflate her left lung."

"Good, that sounds like a plan." Mark responded.

He really liked Stenson's style. Mark thought Stenson was quite a professional and he wasn't impressed with many things about Black males. Stenson was cool, caring, competent and he was a second-generation physician who graduated from Tulane University and Vanderbilt Medical School. Mark would never admit it, but Stenson was one of his role models.

As the doctors connected Caroline to the transport monitors, she looked at Stenson and asked, "Am I going to die?"

Stenson answered, "No sweetheart. But we will have to put a little tube in your chest to help you breath."

Caroline asked him,

"But why am I so cold?"

Stenson answered,

"It's probably because it's so windy up here."

"On the count of three!" Stenson said.

And on three they lifted Caroline to the stretcher, lowered their heads and moved swiftly across the rooftop to the waiting elevator.

The night was very still with only the sounds of a siren in the distance. As they entered the elevator facing the open door Mark pressed the down button and the doors closed as the elevator descended. Stenson turned when he realized Caroline was staring at him. Her eyes more distant, she was much paler and breathing more rapidly. The bloody mist continued to form on her facemask.

Without warning Caroline began to cough violently and as she spoke blood began pouring from her mouth.

Caroline asked again, "Am I going to die?"

Stenson said with assurance, "No sweetheart, you..."

Caroline interrupted and said in a soft resolved voice, "Tell my Momma I love her and I'm sorry. I didn't mean for things to be this way."

The sounds from Caroline's monitor began to scream with a warning of impending doom. Stenson looked at the heart rate monitor and saw it dropping like a skier going down the black slopes of St. Moritz.

Stenson yelled, "Start the chest compressions!"

"Open up the fluids, and give me some epinephrine!"

As the elevator slowly moved downward a battle had begun with the archrival, *Death*. Stenson had often feared having someone arrest in the transport elevator because it was so goddam small.

The anesthesia resident quickly moved to the head of the stretcher, removed Caroline's oxygen mask and in a single motion placed a breathing tube into her throat.

"Looks like she's aspirated, there's food on the vocal cord," the anesthesia resident observed.

Mark jumped onto the stretcher, straddled Caroline and began chest compressions on her motionless body, while Stenson checked her wrist for an elusive pulse. The elevator doors slowly opened as they all, running full stride, hurried the stretcher into the trauma area. The full trauma team was waiting there: laboratory and x-ray personnel and a surgical team including two medical students. Respiratory had a ventilator already set up.

The large room smelled of Clorox and had a sterile appearance. Everyone was gowned in light blue and wore surgical caps and masks. A surgical instrument tray lay open next to an assistant who was waiting to pass any needed tools. Stenson now realized there was more to this injury than a collapsed lung. He felt as if he had crapped on himself, but still appeared calm.

"Okay team let's get busy! This is one patient we can't lose!" said Stenson.

He continued to command, "I need a complete set of blood work including blood type. Cross match four units of packed red blood cells and keep us four units ahead."

"Find me four buttons of platelets. Fuck! bring me four units of red tag blood, we don't have time for a type and cross. We will need fresh frozen plasma and cryo."

Stenson turned his comments to Mark saying, "I hope she isn't hard-core Jehovah Witness because she is about to get a shit-load of blood products."

Stenson knew the consequences should she actually be Jehovah Witness but he didn't care. He just wanted to save her life.

Caroline, still unresponsive, was moved from the transport stretcher to the trauma table and connected to the respirator and monitors.

Winston, a six-foot, two hundred forty pound hospital orderly began rapid chest compressions. He was counting "one, two, three, four; one, two, three, four," during each series of compressions. With each successive series Winston pressed harder and harder watching the monitors for signs of life. But on the third series of compressions Stenson heard a sound that reminded him of walking on fallen branches. He knew that sound.

Stenson directed his voice and anger in Winston's direction. He said, "Winston, you heavy handed son-of-a-bit...!" Stenson caught himself, and slowly said in a quiet voice, "Winston you just broke her ribs. Ease up man and don't hurt us all!"

"Sorry Doc," Winston replied, in an humble voice, as if his feelings were hurt.

Stenson then said compassionately, "Don't be sorry, but please be gentle."

The epinephrine helped some, Caroline's heart rate increased to ninety beats per minute. But she was still unresponsive.

Directing his request to Mark, Stenson said, "Turn her left side up. Give me a knife and rib retractor."

Stenson made a large incision in Caroline's chest wall and whispered, "Shit!"

It was filled with blood. Stenson continued to appear calm but he began to sweat. He knew that he was behind the eight ball and losing a fifteen-year-old was not an option.

He then said to Mark, "Give me a suction catheter and something to clamp off this bleeder."

Mark handed Stenson a suction catheter and clamp. Then asked, "Can you see anything?"

"Not a damn thing. She's bleeding like a stuffed pig and I can't see the source." Stenson replied.

The blood was pooling rapidly in her chest cavity and hampered Stenson's ability to see.

"This goddamn suction isn't working worth a shit." Stenson complained.

"Please work with me. Please, I need your help. If I can't see the source of the bleeding I can't fix it. And if the suction isn't working I can't see."

Stenson then turned to Michelle, the nurse responsible for having the trauma room equipment ready for this type of emergency. Michelle was also All-First-Team-Airhead. She was very kind, but marginally competent at best. Stenson suspected she must have been blowing the hospital administrator to get this lead clinical position.

Michelle said, "Dr. Hawk, ooh, I knew I forgot to do something!"

She rushed over and connected the suction to the wall outlet. Blood from the open chest cavity began running through the tubing into the suction canister the way it once ran through Caroline's veins.

Mark asked Stenson, "Have you cross clamped the aorta?"

Stenson replied, "I'm trying."

Caroline's heartbeat suddenly got slower and slower, then stopped. The heart rate monitor began a loud continuous howling beep, crying almost in agony for the impending loss. Stenson whispered a plea, "No God, not this one, please don't take her! I know we can't save them all but I'm asking you, please don't take her, can't you take someone else? She's so young and we've worked so hard!"

Caroline's skin was the color of ashes, her fingertips blue, her body motionless without respiration or signs of life.

Winston stepped back, as tears rolled past his broad checks, slid down the grooves on the sides of his nose, accumulated, then leaped from his chin onto his lab coat.

In his typical cool calm manner, Stenson turned to the trauma staff and said, "Thank you all for your efforts, we lost this one."

Caroline had not foreseen her misfortune. The odds of taking a small caliber bullet and piercing through a branch of the pulmonary artery had to be pretty low, but she managed to do it. Death was a formidable foe.

Stenson placed the open palm of his hand on Mark's shoulder. In a voice that dreaded the next encounter he said, "Let's go tell the family. I hate this part so much."

"Shit Stenson, we did the best we could do. She had a lethal injury. I'm surprised she didn't die in the 'chopper."

"But she was only fifteen years old!" Stenson said. "That part doesn't sit well with me. I'm sure whatever pissed her off so much that she shot herself wasn't worth the outcome."

Betty and Richard Lewis had just arrived in the Trauma Surgical Waiting Area. As devoted members of the Church of God in Christ, their pastor and other church members were there for support. When Stenson and Mark entered the room both parents stood up. Stenson hated the surgical waiting room, it was poorly lit, with worn carpet and furniture.

CNN News was broadcasting an update on the President's heart attack following the latest terrorist threat in Chicago. The CNN News anchor was saying, "It appears that during a meeting with the Director of Homeland Security the President complained of chest pains and the Whitehouse physician was summoned."

"Mr. and Mrs. Lewis, this is Dr. Mark Bradford and my name is Dr. Stenson Hawk. We are the trauma surgeons who cared for your daughter."

"How long has she been dead?" Mrs. Lewis asked, her voice cracking as her lower lip quivered.

She knew by their solemn faces and the harsh chill she experienced thirty minutes earlier that her only child was gone.

"She passed about thirty minutes ago," answered Stenson.

"She was too young to die, couldn't you do something to save her?" asked Mr. Lewis as he slumped into the worn chair, leaning forward, with both hands covering his face unable to stop the flow of tears.

In a soft, almost tearful voice Stenson replied, "Mr. Lewis she had a gunshot wound that pieced a branch of the main pulmonary artery. We really worked hard but couldn't make a difference. Her blood loss was so great when we got her that I'm surprised she made it off the helicopter."

"I'm sorry young Doctor, I'm sure you did the best you could. She was our little girl, our only child." said Mr. Lewis.

As Stenson and Mark turned to leave, Mrs. Lewis gently grabbed their arms.

"You were the last to see my baby with life, thank you for comforting her as she moved to the next world." She softly kissed the cheek of each physician; embracing them with a hug only a grieving mother could give. As the doctors made their exit the Lewis family huddled in prayer.

"Tell my mother that I'm sorry. I didn't mean for things to end this way." Stenson heard Caroline's words clearly, as if she was speaking directly into his ear. He stopped under the exit sign.

Mark asked, "What's wrong Stenson?"

"I forgot something Caroline wanted me to tell her mother. Give me a minute." Stenson walked back to the Lewis family as they were still huddled in prayer.

The CNN News anchor continued his report on the President: "The President will have repeated angioplasty..."

Staring at the television without breaking his glance Mark said to Stenson when he returned, "I don't think he'll finish this term."

Stenson's response was short and honest, "Who gives a shit? I need a martini."

CHAPTER

t w o

Melanie Walker was striding with the confidence of a model on a Milan runway as she walked to the most important luncheon meeting of her career. She was on top of the world. Melanie had always believed that finishing in the top of her class would propel her to success at some future time. Her hard work in college and graduate school was beginning to pay off much sooner than she expected.

Melanie had lived in Memphis for three years, moving from Atlanta after finishing her academic studies there. She really missed the faster pace of that city, but clearly realized that a position with the investment banking division of McKenzie, Ward and Lawrence was nothing less than a godfather offer; one she couldn't refuse.

As Melanie turned the corner onto Third Street, headed towards the exclusive Metropolitan Club, she thought that perhaps her idea of walking any distance in the middle of a humid July day in Memphis was probably less than wise. She began to perspire and the thought of her hair drooping was affecting her groove in a negative way. After all, she had spent most of the morning in Meg's Salon.

Melanie entered the Toyota Building and found immediate relief in the air conditioned lobby.

"Good afternoon Ms. Walker. You look wonderful in spite of the heat."

"Thanks Norman, I've grown to appreciate a man who can look me right in my eyes and lie with a straight face."

They both laughed.

As Melanie walked toward the elevators she had a feeling of being watched. A quick glance over her shoulder showed Norman admiring her. She was quite fashionably dressed in a St. John suit that fit well and felt good against her tall, slender, athletically built body. Navy wasn't her favorite color but she loved it for business meetings because it gave her a feeling of power and a sense of confidence. She moved swiftly across the marble floor to the elevators, entered with a young man dressed in business attire and ascended to the second floor.

"I wonder who made the decision to place an exclusive restaurant on the second floor of a building with no view of the Mississippi River ?"

Melanie decided to ignore the comment although she agreed with his assessment. He continued, "Apparently the owner kept the top floor for his personal offices and enjoyment. Oh, the benefits of being the boss!"

The elevator doors parted and they both exited toward the dining area where Melanie was greeted by the Maitre d', Pierre.

"Ah, Madame Walker, you look marvelous today. That must be a St. John you're wearing."

With his southern "French" accent, Melanie believed this maitre d' must have been the only one of his kind in Memphis.

"Thank you, Pierre," she said.

"He probably owns the same outfit," she thought.

Melanie was tempted to ask Pierre the name of his hair stylist because his hair always looked better than her own.

"Madame, Mr. Wellington has not yet arrived. Would you like to be seated in the dining area or do you prefer to wait at the bar?"

"Please seat me in the dining area Pierre, it'll give me some time to review a few things."

"Follow me Madame."

Pierre led Melanie to her favorite table located in a far corner of the room. It provided the best view of the passersby on Third Street. As Pierre pulled back Melanie's chair and motioned for her to be seated, she admired his perfectly manicured nails and the beautiful, four-carat diamond pinky ring he wore. Pierre had to be the best groomed and most fastidiously dressed man on the planet. She wanted to ask him who did his nails.

"Thank you Pierre, you always look so nice, your presence makes dining here an extra treat."

Pierre flashed a broad, confident smile which revealed his perfectly capped teeth. He gave an affirmative nod, turned and sashayed away. Melanie thought, I should ask him the name of his dentist.

three

"Dad we just couldn't see a thing and I feel so terrible about it." Stenson said to his father Dr. Abraham Hawk.

"Son, unfortunately this won't be the last patient you'll lose and if you pursue a career in pediatric surgery you'll see younger patients die."

Dr. Abraham Hawk was Stenson's number one fan and role model. The senior Dr. Hawk was a busy general surgeon in Selma, Alabama. He attended the University of Alabama during the mid 1960s when race relations were tense and the memory of Governor George Wallace's stand in the schoolhouse door still resonated throughout the State. Dr. Hawk's experience at that University was so stressful he insisted that, when Stenson and his sister Gina reached college age, they apply only to historically African American universities for their undergraduate studies. Gina attended Spelman College but Stenson refused to follow his father's wishes and, with full academic scholarship in hand, attended Tulane University.

When Dr. Abraham Hawk graduated from the University of Alabama he felt it best to leave the South for his medical education. The two medical schools in Alabama had terrible records for admitting and graduating African Americans. He applied and was accepted to the Medical College of Wisconsin in Milwaukee where he completed medical school and his surgery residency. He met and married Beth Austin, a student nurse who attended Marquette University. She met Abraham Hawk when he visited Greenwood Baptist Church in Milwaukee, where she was a member.

Abraham was invited to a Sunday service by one of the assistant ministers who was also the Chaplain at the Milwaukee Children's Hospital. When Abraham met Beth he called it love at first sight, she called it lust at first sight. They dated for one year, married and the rest is history.

After Abraham finished a grueling five-year general surgery training program, he strongly considered practicing medicine in Wisconsin. While Milwaukee was clearly more liberal than what he'd experienced in Alabama, Abraham knew that in order to impact change and to have a viable practice he must live somewhere with a moderate African American presence. Although eighty-five percent of all the African Americans in Wisconsin lived in Milwaukee they made up less than ten percent of that city's population. So, the demographics of the city reinforced Abraham's belief that he and Beth should be southward bound. He chose Selma, Alabama because of its large African American population, its desperate need for well-trained physicians and its historical significance during the Civil Rights Movement.

Stenson was born soon after his parents settled in Selma and Gina was born four years later.

"Dad, there are only eighty-seven pediatric surgery fellowship slots in the country, which makes my acceptance extremely competitive. What do you think are my chances?"

"Well, the fact that you are my son gives you a major competitive advantage. Secondly, you've always excelled academically and completed your undergraduate studies in three years. Thirdly, your current clinical performance is going quite well and most importantly, you have your mother's eyes."

"Speaking of mother where is she?"

"She has descended on the new K-Mart Super Store armed with a Debit Card and a long list of gardening items."

"Okay, tell her to give me a call or hit me on my hip."

"Hit you on your hip?"

"Yeah Dad, that's hip-hop for page me on my beeper."

"Hip-hop?"

"Dad, I'll break it down to you later, take care. I love you."

"I love you too son, stay strong. Oh, Stenson..."

Stenson stopped mid-motion from hanging up the phone and said, "Yeah, Dad."

"Are you still seeing Melanie?"

"Melanie, Melanie who?"

"Yeah, okay Dr. Funny. You know your mother likes her."

"And you?" asked Stenson.

"Son, you know I try to stay out of your personal relationships, but I must admit I do like her."

"Yes Dad, we go out from time to time. But she's high-spirited, a major challenge and right now I really need someone who is a little less high maintenance. Dad, on another note, have you heard anything from Gina lately?"

"No son, we haven't heard a word. We're not sure where she is."

CHAPTER
four

"*Ms. Walker, my name is Rachel* and I will be serving you today. Would you like to have a beverage while you wait for Mr. Wellington? I have a wonderful Cabernet Sauvignon."

"Yes Rachel, but it's a little too early in the day for me to drink an alcoholic beverage. I'll have a Sprite with a twist of lemon and lime."

"Coming right up, Ms. Walker."

Melanie was a native of San Diego. Her father was a history professor at the University of San Diego and her mother a homemaker. She had no siblings and was a daddy's girl through and through. In fact, she acquired his interest in music and especially enjoyed the jazz of Miles and Coltrane. With the absence of siblings and her intense desire to control 'everything', Stenson diagnosed her as suffering from a severe case of 'OCS', Only Child Syndrome. Her parents migrated from Mississippi to San Diego when Melanie was five years old in order for her father to complete his masters and later earn a doctor of philosophy degree at San Diego State University. Her mother obtained a degree in economics but found the San Diego weather unkind to her severe Rheumatoid arthritis, which limited her ability to work, hence she chose to dedicate her time nurturing their only child.

Growing up on the West Coast gave Melanie a different perspective of the world. She viewed people as people and gave little consideration to race or color. Her beautiful copper-color skin complemented her flowing sandy hair, which made it difficult to label her to any particular ethic group.

Melanie was an excellent example of how Africans Americans come in all hues. Her father constantly shared with her his experiences growing up in Mississippi to keep her anchored in the reality of race in America. Although she received full academic scholarships to Stanford, the University of Southern California and San Diego State University, her father insisted that she attend Spelman College in Atlanta. He thought studying in Atlanta, a major Southern metropolitan city, would be a good change of pace. He also thought an all women's school would create less academic distractions. He had failed to consider the all-male Morehouse College directly across the street from Spelman.

After graduating from Emory University, Melanie had job offers from all the major brokerage and financial firms. She interviewed in New York, San Francisco, Atlanta and Chicago, but decided to settle in Memphis because of the great opportunity at McKenzie, Ward and Lawrence. She was offered a six-figure salary and a wonderful corner office overlooking the Mississippi River at Front Street. Stenson was another reason she was interested in moving to Memphis. Her mother and best girlfriends all warned her not to relocate because of 'a man'. She could honestly say, even though they didn't believe her, that she truly came to Memphis for the job and that Stenson could turn out to be 'the icing on the cake'.

"Ms. Walker." the voice in Melanie's direction was upbeat, crisp and polite.

"Yes."

"Ms. Melanie Walker?" There was a slight Bostonian ring to that polished voice.

"Yes."

"I'm Adam Wellington."

"Mr. Wellington, I am very pleased to meet you, please sit."

He pulled back a chair and guided his six-foot frame into the seat across from her.

"Ms. Walker I am also pleased to meet with you. If my flight had not been delayed in Nashville, I would have arrived earlier."

"Please call me Melanie. Did you fly out of Nashville on Northwest or Delta?"

"I traveled in one of our corporate jets. We just purchased a new Gulfstream and it took our pilots a little longer to do the flight check. But the ride was certainly worth the wait. And please call me Adam, all my friends do."

"Ms. Walker I have your beverage." Rachel placed the glass to the right of Melanie. She then said, "Mr. Wellington my name is Rachel, may I offer you something to settle your thirst and satisfy your taste?"

"Ah, Rachel what shall I have? Let's see, let me have bottled water to satisfy my thirst and a Cosmopolitan Martini with Bombay Sapphire to satisfy my taste."

"Yes sir." Rachel said as she placed menus to their left.

"I'll tell you about our luncheon specials when I return."

"Thank you Rachel." Melanie said.

Adam Wellington was in his mid-fifties, impeccably dressed and youthful. His strong chin and salt and pepper hair complemented his soft blue eyes. He was a distance runner during his college days at Boston University where he majored in chemistry and international finance. He was still an avid runner, which enhanced his lean, athletic build. Accepting the dare of a friend he took the Medical College Admission Test after his junior year in college and performed quite well. After graduating from BU he was accepted at Tufts University School of Medicine where he excelled.

"Melanie, I understand you are a San Diego native."

"Not really. My family moved to San Diego when I was five and I resided there until I went to Atlanta for college and graduate school."

"I must tell you, San Diego is one of my favorite cities. I travel there at least four times a year. I visit a dear friend and business associate who lives in La Jolla where he's involved in foreign currency exchange. My company also has contractual relationships which cover employees of the City of San Diego."

"Impressive." Melanie commented.

"Thank you Melanie, tell me about your business interests. I'm not quite sure how much you already know about CORE but I will bring you up to speed about us shortly."

"Well, as you know from my vitae, my degree is in accounting and my graduate emphasis was finance. With McKenzie, Ward and Lawrence I...."

"Excuse me, Mr. Wellington your water and Cosmopolitan. I'm sorry for interrupting you Ms. Walker, but have you had a chance to review the menu?"

Taking a sip of his water, Adam and Melanie glanced at their menus.

"Adam I'm starved, let's order."

"I wholeheartedly agree, Melanie. Rachel tell us about the luncheon special."

After their orders were placed the conversation took on a more serious business tone.

"As I was saying earlier, I was attracted to McKenzie, Ward and Lawrence because of their investment banking division and the opportunity they offered toward my professional growth," Melanie said.

"In my three years with the company I have participated in three major corporate acquisitions and was the lead investment banker on two independent public offerings; one is on the NYSE and the other is on NASDAQ."

Adam listened attentively, nodding affirmatively to indicate he was pleased with what he was hearing.

"Were all the acquisitions friendly takeovers or were they hostile?"

"Two of the three were hostile, one of them was extremely hostile."

"Tell me about the companies you took public," Adam asked.

"The first company was E-Care, an Internet portal company that was the window for healthcare providers, hospitals, physical therapy services and the like. This portal allowed the entities to immediately verify the insurance status of a patient; in addition to their co-pay, policy coverage and procedure verification. The providers access E-Care for a monthly fee, the cost of software and support services. When providers access E-Care, which includes Medicare and Medicaid, they can immediately get real-time information from over 2,000 insurance carriers. This service is independent of any other type of healthcare service the patient seeks to secure, whether the patient is looking for care in a hospital emergency room or an orthopedic rehabilitation facility."

"The year we took them public their gross revenues were some-where around fifteen million dollars with a net income of $4.7 million. Our opening NYSE stock price was around eight dollars per share and peaked at fourteen dollars on its opening day. It currently trades for $27.50 per share and the fifty-two week low has not been under eighteen dollars per share."

Adam asked, "What is their current price-earnings ratio?"

"It currently fluctuates between fifteen and twenty."

"I see. How did you go about getting institutional support for the company's stock public offering?"

"Our strategy was quite similar to what I would recommend for CORE, that is, a traditional dog and pony show. We visited all the major mutual fund brokers, pension plan administrators and brokerage firms in all the major cities and had our presentation team to do a great sales job."

Rachel arrived with their order.

"Ms. Walker, excuse me please, I have your sea bass grilled with a white sauce and crawfish topping."

The aroma was appetizing and as usual the presentation was excellent.

"Thank you Rachel, this looks wonderful."

Rachel looked toward Mr. Wellington and continued, "You also requested the sea bass."

"Thank you Rachel, I agree with Melanie, this looks delicious. Tell your chef he just made another new friend." As they both enjoyed their meals Melanie continued to give Adam the details of her work experience in the areas of business acquisitions, mergers and public offerings. Adam was impressed that someone so young had such extensive experience in this area of investment banking.

McKenzie, Ward and Lawrence had allowed Melanie to have a lead role in these major ventures. Adam Wellington agreed that Melanie had made the right decision in coming to Memphis.

"Melanie, let me tell you some things about myself and about CORE Healthcare Management Enterprises. When I finished medical training it became apparent to me that the landscape for the practice of medicine was about to make some major and likely irreversible changes."

"There are two things that have always been important to me. One is autonomy and the second is financial independence. Both of which were clearly in danger with the day-to-day practice of medicine. I believe in the saying, 'stick to what you know,' and there are two things that I feel comfortable with, medicine and business.

"Consequently, after I finished medical school and completed a residency in general surgery at Boston City Hospital I decided to get my MBA and go into the business of medicine instead of pursuing the practice of medicine."

"So Adam, after all those years of medical training you didn't practice medicine at all?"

"Not at all. Not for one day. I never practiced medicine and I have never regretted my decision for one minute."

"I drew up a business plan for a physician-owned managed care organization, raised five million dollars from investors and venture capitalists and got started. We were profitable in three years and bought out the venture capitalists in five years. After ten years we have 700,000 clients enrolled in our health plans, 50,000 physicians associated with our provider network, multiple hospitals, outpatient diagnostic services and rehabilitation facilities which total over 250 million dollars in annual revenues."

"Now, we are interested in becoming a member of the New York Stock Exchange. That's why we wanted to talk with you and McKenzie, Ward and Lawrence about leading the public offering for our company."

"Mr. Wellington, I'm sorry, Adam. As you can imagine this would be a great opportunity for us. I appreciate your interest in what we do and I can assure you that we have the infrastructure and experience to make this project a success for everyone." Melanie continued, "At this point I will speak with our CEO about this meeting and get back with you to set up a conference with our IPO team, which includes our marketing and finance departments. We will provide you with the cost for our services including a time frame for the IPO," she said.

"Well Melanie I must admit, you are every bit as impressive as my staff said you would be. And if you don't mind my saying so, you're certainly as beautiful and much easier on the eyes than most investment bankers."

"Thank you Adam. McKenzie, Ward and Lawrence appreciates this opportunity to work with your company and we'll do our best to serve you well. We can help you raise lots and lots of money."

She extended her hand as Adam extended his. Melanie noticed how soft, but strong his handshake felt. This was the reason she had worked so hard. And now she had the opportunity to be treated as an equal, not just a female or an African American token. Melanie realized she could never be a part of the "good old boy" network, but she knew how to be productive in the "good old boy" arena.

"Do you think it will be possible for your team to make a presentation to our staff in a couple of weeks in our Nashville office?"

"Certainly," Melanie responded, " but I will need to speak with your Chief Financial Officer prior to that meeting. There is some financial information we must review in order to project the number of shares to make available. We must have an idea of the amount of capital you want to raise in order, as you know, to determine our opening stock price."

"Archer Garrett is our Chief Financial Officer, he has been with us since the early days. Archer is extremely sharp and will be a great resource person for you. Also, I must be honest with you, our final decision on the brokerage firm we'll use won't be made until we have seen all the presentations. Presently, there're only your firm and the New York-based Kennard and Associates Brokerage Firm being considered."

"Is Mr. Garrett located in your Nashville office?"

"He actually works between our Nashville and San Francisco offices. But he will be in Nashville for your presentation and you can reach him in our San Francisco office early next week for the financial information you need."

Rachel returned with the check and asked Mr. Wellington, "Do you want me to place this check on your account?"

Staring at Melanie with a warm broad smile Adam said, "No Rachel, place it on Ms. Walker's account."

CHAPTER

five

"But Stenson I don't understand why you get so uneasy about M&M conferences." Mark was sincerely concerned about Stenson's discomfort. Stenson disliked the weekly Morbidity and Mortality Surgical Conference, which was usually known as the "M&M Conference". This gathering consisted of the surgery residents who presented surgical cases considered interesting.

"Let's put this whole thing in perspective, Mark. Some of the presentations are worthwhile because they reveal examples of intuitive diagnoses and support our understanding of the state of the art in medical technology when coupled with skillful surgical techniques. Correct?" Stenson was beginning to make his case.

"Correct." Mark replied.

"However," Stenson continued, "some outcomes have been disastrous, a result of negligence or failure to appreciate or incorporate the value of one or more of the aforementioned." They were both silent for a moment, then Stenson added, "Mark, the truth of the matter is these conferences are often the forum for residents to present their clinical screw-ups. They also provide an opportunity for the surgical faculty to 'bend'em over and pump'em' in a public forum."

"In addition to that, other residents can learn from the screw-ups of their peers to develop a healthy fear for the surgical staff. With that in mind do you understand?" Stenson asked, opening his eyes wide as if to offer Mark insight into his thoughts.

"I understand." Mark answered. They entered the auditorium and took their seats in the very back to get a better view of the action.

Stenson thought the academic side of this exercise helped the participants develop quick thinking, thick skin and transient humility. When an intern did well and experienced a good patient outcome there was nothing said. But when interns did poorly and the patient had a bad outcome they stood a better chance of getting out of a Ku Klux Klan rally wearing a Malcolm X tee shirt.

The moderator of the M&M Conference was the Chief of Surgery, Dr. Odellious Brown. Dr. Brown was a basic, down to earth, clinician considered to be a surgeon's surgeon. On the other hand, he was also quite a character.

"Stenson, what is your opinion of Dr. Brown?" Mark asked.

"What do you mean?" Stenson replied, knowing exactly what Mark was asking.

"I mean, does he live up to his reputation as a really good surgeon? And if that's true, why does he present himself as a ghetto cop?"

Stenson always found it interesting that white people think all Black people know each other and can explain why individual Blacks do what they do. But Stenson did know and admired Odellious. He recognized Odellious' strength of character, his willingness to persevere and that he was a highly principled individual. Stenson thought the story of Odellious' upbringing to be an interesting one.

He began by saying, "Well Mark, Odellious grew up in the ghetto of East St. Louis, Illinois and was an honor student in spite of being the warlord for the local Disciples Gang. He was the youngest of three boys reared by a single mother. His two older brothers died while serving long prison terms. One brother was imprisoned for failing to accept a "beat down" from two policemen during a routine traffic stop. He killed one of the policemen with his own nightstick and the other spent eight months in a coma as a result of head trauma. The second brother died while serving time for robbing a string of Seven-Eleven stores."

"I hope he got the full weight of the justice system because no one should ever hit a cop." Mark interjected.

"Well, don't worry. They got the full weight of the justice system alright, but I find it interesting that in our judicial system, some of the CEOs of many Fortune 500 companies steal millions of dollars, erode employees pension plans and bankrupt major corporations without spending one night in jail. And a Black man can get ten years for stealing five dollars from a Seven-Eleven store. You go figure that one."

Odellious received a full academic scholarship to Washington University in St. Louis where he continued through medical school. He was the first in his family to graduate college.

His appearance and demeanor belied his experience and education. On most streets in Memphis, Odellious would surely be mistaken for a drug dealer, gunrunner, pimp or some combination of such thugs. At five feet ten with a rock-hard body, he had an intimidating presence. He often sported a 'do rag', had a front tooth capped with gold, and wore a two-carat diamond earring in each ear. He also wore a dragon tattoo on his right bicep.

On several different occasions the Chairman of Surgery had spoken with Odellious about his appearance. Odellious always had a practical response. Most recently Odellious retorted, "If Albert Einstein's looks didn't stop him from winning a Nobel Prize, my appearance won't stop me from making sound surgical decisions."

Odellious believed his appearance should not be a yardstick used to measure his competence. But in reality he was painfully aware that many of his colleagues could not see beyond his appearance. Stenson appreciated the depth and complexity of this man whose humble beginnings continued to belie his intellectual genius.

CHAPTER

SIX

Dr. Brown entered the auditorium with a cheerful "Good morning doctors", spoken in a smooth, deep baritone voice.

"I am very interested in the cases we are reviewing this morning. Some of you will give us examples of what we should do to maximize patient care. Others will give us examples of the outcomes that result when we fail to view all aspects of the patients' needs, fail to ask the right questions, don't think, don't ask for help or don't realize that we don't know!"

Mark whispered to Stenson, "I think this is going to get ugly! Are we presenting Caroline Lewis' case today?"

"No, she didn't make the list since she had a fatal injury. We didn't screw up, we just experienced a bad outcome."

"Okay," said Odellious, "Our first case will be presented by the Blue Surgical Team. The presenting surgeon is Dr. McAlester."

Odellious motioned to Paul McAlester, a second year surgery resident. McAlester moved cautiously toward the podium as if he were a death row prisoner about to receive a lethal injection. He was a short, rotund young man who wore Poindexter glasses. In spite of his meek appearance he was extremely arrogant and naive.

"Paul suffers from a severe case of 'short dick' syndrome" was a description of him overheard when a young nurse was talking about McAlester to her friend.

"Good morning." McAlester's voice slightly trembled.

"This case is about a thirty-two year old Black male who entered the trauma center with a blunt abdominal injury, secondary to a physical altercation. The injury apparently occurred when the patient was assaulted with a metal baseball bat. Under local anesthesia we made a small abdominal incision and observed what was later determined to be a false-positive abdominal lavage. It led us to believe he was bleeding internally. We thought at this point that the patient had suffered a ruptured spleen. We then conducted an exploratory laparotomy under general anesthesia."

"Dr. McAlester, what were your surgical findings?" Odellious asked.

"The exploration was negative, the spleen was normal, and there were no additional signs of internal bleeding."

"Then why did you do the exploration in the first place?" Odellious' tone was becoming more agitated and aggressive.

"Again Dr. Brown, we misinterpreted the lavage results."

Stenson gave a soft giggle and whispered into Mark's ear, "Fuckup number one."

Odellious asked, "Dr. McAlester, if this patient came in for blunt trauma to the abdomen and underwent exploratory abdominal surgery, why does the case report indicate there was an amputation of his right leg below the knee?"

McAlester attempted an evasive maneuver, "Yes Dr. Brown that is correct, an amputation was performed."

Odellious continued, "Well, goddam Doctor, what happened?"

Mark whispered to Stenson, "This is *really* going to be ugly."

Stenson knew Mark was getting excited because he was starting to repeat himself.

"Well, wh... wh... when the patient..." McAlester was beginning to stutter.

"..wa..was in the trauma ho... hold... holding area we attempted to get central veinous access in the right femoral vein with a large introducer."

"And?" asked Dr.Brown.

"And, I... I... guess we ruptured th... the femoral artery instead."

"What do you mean 'you guess you ruptured the femoral artery'?"

"Well, the intensive care unit nurse said she couldn't feel a pulse in the leg after we finished the surgery."

"And when you completed your physical assessment after surgery what were your findings?"

"The patient had no pulse in that leg."

"Well, if you noted there wasn't a pulse immediately after surgery why couldn't you save his leg?"

"Well, I didn't notice it immediately after surgery."

"I thought you said the ICU nurse called you immediately after surgery."

"She did, but I didn't go and see the patient right then."

Odellious shouted, "Damn McAlester, quit dancing around the question! How long did it take you to get to the patient?"

"Eight hours."

"What? Eight hours!" Odellious spoke just short of a yell.

"Well, yes."

"Is Dr. Stewart your senior resident on this service?"

"Yes."

Looking around the auditorium Odellious asked, "Is she here today?"

"No, Dr. Brown, she called me this morning and told me she wouldn't be able to make M&M because she had a doctor's appointment."

There was a sudden outburst of laughter in the auditorium, it was obvious that McAlester had become the fall guy and unfortunately when it came to Odellious, there would be no sympathy. Odellious was about to turn up the heat.

"Okay McAlester, your chief resident has left you to present this case. Continue the presentation."

"After I evaluated the patient it was obvious there was an injury to one of the femoral vessels. I spoke with Dr. Stewart and she suggested that we get an arteriogram; the results of which showed complete laceration of the femoral artery. The patient was taken back to surgery for exploration and repair of the femoral artery. After seven hours of exploration, the vessel was repaired but since the leg had no blood supply for so long it was dead and we elected to amputate. At this time we...."

"Stop, just stop," Odellious said with controlled anger.

"Let's review this to make sure I didn't miss anything."

McAlester nodded, then said, "Okay Dr. Brown."

"Now, you had a young male without any significant medical or surgical history."

"Yes sir."

"He got in a fight and lost to the baseball bat."

"Yes sir."

"He came to the hospital and you misdiagnosed a spleen injury which resulted in unnecessary abdominal surgery."

"Yes, sir."

"In the process you inserted a large catheter and cut through the femoral artery instead of placing the catheter in the femoral vein."

"No sir."

"What do you mean 'No sir'? What did I misunderstand?"

McAlester, whimpering as if being brutally cross-examined by Johnny Cochran, broke down on the witness stand and confessed.

"Dr. Stewart cut through the femoral artery, I didn't. She was trying to do the femoral vein central line, not me."

Odellious asked, "But weren't you there?"

"Yes sir."

"Didn't the ICU nurse page you to come see the patient?"

"Yes sir."

"So what in hell were you doing that was so important you couldn't go and check on a patient."

"We were making rounds and then I had clinic."

"Is that a good reason?"

"No sir."

"Continue."

"When we realized the leg had no blood supply for more than eight hours we initially decided to do a hip disarticulation but...."

"What? A hip disarticulation! I guess that was Dr. Stewart's great idea too."

"No, actually that was my idea." McAlister said with a glimpse of pride.

"That was a dumb idea! Thank God your senior resident killed that idea."

"Well Dr. Brown, she really didn't kill it."

"Have you or Dr. Stewart ever done a hip disarticulation?"

"No, but we called the junior orthopedic surgery resident who had read about it, because he had a case scheduled at the Veterans Administration Hospital."

"You called the junior ortho resident who had done one of these procedures before?"

"Well, yes, we called him but he hadn't done one either. He had read about it for a case he had scheduled at the VA, but his case was cancelled and he never got to do one."

"What happened next?"

"The junior orthropedic resident scrubbed in with us but he and Dr. Stewart couldn't agree on the incision site."

"What happened next?"

"We sent a senior medical student to get a surgery textbook so that we could review the anatomy for the incision site and ..."

"Wait, Wait!" At this point Odellious was screaming. His eyes were bulging and his ears were red.

"You sent a medical student to get a book for you to review while the patient is asleep under general anesthesia?"

"Yes sir."

"Why didn't you contact the attending Surgeon on Call?"

"Well after we couldn't agree on the incision site we..."

"Even after reviewing the anatomy you still couldn't agree on the incision site?"

"No sir"

"Well how in hell did you end up amputating this patient's leg?"

"The attending anesthesiologist complained to our attending surgeon that we had been in the operating room for four hours with an anesthetized patient and hadn't made any progress. Dr. Westborough told us not to do anything until he got there."

"When he arrived he suggested we do a below the knee amputation which would allow better rehabilitation with a leg prosthesis."

Sounding sarcastic Odellious said, "Now let me make sure I got this straight. This patient came into the hospital with two legs and a suspected blunt trauma. But left with an abdominal incision that did not reveal any abdominal injury, and one leg because somebody screwed up and lacerated an artery. This occurred because you did not respond in a timely manner when the nurse asked for the injury to be evaluated."

"In all honesty sir that sums it up."

"Your honesty is admirable but your poor clinical judgment has caused irreversible harm to a patient. This is unacceptable and I will recommend that your entire team be placed on probationary status. Furthermore Dr. Stewart, your senior surgery resident, will be required to complete an additional six months of training which will delay her graduation date."

The stark quietness in the auditorium created the stillness of a petrified forest. This was by far the most pissed off Stenson had ever seen Odellious, who was so angry he began to tremble.

"Next case," said Odellious.

It was late afternoon when Mark and Stenson walked out of the medical center toward the physicians' parking lot. They had been in the hospital for a total of thirty-eight hours and had slept only two of them. After reporting to the arriving Call Team they were both eager to leave the hospital and relax.

Stenson said to Mark, "Hey man, what about stopping down at Jullian's for a beer?"

Mark replied, "No can do man, I haven't seen my wife and kids in two days. If I don't go straight home I'll get my ass kicked. My wife has already placed a picture of me over the kids' beds so they won't forget what I look like."

Mark's wife Karen was also a physician. She completed her residency in pediatrics and became pregnant shortly thereafter. With the birth of their twin boys, she traded her stethoscope for a baby stroller.

"That's fine. I was told that when you give up your player card and get married, life is never the same. All control is lost."

"It can be a struggle for power. That's why I periodically walk around the house butt naked so my wife can see who has the penis," Mark replied.

"Okay, let's hookup next time," Stenson said, "I think I'll go home and get some sleep because tomorrow will be a busy day for me. In addition to visiting my barber I'm having dinner with Melanie tomorrow night. Apparently she's got some big project she's excited about."

"This has got to be the first girl that you've ever dated for more than six months," Marked observed.

"No, the second," Stenson countered, "I dated Vickie Smith for seven months when I was in the sixth grade."

"Where are you guys going for dinner?" Marked asked.

"As a matter of fact I'm going to prepare dinner at my apartment?"

"Bullshit!"

"No shit."

"She must have pussy-whipped you pretty good."

"Pussy-whipped? When did white guys start talking about 'pussy-whipped'?"

"When we started hanging out with Black guys." Mark said with a chuckle.

"Well, not that it's any of your business, but we aren't having sex right now," Stenson said in a quiet voice.

"What do you mean you aren't having sex right now? What happened? Did she stop because of your size?"

Mark asked as he took his forefinger and thumb to show a two-inch circle.

"Now that's funny, Mark," Stenson said in a dry, sarcastic tone.

"What I mean is that we haven't had sex at all and she isn't interested in much more than my friendship. She wants to be a virgin until she gets married."

Mark answered, "You have got to be kidding."

"No, I'm afraid not. But right now it's alright with me, it really is. I think I'm curious to see what the future holds."

"If my wife had wanted to stay a virgin until she got married she wouldn't be my wife," Mark continued.

"Mark, I never thought I would have hung in this long. But she is someone very special."

They arrived at Mark's car first. Stenson said, "Okay man, be good. Give the boys a big hug and tell the wifey I said hello."

"Have a nice evening and get some rest while you can. It's not often we get time off," Mark said as he extended his hand, which was embraced by Stenson as they looked at each other and smiled.

"Peace," they said in unison.

CHAPTER

seven

Impulse Barbershop was located in the heart of the North Memphis 'hood at the corner of Chelsea and Hollywood. Stenson had been a customer there for three years because he believed such an environment offered an opportunity for him to stay in touch with the brothers. He was provided an escape from the sometimes plantation-like environment of the medical center. Although he often wore medical scrubs when he went for a hair cut, only Stenson's barber knew he was a physician. The other barbers and patrons thought Stenson was a drug dealer since he drove a BMW and gave large tips. The real purpose of his tips was to avoid long waits to get into his barber's chair.

As he drove down Chelsea Avenue Stenson noticed how much the area had deteriorated. Most of the thriving retail stores were long gone and had been replaced by liquor stores and pawnshops. The retail stores followed the white Memphians' migration to the East Memphis, Cordova and Germantown suburbs and left behind poverty, crime and disenfranchisement. But strangely enough Stenson found more comfort here, although it was very different from the environment provided him by his parents.

His car slowed to a stop in front of the barbershop and as usual there were young African American men in front of the shop. They were going though their rap lyrics; each with aspirations of becoming the next Nelly or Tupac. Stenson stopped for a quick listen to the rhymes and thought about the conversations he and his father had about music or, as the senior

Dr. Hawk would say, the "deterioration of music." His father thought little talent was required to become a rapper. He felt that creativity was required for the old love ballads. And that the skills, discipline and dedication required to be a great musician had been lost to the quick-fix of sampling music and electronic drum machines.

"Wassup?" was the friendly greeting coming from one of the would-be rap superstars.

"Not much man, it's all good," was Stenson's reply as he entered the barbershop. As expected on a Saturday, nearly every chair was filled with brothers sporting a variety of hairstyles: braids, fades, locks, waves and jheri curls.

"Hey Doc, you need a cut?" asked Zeke. Zeke was Stenson's barber. He was also a Memphis ex-basketball great. In high school he scored 80 points in one game. But he was also a casualty of Proposition 48, which required high school athletes to achieve a minimum score on the college admission test. Since Zeke finished high school reading on an eight-grade level, that promising college and NBA career never materialized.

Stenson asked, "Zeke how many heads do you have in front of me?"

"Doc you'll be the next one in the chair."

Stenson knew by the number of people in the shop that, under normal conditions, there must be at least three people ahead of him. But he always gave Zeke a ten-dollar tip which insured he would be next up.

The Impulse Barber Shop was a place were the brothers gathered to discuss current events. While they talked about local and national news, contrary to the stereotypical thinking, it was surprising how many of the brothers were well versed and had an opinion on international situations. Impulse was also a place where customers could purchase anything from a laptop computer to Viagra, which one brother was selling for five dollars a pill. As he pitched it, "Man that's a fifty percent discount from what you'd pay at any drugstore, plus you don't need a prescription!"

The Viagra was selling like hotcakes! But he failed to warn his customers of the side effects; such as priapism, a painful erection which was more common in his younger customers. There were also pictures of used cars and homes for sale. Canali suits and Donald J.Pliner women's shoes were still neatly packaged with price tags attached.

Zeke, talking openly to other patrons of the shop, said, "I never thought Jordan should have come back, because I knew he couldn't play with the young guys. It's hard for bald headed guys like Jordan and Malone to keep up with the young guys with braids and Afros. It's still true today, Malone couldn't do a thing to help the Lakers win, you have to have braids or a fro."

"But Shaq don't have no 'fro or braids."

One of the patrons sitting in a chair across the room interjected.

"But Shaq is Shaq; and as long as Shaq stays Shaq he won't need no braids or a 'fro. But when that changes he may need braids or a 'fro."

Zeke was in the last phase of placing a relaxer into an older gentleman's hair. He said to Stenson, "Doc, I'm finished with this part, you're next up." The older gentleman, his hair covered with a white, funky smelling paste, put on a plastic cap and took a seat next to Stenson. Stenson wished someone would tell him that the wet, greasy look ended twenty years ago and that jheri curls where out too.

Stenson stepped up and sat in the barber's chair and Zeke draped a cloth over him to keep hair off his scrubs.

"Zeke, what's been happening man?" asked Stenson.

"Not much Doc, not much. Buzzard luck, I can't kill nothing and won't nothing die."

Stenson continued, "How's the family?"

"Fine Doc, the kids are great and the wife hasn't complained this week, so I'm doing pretty good."

That was one of the things Stenson admired about Zeke. He had three sons under the age of four, his wife was unemployed and he didn't make very much money as a barber, but he always appeared upbeat, clean cut and devoted to his family. Zeke said, "Doc, what do you think about reparations for Blacks? I mean, you know the Japanese got paid for getting locked up in concentration camps and Germany paid the Jews for the Holocaust so why shouldn't we get something since we picked cotton for free, built Washington, DC and shit like that?"

"I, I, I'll tell you wh..., wh..., why we shouldn't ge...,ge...,get paid anything," stuttered Serief Mohammed, a political science major on scholarship at Lemoyne-Owen College. He was interested in becoming a lawyer.

"If we take mo...,mon..., money for slavery, then i..., it lets the white man feel like th..., th...,they have done their part and we would have no argument fo..., for job equality or affirmative action."

Serief always had good points but listening to him talk was almost painful.

"Sec..., sec..., secondly," he continued, after pausing to take a deep breath as if talking was a tiresome effort.

"I believe the President would rather give money to Middle East terrorist organizations than to de..., des..., descendents of slaves."

Zeke asked Stenson, "Doc how do you want your cut?"

"Give me a close fade, no line across the front."

"Do you want a shave?"

Stenson hadn't shaved in over a week and looked it. Furthermore, he had been in the hospital for the last two days. Zeke was a great barber but his shaving blades were quite dull and often left Stenson with severe cuts and bumps.

"Nah Zeke, I'll shave when I get home."

"Man, Uncle Sam needs to pay us for that slavery time!" A patron in the barber's chair next to Stenson added.

"Just think about it Man! Cotton was the largest domestic product at the time, and it was all harvested with free labor. It would be like Bill Gates and Microsoft generating all their money but not having to pay their employees a salary, pension, healthcare or disability. We got only room and board and we grew our own food. Black people built the Whitehouse and all that other shit in Washington with free labor. And labor costs can be as much as fifty percent of the cost of a project."

Zeke asked Stenson, "Doc, are you interested in a desktop computer or a digital camera? I know a dude who can give you a good deal on them and they are still in the box."

Stenson replied, "Nah Zeke, I'm straight on both right now. But if I hear of somebody with a need for such items I'll send them your way."

Zeke said, "Cool."

Zeke was finishing with Stenson's hair when a loud conversation in the far corner of the shop gathered everyone's attention.

Bopeep, one of the local, small time drug dealers had just entered with his nine months pregnant girlfriend. The girlfriend, Tracy, had once dated AJ, the barber who cut Bopeep's hair. Furthermore, AJ and Bopeep were first cousins but far from close relatives. Bopeep sold AJ his old Lexus 400 but on the day money changed hands Bopeep told AJ he had forgotten to bring the car title. Two days later one of Bopeep's runners took the Lexus from AJ's driveway, to a 3rd Street auto dealer and, with car title in hand, sold it.

AJ didn't actually know what happened until six months later. Bopeep walked away with a total of $28,000.00 on the deal and never acknowledged any involvement with the car swindle.

"AJ, how many people you got in front of me?" Bopeep asked in his deep hustler voice. Dressed in his typical hip-hop FUBU gear, he had his girlfriend Tracy dressed in Burberry maternity wear sitting to his left.

"When I finish this guy in the chair you'll be next up."

"Cool," Bopeep replied.

"AJ," Tracy called in her soft sexy voice,"how long you been out?" She asked.

"Two months," AJ replied.

AJ had served a thirty-day sentence for driving with a suspended Driver's License.

"I heard you had a hard time down in city jail."

"Hey babe, dig that's behind me now. I don't want to talk about it."

Tracy persisted.

"AJ, is it true what I heard that...." AJ quickly interrupted.

"Tracy, is it true your sister still a crack head walking on 2nd and Vance at night? And is it true you not real sure who yo' baby daddy?"

With that statement it was on.

Bopeep yelled, "Yo' nigga! Why you trying to dis' my lady like dat?"

"I ain't yo' nigga and yo' bitch ain't no lady, she was just trying to dis' me."

Tracy catapulted from her chair. With both hands on her pregnant hips, eyes blazing and neck extended, her head began to rock from side to side as she spoke.

"AJ, who you calling a bitch, you the bitch ass, I know what happen to you in city jail. You punk ass motherfucker."

Bopeep piped in, "And if you don't 'pologize right now I'll give you de same thing you got in jail."

"Oh shit." Zeke said "He could have said anything but that!"

AJ moved across the room with the speed reminiscent of a Sugar Ray Leonard fight and before anyone could mentally process what they were seeing AJ was on top of Bopeep beating him like a drum. Tracy let out a piercing scream and grabbed her pregnant stomach. Water began flowing down her legs like she was urinating on herself. The excitement had pushed Tracy into labor and her water sac had broken. AJ and Bopeep were rolling around on the floor like eight-year-olds in a schoolyard fight. Stenson, Zeke and Warren were trying to pull them apart. By this time Tracy had fallen to the floor screaming with labor pain. Stenson was thinking, this is all I need on my only day off: to be caught in a fight in a barbershop with a pregnant woman in labor.

Warren, one of the barbers said, "Okay guys, cut this shit out," as he wrapped both his arms around AJ pulling him up backwards from the floor. Bopeep then swung, trying to take a sucker punch advantage, but Zeke caught his arm before it could find its target. Stenson found some satisfaction in this fight, although it was unfortunate to see two grown men fighting for no reason. But it was refreshing to see fists used instead of guns.

"Ahahahahah!" yelled Tracy, who had been forgotten in all the commotion.

eight

She lay on the floor, her pants were becoming soiled with blood as well as amniotic fluid. Stenson shouted, "Someone call 911 fast!"

He forgot he was in a barbershop.

"Someone call 911 immediately!" He said again.

Mohammed picked up the phone and dialed 911 quickly. When the operator answered he began to give the scenario. "I,I,I neeeeed a,a,a..."

Mohammed always stuttered worst when he got excited. And Stenson thought this was the last person who should be giving directions.

Stenson said, "Goddam it, somebody take the phone from Mohammed and get an ambulance in a hurry! Please!"

By this time Bopeep and AJ were completely separated.

Both were breathing deeply, their faces bruised with perspiration flowing. Tracy was still lying on the floor, the vaginal bleeding had become alarmingly impressive and visible to all. As Bopeep watched he began to sway back and forth. He wanted to give the impression of being a rough neck but always fainted at the sight of blood. This time would be no exception. AJ reached for his cousin but it was too late. As Bopeep's head hit the floor with a thud, there was a slow trickle of urine in his pants.

AJ began to laugh as he said to Zeke, "I'll never have to worry 'bout Bopeep dis'ing me no more. After fainting and peeing in his pants he won't be back here for a haircut again soon."

Warren, Ike and Mohammed carried Tracy to a sofa in the back of the shop. Stenson said to Tracy, "I'm going to have to take your panties off and examine you, is that okay?"

Tracy yelled, "Okay, okay, okay. Ahahahahah please help me."

She was beginning to perspire. Stenson checked her pulse, her heart was beating very fast. He hoped the rapid heart rate was due to pain and not because of blood loss.

"Warren, give me any type of towel, sheet, blanket and any type of clean gloves you can find." Stenson requested.

"I know you don't expect me to have anything sterile," said Warren.

"Where are those slow ass paramedics?" Stenson asked.

Tracy was experiencing either placental previa or placental abruption, either of which could lead to her and the baby's death. Without an ultrasound machine it was impossible to make a definitive diagnosis and it was unlikely the baby would wait until the paramedics arrived. Stenson knew he must deliver Tracy there, although he had only done four months training in obstetrics as a medical student and one month during his general surgery residency. He hated obstetrics , the screaming women who rarely attended birthing classes frequently had unrealistic expectations of interventional pain relief.

It was difficult to comfort Tracy as she lay on the couch which was old, lumpy and way past due in its need for a good cleaning. The room was small with a snack machine and an adjacent restroom; a running toilet could be heard. The lighting was extremely poor and there was nothing sterile or private about it. Stenson now wished he had done more obstetrics, but was comforted by the thought that many babies are born in far worse environments than this and survived just fine.

Stenson said, "Okay Tracy, I want you to take slow deep breaths, because the contractions will become more frequent and painful and we don't have any medication. I'm going to do a vaginal exam to determine how dilated is your cervix."

Zeke entered with a box of plastic gloves.

"Here you go, Doc."

Tracy asked, "Now who did you say you are? I just can't let anybody stick their hand up my pussahahahahahahah."

The contractions were beginning to come closer together and as Stenson placed his hand on Tracy's stomach he could tell the pains were getting stronger. Stenson said softly, "Listen I'm a doctor."

Tracy asked, "What kinda doctor are youuuu ahahahahahaha?"

Zeke said in an impatient voice, "Tracy, cut the shit and let Doc help you!"

Tracy asked, "Why does it hurt so much and why am I bleeding like this?"

Stenson said in a troubled voice, "I think something bad is going on, but if you relax and listen closely we can get through this."

Warren walked over and closed the door because a crowd was gathering to observe. Stenson gently lifted Tracy's dress and removed her stained underwear. Mohammed brought in a pan of water that he had warmed in the microwave.

"Oh shit!"

Which was an appropriate response that Stenson gave to what he was observing.

Zeke asked, "Doc is that foot supposed to be hanging out like that?"

When Stenson removed Tracy's underwear there was a foot protruding from her vagina, instead of the baby's head. The baby was breeched, a bad situation in a hospital and a nightmare situation in a barbershop. Stenson had limited obstetric experience anyway, plus he had seen only one and never done a vaginal breech delivery. Stenson tried to push the foot back into the vagina but it didn't work. This could have brought him a little more time.

"Okay," he thought.

He was accepting the fact that this was turning into a bad day. He was going to have to deliver this baby.

Stenson told Tracy to relax, then said, "Your baby is coming out the wrong way."

Tracy raised her head to ask, "Whatcha mean the wrong way?"

"Feet first, ass backwards." Stenson firmly responded.

He reached into the vaginal vault to search for the second foot. Moisture was dripping from his forehead as if he had entered a steam sauna. The back of his shirt and underarms were soaked with sweat. There was absolutely no good reason to take on this kind of medical liability. He was clearly in what he perceived to be a lose-lose situation and over his head.

"Call 911 again," he yelled pausing only to look at the time.

Certainly, the likelihood of Tracy having insurance was small and a claim would be denied because the delivery was taking place in a barbershop. As a resident he couldn't charge for anything anyway. But if he screwed this up, he was sure Tracy would sue the hell out of him. Stenson believed half of all patients silently hoped for poor or less than adequate medical outcome, just so they can sue a physician. For some, a big medical settlement is better than hitting the lottery. Stenson continued, "Tracy, I'm going to need your undivided attention. Spread your legs and take slow deep breaths."

Tracy responded as she was directed.

Zeke hurried into the room with a pot of steaming water.

"Doc, I heated this up in the microwave. I cleaned this pot as best I could. I keep my relaxer in it."

Reaching further in, Stenson located the second foot and pulled it down. By this time Bopeep had recovered and was standing in the doorway looking at the two feet protruding from Tracy's vagina.

Bopeep yelled, "Oh, shit! I, I, I...".

There was a loud thud and once again Bopeep was on the floor with urine running down his pants legs.

Zeke complained, "I hate a bitch ass nigga!" He was looking at Bopeep and shaking his head.

Stenson said, "Okay, I think the next thing is to grab both feet," he was talking to himself with Zeke standing close by and nodding affirmatively, "and pull until the waist appears."

Stenson gently pulled both feet, which rested comfortably in one hand.

"Tracy, it's a boy." Stenson said.

"A boy, I wanted a girl. The ultrasound said it was gonna to be a girl." A weak Tracy complained.

"Do you want me to put it back?" Stenson asked.

"Do what? You out yo' goddamm,.." Tracy uttered, and Stenson interrupted, "Tracy. Okay, okay. I was only kidding." Chuckled Stenson.

"Doc what will you do next?" Zeke asked as if he might have the answer.

"I think the next thing is to find the shoulders. But I don't remember if it makes a difference if the baby's right or left shoulder comes first," said Stenson.

"Does it make a difference Doc?" asked Zeke.

"Well, one major complication, if I remember correctly, is that a shoulder fracture could leave the baby unable to use his arm for life." Stenson said.

"You need to make up your mind down there. If you done forgot, 'cause these pains is kicking my ass."

Tracy's words were interspersed with blowing and deep breathing.

"I'm not going to sue you. Just get the damn baby out, shit!"

Stenson said, "It seems like most things in life are geared towards the right."

Zeke replied, "Yeah, Doc that's true. Desks are generally designed for right-handed people, postage stamps are usually put on the upper right corner of an envelope, we can legally turn right on red when driving and stuff like that."

Stenson said, "I'm left-handed and always thought that shit was a little unfair."

He continued, "Zeke, with your sound scientific logic I guess I'll pull the right shoulder down first."

Stenson slowly pulled down the right shoulder and the left followed, much easier than he thought.

"Ah, ah, ah, ah!"

Tracy had lost her concentration and was screaming at the top of her voice.

"Tracy I know those shoulders coming out had to hurt, but I still have to get the baby's head out."

Stenson then rotated the baby's body and reached up to feel the face. He was able to touch the baby's chin and pull it down towards the chest. He pulled the body but the head wouldn't budge. It was stuck. Stenson was certain that Tracy's pelvis was large enough for the delivery but the head wouldn't move.

"What's taking so long? Please hurry up, please, please."

Tracy was beginning to lose control.

Stenson looked to the floor at Bopeep's disproportionately large head and made the diagnosis. Like father, like son. The baby was big-headed.

"Zeke, I need you to get a pair of scissors, take the shoe strings out of your sneakers, place them in water and microwave them all for three minutes. Also, send Mohammed to the drugstore across the street for sterile dressing and Ambersol toothache medicine."

"Ambersol toothache medicine?"

"Yeah, get that and some insulin syringes."

"Oookay, Doc!" Mohammed was really excited.

"Go with him to help translate," Stenson said to Warren.

Warren gave an affirmative thumbs-up and exited the barbershop with Mohammed. The legs, waist and shoulders were out as Stenson palpitated the umbilical cord. The baby still had a strong pulse. Mohammed and Warren returned so fast that Stenson knew they must have skipped the checkout line.

"Okay Doc, we hooked you up. We got two of everything you ask'd for."

Stenson said, "Thanks guys, Zeke let me have the sterile scissors and some alcohol."

"I only have the rubbing alcohol that I use after a haircut." Zeke replied.

"That's fine, it's better than nothing."

Stenson opened the sterile dressing, soaked it with alcohol and wiped the area of Tracy's vagina. He drew the Ambersol, which is a local anesthetic, into several insulin syringes.

"Tracy, the baby's head is too big to get through the birth canal, so I'm going to numb your vaginal area and make a small incision to deliver the baby."

"I don't give a shit, ahahahahah."

She was breathing steadily between contractions by now, but still screaming at the top of her voice.

"I just want to get this over and get this damn baby out of meeeeeeee!"

Stenson took the Ambersol and injected it right below the space between the vagina and the rectum. He took the sterilized scissors and cut the skin. Tracy screamed even louder.

"I guess the Ambersol didn't work as well as I thought." Blood began to pool below Tracy. Stenson again felt the baby's chin; and he grabbed the chin to flex his head. Then Stenson pulled the baby straight down. Tracy gave a loud ear-piercing scream and the baby popped out. The bluish color of the baby indicated decreased oxygen. Stenson took Zeke's sterilized shoestrings and tied them around the umbilical cord, cut it, wiped the baby's face and wiped the baby's mouth with his finger to remove any birth material. The door to the small room suddenly flew open.

"Oh, shit!" said a voice from the rear of the room. Stenson turned, there were two paramedics standing in the doorway with their mouths open in shock.

"Give me a suction bulb and some oxygen!" Stenson shouted. Fumbling through an equipment box a paramedic produced a large suction bulb, while the second paramedic scrambled to get the oxygen tank. Stenson suctioned the infant then began breathing into his mouth while gently but aggressively rubbing the baby's chest and tapping the bottom of the baby's feet.

"How is my baby, is he alright? Is he? Is he alright?" The baby began breathing on his own, he coughed and let out a loud cry.

"Tracy, I think we made it. The baby's color is much better. Congratulations! You have a wonderful baby boy," said Stenson.

Then Stenson slowly pulled on the umbilical cord, delivering the placenta. The paramedics wrapped Tracy and the baby in warm blankets. Transported them to a stretcher and placed them in the ambulance. Tracy looked at Stenson as she was being loaded into the ambulance and asked, "Are you going to ride to the hospital with us?"

"No, you guys should be fine now. I've already spoken with the obstetrician on call and gave her a report on our adventure. She will meet you in the Emergency Room when you arrive. I just spoke with the pediatrician who will care for your baby. He will also be in the Emergency Room when you arrive."

"I don't know how I can thank you. It was a blessing that you was here today, 'cause Bopeep was fucking worthless in this situation. Has he woke up yet?"

"Last I looked, he was sitting in a chair and AJ was giving him a pretty hard time."

"Have you selected a name for the baby?" asked Stenson.

"Yep, I sho' did," replied Tracy.

"And what will be the baby's name?"

Tracy produced a broad smile revealing a gold front tooth with a "T" on it that Stenson had not previously noticed.

"I want my son to be smart and help people. His name will be Stenson."

CHAPTER

nine

"Stenson? You've got to be kidding me." Smiled Melanie, with the excitement of a schoolgirl on her first date.

"No, I am serious, she went into active labor right there in the barber shop." Stenson said into his cell phone as he drove to pick up items for their dinner.

Melanie opened her refrigerator in search of a strawberry smoothie to quench the thirst she had developed after her run. When the phone rang she new it was Stenson. The phone always sounded a little "happier" when Stenson called.

"And was breeched?" Melanie asked.

"Yes, and was breeched."

"Stenson, you're a surgeon. When's the last time you delivered a baby?"

"A baby? Oh, perhaps three or four years ago. A breeched baby, never."

"And everything turned out okay?"

"Yep, everything turned out fine."

"God is good."

"Yep, all the time."

"Well, what time and what is for dinner, I plan to be starving."

"Must you be starving to enjoy my cooking?"

"Not exactly, but being hungry can make some meals more tolerable."

She said in a humorous tone with a soft laugh that followed. Stenson loved Melanie's sense of humor and her free spirited, lighthearted laughter.

"I have a coupla more stops to make. Dinner will be the chef's surprise and the time of dinner is 1900 hours.

"Thank you Doctor, I will see you at seven. I'll bring the wine."

"Nope, I already have the wine. You just bring yourself and a hearty appetite."

"Yes, Doctor."

"You just spoke two of my favorite words, 'yes' and 'Doctor'." Stenson ended the call and sped towards the market to get the items on his dinner shopping list.

T his was the first time Stenson had prepared a meal for Melanie so he wanted everything to be perfect. His mother, an excellent cook in her on right, had provided him with suggestions for everything from the table setting and wines to appetizers through dessert. She said to him, "Now Stenson, remember, you must have fresh vegetables, meat that has never been frozen and wine which complements but does not dominate."

He also wanted the music and atmosphere to create an ambience that was secure yet seductive. He wanted Melanie to feel comfortable alone with him in his apartment. Although they had known each other for a long time Melanie had never spent an evening alone with him in his apartment. There was always someone else; either she came with a girlfriend or Stenson invited another couple over. Melanie liked it that way. When other people were around it eased the sexual tension she felt when alone with Stenson.

When the doorbell rang, Stenson looked at the clock on the microwave oven. It was 6:55 pm and as usual Melanie was on time. Stenson rushed over to the CD player and put in a disc he had recently burned that contained a mixture of Melanie's favorite jazz and R&B songs. The doorbell rang a second time as he walked across the room, but before opening the door he looked through the peephole, and even with the distorted view of her in blue jeans and a sweatshirt, Melanie's beauty was apparent.

"Welcome." Stenson said as he opened the door bowing and motioning her in at the same time.

"Am I too early?"

"No, not at all. I'm running a little late because it took longer than I thought for the bread to rise."

Melanie entered and was immediately impressed by the wonderful aroma from the kitchen. Playing softly in the background was an old Dusty Springfield tune she had not heard in years. She could not resist the urge to sing along, "I can hardly wait to hold you, feel my arms around you. How long I have waited, waited just to love you now that I have found you..."

"So you like that huh?" asked Stenson.

"That's a classic and one of my favorites. My dad played it all the time when I was growing up. How did you find it?"

"I downloaded it from the net. Come on into the kitchen, dinner is almost ready."

Melanie loved Stenson's apartment. Located in an old warehouse in the downtown section of Memphis, the large loft apartment was quite spacious with huge floor to ceiling windows that gave a breathtaking view of the Mississippi River. She had never asked, but Melanie was sure Stenson's mother had given him a hand with the decorating. It was masculine but fashionable in colors in a range of soft earth tones. A wonderful array of paintings from Art Bacon to Tolliver to Lashaun Beale; sculptures by Ed Dwight and beautiful pottery by Charles Smith enhanced the decor.

Since Stenson spent most of his free weekends moonlighting in rural hospital emergency rooms in neighboring Arkansas and Mississippi, he was able to double his resident salary and his standard of living.

"Stenson your apartment is so nice, and the food smells so good! What in the world are you cooking? I'm going to need a bib to catch my drooling."

"Well my dear Melanie," Stenson said in a mocking French accent.

"Tonight I have prepared for you a wonderful five course meal. We will start with lobster bisque, crab cakes, and a mixed green salad with homemade raspberry vinaigrette."

"Stenson, you have got to be kidding."

Ignoring her comment he continued:

"Our entrée will be roasted rack of lamb with grilled potatoes and we'll have vanilla bean creme brulee with fruit topping for dessert."

Melanie followed Stenson into the dining area. He had selected a bottle of Australian Merlot and motioned her to the seat across from him.

The evening was filled with wonderful music and elegant dining. It was the first time the two had spent this amount of time together without either Stenson getting a page from the hospital or Melanie being side tracked by a late business meeting.

"So tell me about this big project of yours."

"Have you heard of CORE Healthcare?"

"Yeah, I think so. If I remember correctly, they are the largest healthcare management company in the State of Tennessee."

Melanie responded, "Not quite. They're the largest healthcare management company in the Southeast!"

"That's right. They recently took over three managed- care companies which gives them the largest number of patients, or as they say 'covered lives', the largest number of hospitals and more physicians of any healthcare company in the Southeast."

"Well, yesterday I met for lunch at the Metropolitan Club with their president and CEO."

"Really?"

"Really. I met with him to discuss the possibility of taking their company public on the New York Stock Exchange."

"Get the fuck outa here!"

"No really, I'm serious. If we are selected, three of us from McKenzie, Ward, and Lawrence will meet with them in Nashville in about two weeks to close the deal."

"Baby, that's outstanding! How much money will be generated on this deal for your company?"

"Well, usually we get our expenses and we work on an hourly basis. We also get a percentage of the capital raised which averages three percent. So if we raise, through the public offering, somewhere around one hundred and fifty million dollars our company can generate over three million dollars in billing. Additionally, I should receive a nice bonus, anywhere from one hundred to one hundred and fifty thousand dollars."

"I knew I chose the wrong profession." Stenson said as he passed the bread and poured more wine.

"That's enough about my work. Tell me what's going on in your world. What's your next surgery rotation? How is the process going for your pediatric surgery fellowship? What's the update with Gina and how are your mom and dad?"

"Mom and Dad are fine. He's slowed down and is only doing routine general surgery on hernias, gallbladders, and stuff like that. He has also stopped taking emergency room calls."

"Is he still thinking about politics?" Melanie asked.

"I think so. He believes Selma is about twenty years behind the rest of the country and he thinks part of that is the result of Selma's political leaders."

"What's going on with Gina? I lost touch with her right after we graduated but I think of her often. I really thank her for making it possible for me to meet you."

"I haven't heard from Gina in over a year and I have not seen her for over two years. Mom spoke with her doctor in New York and was told she didn't follow through on her chemotherapy. Gina had missed her last seven appointments."

"Is she still in New York?" Melanie asked.

"We don't really know. My father has a private investigator looking for her. There is the possibility she is already dead."

Stenson got up from his chair and began to remove the dishes from the table. He said, "Now it's time for my favorite part of the meal." "What's that?" Melanie asked.

"Dessert!"

"So Stenson, what's going on with your pediatric surgery fellowship?"

"I've finished the application process and now I'm just waiting to see if I can get an interview somewhere."

"Do you have a preference as to where you'd like to go?"

"Well, you know getting accepted is quite competitive since there're only a few programs where pediatric surgeons are trained. So I'll take any place that takes me. I've always wanted to train somewhere in Boston or Baltimore so I've applied to Massachusetts General Hospital and John Hopkins in Baltimore."

"Have you looked into any West Coast programs?"

"It's interesting that you should mention the West Coast. I had considered looking at your home area."

"San Diego?"

"No, I applied to UCSF, the University of California San Francisco, but I didn't apply to the University of San Diego, because my time for applying was limited and getting a placement is so competitive."

"I'd love for you to consider San Diego, my parents would love having you in the area."

"But you also know that my parents would love for me to go to the University of Alabama at Birmingham. Birmingham would be less than a two-hour drive from Selma. So I applied there as well."

"That means you'll be leaving Memphis."

"It looks that way."

Stenson lit the small torch to caramelize the Creme Brulee.

"No." Melanie said with strong conviction.

"No what?"

"I know this is not the first time you've tried this."

But she really knew he was not experimenting with his cooking, and that is what made Stenson so special to her. He was a talented man of many interests as well as a gifted surgeon. Melanie was hopeful that he would complete his pediatric surgery fellowship, because it was what he wanted to do and he would be one of less than one hundred African American pediatric surgeons in the United States. He was devoted to his friends and family; he was honest, dependable, athletic and looked good in both Armani and FUBU. He was also a damn good cook. His mother had prepared him well. But Stenson was certainly a ladies' man and Melanie was well aware of his conquests. She had no intentions of making his or anyone's Conquered List.

There was an unarguable chemistry between them and a number of her girlfriends had said she should "give him some", but she was committed to wait until marriage. She figured, if she had waited this long, waiting a little longer wouldn't make any difference.

"Actually it is. I thought I'd try something new for you," he replied.

The best romance novelist could not have written the rest of the evening. The lighting in Stenson's apartment set the tone for enjoying the wine and wonderful music, which continued song after song after song. As Stenson moved closer to Melanie and replenished her wine, they looked out over the Mississippi River as "A Wonderful World" by Louis Armstrong began playing in the background.

"Melanie."

Her heart began to race. It always raced when Stenson called her name in his soft, sweet tone.

"Melanie, now that all things are falling in place for you, don't you think it's time for you to develop a relationship?"

"Maybe," she said, "Do you have someone you'd like to recommend?"

"Melanie, you know I've been interested in you since your days at Spelman, and you haven't given me a minute of your romantic time. At first I thought it was because you weren't sure I'd finish medical school. But when that happened I accepted the brutal reality that maybe, just maybe I don't turn you on. I figured if you didn't like me, you must like girls."

Stenson broke into his trademark full laugh. Melanie reached out and smacked him softly on the head.

"Don't play, you know I don't roll like that."

"Melanie, you don't roll at all."

"Stenson, listen to me. I think you are wonderful and you're one of my best friends and advisors. You're everything I love and admire in a man. But I don't think you're ready for a commitment and I wouldn't want intimacy or the lack there of, to change what we have. It's too precious to me."

"But I think I'm ready, can't we just take this thing day by day?"

"Stenson be patient, when the time is right we will both know. Right now I don't share your optimism and I believe we'll only get one shot at this. So, I want to do the best I can to create an environment that will be conducive to a successful, long relationship. I don't think I feel what you feel right now, but when the time is right I will."

She was so practical, so smart, so much of what he needed and wanted. He could wait.

CHAPTER

t e n

Three Years Earlier

Gina was Stenson's only sister. She and Melanie had shared an apartment during their senior year at Spelman College. But Gina was attracted for some reason to the seedier side of Atlanta. She experimented with marijuana during her freshman year. Midway through her junior year she was using cocaine to the tune of two hundred dollars a day and spending the weekends dancing at an Atlanta Gentleman's club to support her habit. In spite of all this Gina never missed her classes or made poor grades in her courses. In fact, she made grades that allowed her to graduate from Spelman with honors. Throughout this time she kept her activities and habits a secret from her family and friends.

But Gina had a life-altering experience on her graduation night. Her regular dealer, Peter Pan, had called her the night before her graduation. He said, "Gina, I'm having a few friends over tomorrow evening. Why don't you stop by after your graduation and I'll let you have a free one-on-one."

"Sounds great, I'll be over right after I get my diploma," Gina said with anticipation.

Following the graduation ceremony she told her family she wanted to do some quick shopping and she would meet them later at her apartment. She drove to Southwest Atlanta, where high crime areas interface with upscale institutions of higher learning. This is where she'd meet Peter Pan, her regular supplier of all the illegal intoxicates her body and mind desired.

Upon arrival at the smoked-filled apartment Gina immediately felt uneasy. Although Peter Pan had always been respectful of her there were three other guys in the room who were watching her as if she were a piece of meat and they were hungry dogs. The only other female in the room was focused on getting the last hit of crack in a glass pipe. Her eyes were shallow and empty. She was small and appeared to be in greater need of a Happy Meal than a high.

In the far corner of the room sat a figure who had a small, almost pre-pubic frame. He was holding a lighter, the flame of which was heating the underbelly of a spoon. He drew the contents in a small syringe to inject the substance into his tourniquet-tied left arm. When he raised his head and made eye contact with Gina, she realized this child could be no more than ten years old!

"What is this world coming to?" she thought. But this did nothing to subdue her need for the illegal intoxicating high. Peter Pan came into the room and greeted her, "Come on Gina, I have a special one-on-one for you in the back room."

That special one-on-one was uncut, almost pure. It gave Gina a high that she had not felt since the very first time. Peter Pan opened a bottle of champagne and poured them a toast to the future. The room began to spin, her vision became blurred and as she fell to the floor everything appeared to move in slow motion. Her head met the floor with a loud thud and no pain.

Gina awakened about ten hours later with a severe headache. As she surveyed the room she caught the image of Peter Pan over in a corner slumped in a chair with a 40 ounce in his hand. He appeared to be unclothed from the waist down and breathing shallow. Gina noticed she was lying on a small mattress with a soiled sheet. But she panicked when she saw the small patches of dried blood and semen from her rectum and vaginal area. She touched her face, which appeared swollen, and she could taste the blood in her mouth. But she was unable to open it. She wasn't sure if the intense pain was clearing her head or making her confused. Gina finally stumbled to a telephone and called Stenson.

Gina's surgery lasted eight hours. She had been raped and sodomized with a foreign object that created a fourth degree rectal tear and vaginal fistula. She had been beaten severely about her face and left with a fractured mandible and orbit. She spent two weeks in the hospital and drank through a straw for a month. Gina was never the same after that. She bounced from city to city, job to job and relationship to relationship.

If things were not tough enough almost one year to the date of the rape and beating she began to feel different. Her energy level was low. She had night sweats, shortness of breath and a fifteen-pound weight loss over one month. When she finally visited her doctor for a routine exam he noted several swollen lymph nodes in her neck and femoral area. After describing her additional symptoms, her physician suggested a complete workup including chest x-ray and bone marrow evaluation. Her worst fear was to be HIV positive. Which she believed would be the final insult her body and soul could suffer from that still cloudy evening with Peter Pan.

When the phone call came from her doctor's office his voice was soft and more compassionate than she expected.

"Gina I have some good news and some not so good news." She braced herself.

"Your HIV test was negative but your blood count and bone marrow were abnormal. It appears you have Large Cell Lymphoma."

"What's a lymphoma, Doc?"

"It's a form of cancer that lives in the lymphatic system."

"Well Doc, which is worst HIV or lymphoma?" Gina asked in her typical upbeat tone.

"Gina, there's not a cure for either, but you would probably live longer if you had HIV."

This was the shot in the head. She continued her nomad lifestyle, but was not compliant with her chemotherapy or medical follow-up; she accepted that early death was her destiny. She would never marry, never have children or experience a true career. By all likelihood she would live less than two years.

eleven

Stenson had a rare Sunday off. But even on his off days he was unable to sleep late. He was up at 6:30am and completed five miles on his treadmill plus thirty minutes of weight training. He then sorted through his mail as he reminisced about the memorable dinner he shared with Melanie. He hoped her trip would be more successful than she could expect.

Halfway through his pile of mail, Stenson's attention focused on three large business envelopes and his heart began to race. One of them was from Johns Hopkins University, the others from the University of Alabama in Birmingham and the University of California at San Francisco.

Each letter was from a Department of Pediatric Surgery. His first choice was the University of Alabama in Birmingham; it had a great pediatric surgery program and was in close proximity to both Selma and Memphis. It would give him a great clinical experience and allow him time for research. Birmingham had demographics similar to Memphis, except for professional basketball. Johns Hopkins would also be a great place to study. The major downside was that he really wasn't very fond of Baltimore. But pediatric surgery fellowship spots were very few and so very competitive that he would go anywhere he was accepted.

He held the letters up to the light to see if he could read "Congratulations!" or "We regret..." He could see neither. So he opened the letter from UAB first.

Dr. Hawk:

We have reviewed your application to the University Of Alabama/Birmingham pediatric surgery fellowship program and invite you to schedule an interview with us....

He quickly opened the second letter and again was overjoyed with its content.

"Interviews at both UAB and Johns Hopkins, fantastic!" he thought. And there was also a third letter. He picked up the receiver to call his parents, dialed their number and placed the receiver to his ear without hearing a ring.

"Hello, Stenson?"

"Mom, I didn't hear the phone ring."

"As I was waiting for your phone to ring I could hear you dialing."

"I was calling to give you the good news."

"And what is that good news my dear?"

"Mom, I just received letters inviting me for interviews at UAB and Hopkins."

"Oh, my son, that is wonderful! Your father will be very pleased. When will you go for these interviews?"

"I just got the letters today, so I'll probably try to arrange something in the next couple of weeks."

"I'm sure they must be fighting over you son," said his Mrs. Hawk, spoken like a loving mother.

"Stenson, we are so proud of you. Listen, the reason for my call is to give you an update on Gina."

"Did she call you?"

"No, but as you know your father and I hired a private investigator who believes she has left New York and is in New Orleans."

"New Orleans? Why would Gina be in New Orleans?"

"Apparently, the investigator was able to go through some of the belongings left in her New York apartment. There were three letters with New Orleans postmarks, but no return addresses. They were all from the same person. Someone called James."

"Do you have a last name for him?"

"I don't remember the last name right off, but it did have a Creole sound to it. Has she ever mentioned any acquaintance who has a French surname and currently lives in New Orleans?"

"No, never. And she has never mentioned anything about New Orleans."

"Stenson, hold for your father he wants to talk with you."

"Hey son, I overheard the good news. I told you things would be fine."

"I'm hoping to get accepted at UAB, it would be good to get closer to home."

"We would like that as well."

"Dad what do you make of this update on Gina?"

"Stenson, I don't get my hopes up. I just pray she is still alive and that we will be able to help her before it's too late."

"Dad, I think it may already be to late."

"I know."

twelve

Melanie entered her office the following Wednesday morning and placed her briefcase on her desk, turned on her computer and kicked up her feet.

"Melanie," her secretary's voice reflected the extra shot of espresso she had ordered in her white chocolate mocha at Starbucks that morning.

"Yes?"

"Mr. Bailey is on line one."

Frank Bailey was Senior Vice-President at McKenzie, Ward and Lawrence and was instrumental in recruiting Melanie.

"Good morning young lady."

"Good morning Frank."

"Melanie, I just received an email from Adam Wellington, who informed me that we have been officially selected to take them to the New York Stock Exchange."

"Frank, let me put you on the speaker." She got up from her desk and walked over to a set of golf clubs she kept in the far corner of her office.

" Melanie, what are you doing? Did you hear me say we got the go ahead from CORE?

"Frank, I heard you and I'm ecstatic about the good news. Now I must complete my celebration dance."

"Your celebration dance?"

"Yeah, just a second," she said as she pulled a Titanium putter and a golf ball from her golf bag. Then she walked over to a small putting green, dropped the ball and took the stance her father insisted was the same as Tiger Woods. She also followed her father's instruction to putt "through the ball" and made contact.

"Melanie, are you doing that putting thing again?"

The golf ball rolled in a perfectly straight line and fell into the cup, just as it had with each successful deal since she joined Mackenzie, Ward and Lawrence.

"Did you make the putt?"

"Every time!" Melanie's voice sounded confident as she said, "Okay Frank, what shall we do next?"

"Our presentation committee will hold its first meeting at seven o'clock in the morning to begin preparations," he said.

"When will we leave and what will be our travel presentation route?"

"We will have two weeks to prepare for a meeting in Nashville with the CORE executives. At that meeting we will discuss our travel schedule to Europe and major cities here in the United States. I know we'll travel to Amsterdam as our first stop. Then we'll hit London, San Francisco, Chicago and finish up in Atlanta."

"Any particular reason for that order?"

"We must address the European investors and, while not participating in the Euro currency, London is still a very strong investor in the American market. The Amsterdam and London run will allow us to smooth out our presentation before we get to the States."

"When will we meet the CORE presentation team?" asked Melanie.

"Well, I spoke with Archer Garrett and he's sending a copy of their team makeup and complete financials for the last five years and they are sending their corporate jet to fly us to their Nashville offices."

"Are you kidding me?" The excitement in Melanie's voice was off the scale.

"No my dear, you've made the major leagues."

"Okay, Frank I really have to go now."

"Are you leaving to start packing?"

"No, this is so good I must make a few phone calls."

Melanie then shared the news with her mother and father in San

Diego. She felt good knowing that she had made them proud.

On her drive home Melanie paged Stenson but he had not yet returned her call. Today was clinic day and he was probably still seeing patients. She really wanted to share this news with him before she became consumed in planning for their presentation and her travel to Nashville. When her cell phone rang, Melanie looked at the caller ID and her heart raced. It was Stenson.

"Stenson!" she said.

"You know sometimes I hate caller ID. It's impossible to surprise anybody with that thing. But can you tell me why it never works when the bill collectors call?"

Ignoring his humor Melanie proceeded to share the highlights of her day.

"When are you leaving and for how long?" Stenson asked with a ring of disappointment in his voice.

She told him about their plans and said, "Can you believe that within the next month we'll be making our presentation to some of the leading financiers in Europe?"

"So Melanie how long will you be in Europe?" Stenson asked.

"Well, if all goes as planned we should be back in the States within two weeks after departure. But I'll be better able to tell you when we get back from Nashville."

"Will I see you before you leave?"

"I'd love to Stenson but I have so much to do I can't see where I'll have the time. Please understand."

"I do, but that still doesn't mean I like it."

"Stenson, do you think you could meet me in San Francisco if I give you enough notice to get coverage?"

This was a major breakthrough in their relationship. Stenson had wished for an opportunity to explore a major city with Melanie. He had never been to San Francisco and certainly would not miss the opportunity to visit it with her.

"Are you sure you want me to visit you there?"

"Yes, I think it would be nice for us to hang out there. My parents will be there..."

"What, your parents?" Melanie burst into laughter. Stenson sounded like a little boy after discovering someone had stolen his bicycle.

"Just kidding, my parents won't be there. But don't get any ideas. I just thought it might be good for you to get away for a couple of days. You need a break."

"I know what the deal is, so I won't get my hopes up. Call me whenever and as often as you can."

"I will. Take care."

"Take care."

Later that afternoon in Veracruz, Mexico Phoenix walked across the beautifully decorated suite of the Porta Oaxaca Resort to silence the annoying ringing of the telephone.

"Salut!," said Phoenix.

"They will be leaving for Amsterdam in approximately four weeks."

"Are you sure she is the one?"

"I'm sure."

"Have you made sure everything is in order?"

"I will do a final review before they arrive."

"Will the others traveling with her present a problem?"

"Not at all, I will plan carefully."

"Have the private investigators completed a thorough background check on her?"

"Qui, I have included her family, close friends, their families, anyone and everyone who may benefit us."

"Au revoir!" said Phoenix.

Replacing the phone on the receiver and enjoying the sound of the blue waves rolling in from the Gulf of Mexico, Phoenix smiled. The broad smile continued while lighting a fine Cuban cigar. Great anticipation of what was to come highlighted Phoenix's face. The thought of acquiring a major American company was important to Phoenix, but that was not the paramount focus of this plan.

thirteen

So much work had been done over the past couple of weeks to prepare their presentation that Melanie could hardly believe she was entering the first phase of her whirlwind travel.

"Melanie, it is an absolutely beautiful day! Not one cloud in the sky. I wish I were flying with you to Nashville," said Kathy, talking to Melanie on her cell phone.

She was one of Melanie's best friends since Melanie moved to Memphis.

"Girl it is a beautiful day," responded Melanie as she approached the Memphis International Airport.

Kathy asked, "Is this your first trip on a private jet?"

"No, actually it is my second. My first trip was a business flight to Scottsdale, Arizona."

"Okay, now where are you staying in Nashville and when are you traveling to Europe?"

"Kathy, this is all business. I won't know my precise travel plans until the meeting in Nashville. I'll call you when I get back from Nashville. But I must go now. I'm almost at the airport."

"Okay girl, I'll talk with you when you get back."

"Right, goodbye." said Melanie.

"Bye," answered Kathy in a dejected voice.

As Melanie approached the Memphis International Airport, she thought about how fortunate she had been over the past few years.

Everything was going well, maybe it was time to make a commitment with Stenson, but if she did he would have to marry her. As she pulled into the private flight area the thought of not having to go through all the tight airport security and delays brought her solace.

Only three of them would make the Nashville trip. Frank and Jim Little were in the parking lot when she arrived.

"Well, well, well, if it isn't our golden child. I knew you would be on time for our big event," said Jim Little. He was the lead analyst for McKenzie, Ward and Lawrence.

"I'm always on time," Melanie responded.

Jim had resented Melanie since day one. He viewed her as a quota, and thought she satisfied two minorities because she was an African American and a woman. In his opinion, her studies in higher education, her training and experience had no real merit. He thought her degree from Emory University was certainly a token and the Spelman College degree was a gift. Melanie was well aware of his feelings, which had no impact on her. She viewed him as a rich, good-old-boy; an educated red neck. She also thought he was the kind of white boy who would perpetuate such anti-quated thinking into the twenty-first century and beyond.

Melanie turned her attention to Frank and said, "Have you flown out of here before?"

"Several times, let's go into the Lobby Entrance so an attendant can tell us from which hanger we'll be flying."

Melanie removed her brief case, locked her car and they started walking towards the entrance.

"Melanie, did you get my email that included the final set of CORE's financials?" asked Jim.

"Absolutely. I check my email every night since you often find it inconvenient to notify me about important mail during regular business hours. I have also given the financials a thorough review."

"Jim you said you had told Melanie about that information..." Frank began, but was interrupted by Melanie.

"Oh, that's okay Frank, we both know what the situation is."

The Receptionist in the lobby greeted them.

"Good morning, you must be Ms. Walker, Mr. Bailey and Mr.Little." They nodded affirmatively.

"Ya'll leaving from Station Ten. Is this all the luggage ya'll carryin' on board?"

They nodded affirmatively. Their carryon briefcases were checked and their identification verified.

"The Sky Cap'll shuttle you to th' plane, if ya'll don't have no questions, have a great day."

Each of them smiled at the Receptionist. A Sky Cap transported them in a small taxi to Station Ten, where they would board CORE's Gulfstream for their trip to Nashville. They were about to experience the very best in corporate air travel.

"Good morning, please watch your step." A tall, shapely blonde with a German accent greeted them.

"I'm Gretchen, your flight attendant for this trip. Please be seated and I will take your breakfast orders."

"This is an unbelievable fuselage. The leather and wood trim are the best I've ever seen and I've seen some good ones." Jim said with excitement as his hand moved slowly over the back of his seat.

The interior of the aircraft was nothing short of elegant; there were large individual captain's seats and a large leather sofa in the back of the craft. Each seat had individual monitors with headsets for viewing DVDs or playing video games. As the plane taxied down the runway a voice filled the cabin.

"Good morning, this is your Captain speaking. We have a wonderful day for travel. Gretchen will prepare an appetizing breakfast for you as we cruise to Nashville. Our flight time is forty-five minutes. Enjoy."

"Melanie, I have reviewed the financials sent by CORE and they appear to have been extremely profitable during the last five years." Observed Frank.

"That's putting it mildly," said Melanie.

Then Jim joined in the conversation.

"It appears as if CORE began providing health insurance coverage in the Nashville and Memphis areas. They started in the Memphis area with coverage for Federal Express, AutoZone, and government employees at all levels."

Melanie continued, "But what really set them apart was their creatively developed insurance coverage plans for small business owners who hired less than ten employees."

"I see you did review my email. Anyway, that's true, but what they also did was develop relationships in the State Senate, particularly with members of the Health and Human Resources Board," added Jim.

Gretchen began serving Eggs Benedict with fruit and fresh squeezed orange juice.

"I don't think I'm quite clear on that," said Frank.

"Okay, this is the kicker." Jim said, "the State of Tennessee has a healthcare program for Medicaid and Medicare, which was designed to provide healthcare for everyone in the State who could not afford it. It was set up so the State would make monthly, multi-million dollar, guaranteed payments to these managed care companies or MCO's so they would provide the health coverage."

"Coffee or Tea?" offered Gretchen.

"Yes, coffee for all of us, with caffeine," said Frank.

Jim continued, "Then the managed-care companies contracted with doctors, hospitals, pharmaceuticals and others to provide these services."

"CORE then acquired all the large managed-care companies in the State, some were taken through hostile takeovers, then CORE used its political contacts to have the State Health and Human Resource Committee give them an exclusive arrangement."

"Who oversees that board?" asked Frank.

"Senator Colin Daniels," responded Jim.

"Okay," said Melanie, "next, CORE went into the Central and East Tennessee markets and provided healthcare coverage for all the major companies including employees of academic institutions such as Vanderbilt and Meharry."

"This blue print was later applied to Georgia, Alabama, Louisiana, Mississippi and Texas. Thus making CORE the largest managed care company in the Southeast and certainly a significant part of the Southwest," added Jim.

"Now CORE is looking at the West Coast market," said Melanie, "which has caused a need for their San Francisco office to raise money in this public offering. Raising two hundred fifty million dollars will allow them to become the eight hundred pound Gorilla in the competitive West Coast healthcare arena."

As the threesome finished their breakfast a familiar voice filled the cabin.

"This is your Captain again. We will be landing shortly so please prepare yourselves. There will be a driver on the ground to transport you to the CORE Office Building. Thank you for allowing the CORE air team to be of service to you. Enjoy your stay in Nashville."

fourteen

Stenson and Odellious were looking through the one-way glass window outside the operating room as an anesthesiologist and a resident proceeded to put a patient to sleep. Odellious said to Stenson, "Let's scrub."

They moved towards the large metal sinks and began to wash their hands when Stenson asked, "So what did the CT scan show on this guy?"

Odellious replied, "He's got a dissecting abdominal aneurysm."

"What happened?" Stenson asked.

"Well, if you're drunk out of your fucking mind, driving along at twice the speed limit without a seat belt, lose control of your car in a curve, become airborne and hit the side of a building, you'd get a dissecting abdominal aneurysm too."

They walked backwards through the doors that led into the operating room, keeping their hands slightly elevated to maintain sterility as they moved into the operating suite. The radio could be heard in the background blasting Sting's "If you love somebody, if you love somebody, set them free, free, free, set them free."

The patient's heart rate was a continuous, monitored beat almost in rhythm with the music. The ventilator was supporting his breathing and invasive lines were being used to monitor his heart, blood pressure and other body functions. The circulating nurse walked over with a light blue surgical gown for each of them. Holding their hands above their waists, each doctor simultaneously slid in both arms. This routine was followed with the circulating nurse's application of a glove to each of the doctors' hands.

"Odellious, I've got some good news." Stenson said with a slight grin.

He turned to face Stenson and, with one eyebrow raised asked, "What's up young doctor?"

The nurse tied Odellious' gown from behind and it fit snuggly over his muscular frame. She then tied Stenson's gown.

"I have interviews for pediatric fellowships at UAB, Hopkins, and UCSF."

"Ah baby, exceptional, exceptional! So you got one at UCSF?"

"Can you believe it? The University of California at San Francisco." Stenson tried to conceal his excitement.

"Dude," Odellious' voice was soft yet vibrant, "Of course I can believe it. You have all the right tools for success. What you have accomplished is not an accident; it is by the design of your parents. You are where you're suppose to be at this time in your life."

Looking over the drapes towards the anesthesiologist who stood at the head of the table Odellious asked, while nodding his head in the direction of the patient, "How is he doing?"

"It was pretty rocky when we first put him to sleep. His blood pressure was all over the place, so I have him on some pressers and started some blood so I think he'll be okay."

"Can I make the incision?"

"Cut," said the anesthesiologist.

"Knife please," requested Odellious.

The surgical assistant placed the knife in Odellious' hand. He then made a straight midline incision extending the entire distance of the abdomen.

"He's moving," said Stenson.

Odellious looked over the drapes at the anesthesiologist, sitting on a stool with his feet on the anesthesia machine, reading the *Wall Street Journal*.

"Hey, did you hear us? He's moving." Odellious said again.

"He can't be moving I just gave him a full dose of muscle relaxants."

Suddenly the patient lifted his right hand and attempted to pull out his breathing tube. He was also bending his knees in an effort to move off the surgical table. Odellious, Stenson and the surgical assistant were leaning across the patient to keep him down and at the same time tried to keep the instruments from becoming contaminated.

"Okay, okay, okay. I'll have him back down in a second."

The anesthesiologist then drew up a milky solution and injected it into the patient's IV. Within seconds he was still and the surgery continued.

Odellious and Stenson moved with almost motionless surgical speed. They had worked together long enough for little need to speak. Each knew the other's next surgical movement. The surgery was completed in four hours.

"That went pretty smooth." Odellious said as they moved toward the Doctor's Lounge adjacent to the operating suites.

"I'm going to admit this patient to the Intensive Care Unit for the next couple of days, if that's fine with you," said Stenson to Odellious.

"Of course, let me ask you a question."

"Sure."

"What's up man? You seem to be on the edgy side and it doesn't appear to be about the fellowship shit 'cause you're about assured of a spot somewhere. What else is happening to cause what I am feeling?" asked Odellious.

"Well, I'm not as sure as you are about my success. Look at you, you're the best surgeon on this staff and you've had a hell of a time trying to get a cardiac surgery fellowship."

Odellious had been aggressively recruited to apply to a number of cardiac surgery programs but after each interview he was never accepted.

"Look Dude, we all know or should know how the system works. America isn't as much about race today as it is about economics and social class. You dig?"

Odellious sat at the dictation station but continued to talk, "You see bro, you've got the right pedigree; both your parents are educated, your father's a doc and your sis finished Spelman. It's all good, you speak the language well and you've got that All American glow. You crossover well and you're smart. There is no reason, none, why you can't reach the mountaintop."

"But," Stenson interrupted.

"Hold on Doc, there are no 'buts'. I understand why I haven't gotten a cardiac surgery fellowship. I don't have all the right boxes checked because I haven't been able to change who I am."

Odellious took both of his hands and motioned from his head downward. "My look reflects the roots of my life."

There was silence, then he continued, "Stenson, I've done well to get this far with my history. My role is not to increase my success because I don't have the pedigree to go farther. I came from the other side of the track, but I do want the younger brothers to feel me when I tell them that understanding the inner person is just as important as what they see on the outside. What I like about you Stenson is that what you see inside me is more important than what you see on the outside. With you, I'm given respect; with others I must demand it."

"Odellious, you can still do your thing if you are willing to change some things."

"But that's it Dude, I don't want to change shit and it took me a very long time to realize that. But it's cool with me now. What rubs me is the young brothers, with tattoos, earrings, body piercing and shit, who have three or four baby's mommas and read at a sixth-grade level. You can't look like that if you're not an entertainer, athlete or..."

Stenson interrupted and said.

"But Odellious, you have tattoos and earrings."

"Yeah Doc, but all my children are with my wife and furthermore, I'm a smart, educated motherfucker who can operate his ass off!" He said with a wide smile, extending his closed fist for Stenson to meet with his.

He continued, "But understand Stenson, my role is a support role. I lead my life in a manner from which others can benefit. I want you and the other young docs to be able to stand on my shoulders. Your success is my success. That's why I wrote the letter of recommendation for you and..."

"And I appreciate it big time. Your letter provided my strongest support."

"I called it like it is. Stenson, on the other side, how's your little investment banker?"

"Well man, Melanie has some big things on the table. She is flying high right now and I mean it literally."

CHAPTER

fifteen

The Gulfstream made a soft landing at the Nashville International airport.

"Are you surprised that they didn't send anyone to fly over with us?" Melanie asked Frank.

"No, the reason is probably to allow us time for a private conference prior to the meeting. Since everything is already covered on our end, the meeting should go much faster." Frank responded.

As they departed from the plane the flight crew thanked each of them and again wished them a good Nashville stay.

"These guys believe in first class service," Jim said as he nodded his head toward the black stretch limousine waiting for them. The chauffeur was holding the rear door open.

"Good morning."

The chauffeur spoke and nodded his head simultaneously. As soon as everyone was seated, the limousine moved swiftly through the city and took them to the CORE office complex on West End Avenue, an area of Nashville near Vanderbilt University. The phone in the limousine rang and Melanie answered it.

"Hello, this is Melanie Walker."

"Well, good morning Melanie....", The Bostonian accent sounded familiar to her. "This is Adam Wellington."

"Mr. Wellington how are..."

"Melanie, I asked you to please call me Adam."

"Adam, how are you?"

"Fine thank you, I hope the trip was pleasant for you and your associates."

"Yes indeed. We could easily become spoiled with such travel accommodations."

"Great, if you need any items prior to our meeting please tell our driver and he will stop for you."

"Thank you very much, but we reviewed the major items prior to leaving Memphis, so our meeting should proceed swiftly."

"Well enough. We shall see you shortly."

"Goodbye."

"Goodbye."

Melanie replaced the phone on its receiver and looked up to see Jim and Frank both staring at her with cracked smiles.

"What are you two smirking about?" Melanie asked.

"You're on first name basis with the CEO already?" inquired Jim.

"Please, now you know that is no big deal."

"Whatever we need to do within reason to keep good customer confidence is always wise," said Frank.

The limousine turned off Broadway onto a private street. Slowing at the security guard station, the driver lowered his window and displayed his identification. A courteous smile, nod of the head and speaking like a Walmart greeter, the guard said:

"Have a good day."

Opening with the speed of a turtle, the ornate wrought iron gates parted and the guard motioned them through. Repeating the Walmart greeting in case they missed it the first time, he said again, "Have a good day."

The complex was landscaped with azaleas, Bradford pear trees and a wonderful array of roses and other shrubs. A family of ducks slowly made their way across the road to a small pond located on the grounds of the complex. Jim, Melanie and Frank gathered their belongings as the limousine slowly came to a stop in front of the CORE Office Complex. Frank said, "Okay team, now its time for the main event."

The limo door swung open and each of them, with briefcase in hand, made their exit. They entered the marbled-floor lobby, which was a huge open foyer with floor to ceiling windows of plate glass. It provided a pleasant view of the duck pond and rose gardens. A large, gold-plated CORE logo was centered behind the receptionist desk. Below it was the motto:

"Providing Healthcare to the World."

"Good morning, are you the guests we're expecting from Memphis?" The mid-aged, gray haired receptionist asked in her almost country western tone.

"Yes," said Frank, "we're here to meet with Mr. Wellington and his staff."

"They're expectin' you. Take the elevators on your right to the seventh floor, then go left and you'll find 'em waitin' for you in the Board Room."

The glass elevators enhanced the beauty of the atrium, foliage and sitting areas. Few people were seen in the lobby, using the elevators, or walking about on the different floors as the elevator ascended to the seventh floor. Melanie thought this seemed quite unusual for the number of employees one would expect to see working for a corporation the size of CORE. It was almost as if it were a holiday and everyone was away. When the elevator opened on the seventh floor they stepped out.

Standing at the end of the hallway was Adam Wellington shaking hands with a similarly tall, well-dressed figure.

"Thank you Senator, we appreciate your support," Adam said.

As the Senator turned and walked towards them his face looked familiar to Melanie.

"Good morning Senator Daniels," Frank said.

With a broad smile the Senator responded, "Good morning, how is everyone doing today?"

"Fine Senator, thank you," said Frank.

Senator Colin Daniels was the Tennessee State Senator from Davidson County. He was a member of an extremely powerful and influential Nashville political family. He was chairman of the Senate's Health Care Committee and oversaw a number of State managed-care contracts, and CORE had been the recipient of contracts totaling over a hundred million dollars. The Senator was also known to be quite a ladies' man, which contributed to the failure of three of his marriages. The media was currently reporting turmoil in his fourth. The Senator picked up his pace to a brisk stride to catch the elevator before the doors closed and disappeared inside.

"Good morning, good morning!" His voice full of excitement as Adam extended handshakes to the trio.

"So that was Senator Daniels," observed Melanie.

"I assumed you were already acquainted with Senator Daniels. He's one of the longest serving State Senators and I'm sure your firm contributes to his campaigns."

"No, policy does not allow us to make political contributions and I've never actually met him, although I did recognize him," said Melanie.

Adam hastened to apologize, "I'm sorry, I should have introduced you. The Senator has been a great supporter of CORE in the legislature here in Nashville and we truly appreciate him. Please come in and meet our team."

They walked through large mahogany doors, which automatically opened as they approached, into a spacious boardroom. Three walls were paneled in a dark stained oak and the other wall was floor-to-ceiling, plate-glass windows like those in the foyer. The family of ducks could be seen gliding across the water of the large pond.

When they had all entered the boardroom Adam said, "Please meet the team that will be traveling with you to solicit support for our public offering. You've already been in contact with Archer Garrett, our CFO." Archer was a man in his mid-fifties; his hair without evidence of thinning. He was a shrewd financier and close confidant of Adam's and had been with CORE since its inception.

"Karen Cohen is our senior vice-president of Marketing," Adam continued.

Melanie didn't expect to see another African American but was pleasantly surprised to see another woman.

"And last, but by no means least, please let me introduce you to our chief operating officer and the heart of our operation, Lance Garrison, whom I met during my Boston day."

They all took seats at the large oval table. Lance led the meeting by reviewing the history of CORE, its financial performance over the previous five years, its limited debt, and projected revenues over the next five years. Karen Cohen discussed the marketing plans. While the meeting was to only take a few hours it was becoming quite clear, early during the day, that it might extend well into the night.

"So team," Lance reported, "I believe when we go to the public market, CORE should open with a stock value of eighteen to twenty-two dollars a share. The stock value would allow us to raise over eighty million dollars in the first phase of our public offering."

Melanie spoke then, "Lance," she said, "you have provided us an excellent overview and insight into the history and projected growth of CORE. But I must tell you, I've looked through your numbers and while they are extremely attractive," Melanie paused as if searching for the politically correct, non-offensive thing to say, "I don't understand how CORE has managed to be so profitable even with your low administrative cost. It appears that..."

Adam quickly interrupted. "Melanie as you may have noticed in the financial report our pharmaceutical division is very much our cash cow."

"Yes Adam, I have some questions about that."

But Adam interrupted again, "We have developed a unique method of supplying our enrollees with their prescription medication. For people receiving their insurance through Blue Cross Blue Shield, Aetna, Cigna, and similar companies, they take their prescriptions to a drugstore to be filled. What we do here at CORE is cut out the middleman—the drug store. We own satellite pharmacy distribution stores so..."

Melanie interrupted then, "So this allows CORE to reduce one of its major expenses."

"Correct," said Adam, "By handling our own pharmaceutical distributions we are able to generate significant profits and more effectively control our pharmaceutical costs."

Melanie added, "Which are some of your major costs?"

"Correct," Adam said with a nod of his head.

"But Adam, I can't quite put my finger on it but these numbers cause me some discomfort. I still have some concerns that by opening at such a stock value we may be over pricing ourselves. A price of fifteen to eighteen dollars a share might be more in line with the current market."

"We've had a number of evaluations from three major accounting firms in addition to two brokerage firms that shared some of your concerns, Melanie. But they believe we can make this thing work," Adam concluded.

Lance supported Adam by saying, "I'm comfortable with this market price. Anything less will not allow us to accomplish our goal of two hundred fifty million dollars or more."

Jim then spoke, "We have made arrangements to meet with the potential brokerage and mutual fund investors in each designated city. Our largest investors will be here in the United Sates. Therefore, we will start our tour in Europe in order to work out any kinks in our presentation. When we hit San Francisco, Chicago and Atlanta we should be pretty tight."

"Well, I am quite excited about the opportunity ahead of us. I know that it's late, but we will get you back to Memphis tonight," said Adam.

"Of course," said Frank, "having your own corporate jet is certainly advantageous when one must travel at the end of such a productive meeting."

"You're absolutely correct," Adam responded.

"It is my understanding that you will be flying from Memphis to Amsterdam on Saturday. Is that correct?"

"Yes," Frank replied, "that is our current flight plan."

"Then we will meet you in Amsterdam and we'll travel together for the European tour. Our corporate jet can comfortably accommodate us all and it will be more conducive for travel. We could probably visit more than one city in a day but we won't rush our travel."

"Sounds good," said Melanie, "we'll see you guys in Amsterdam."

They all stood and shook hands. The crescent moon and bright stars that lit the night sky added a sense of celebration. The flight back to Memphis was very relaxing but Melanie knew the next few days would be the most important of her career; she couldn't wait to tell Stenson.

They slept soundly on the flight following a round of Champagne to celebrate. When Melanie arrived at her home it was well after midnight. She checked her answering machine and the only message was from her mother. She knew if Stenson was at home he would be asleep, hopefully alone. It was best to page him, that way if he was busy she wouldn't feel as if she had disturbed him. She dialed the number and placed her phone back on the receiver; it rang in less than ten minutes.

"Hello."

"Melanie what are you doing up this time of morning. Is something wrong?"

"No Stenson, not at all. Actually everything is fine; I'm just getting back in from Nashville. Did I call too late?"

"No, I'm on call here at the hospital. Well, how did it go?"

"Quite well, but it took much longer than expected. I'll be leaving for Amsterdam in a few days. The CORE executives will meet us there."

"Why aren't the members of the Memphis team flying over to Amsterdam with them?"

"I'm not sure, they didn't invite us to fly with them and we didn't ask."

"I see."

"Look Stenson, this is actually why I called. We should be in San Francisco by the end of next week. Will you still be able to meet me there?"

"I'm glad you asked." Stenson replied, "I got Mark to cover for me so I'll be there with bells on."

"Great! I will stay at the Park Fifty-Five Hotel off Market Street. When you make your flight reservations email me so I can arrange for someone to meet you at the airport."

"I'll just take a shuttle to the hotel."

"Are you sure you don't mind?"

" Yes, I'm sure. As a side note, I'm now preparing for my interview at UAB."

"Stenson that's wonderful." Melanie said, not meaning it, because it meant taking him away from her.

Stenson's leaving Memphis to take a pediatric surgery fellowship never set well with Melanie. But she was happy about the fellowship for him because that was what he wanted.

"By the way Melanie, when are you leaving for Amsterdam?"

"We're to meet up with Adam Wellington and his entourage on Sunday, but we will be busy refining our presentation until then."

"Have a safe and successful trip. I'll see you real soon," said Stenson.

"OK," said Melanie, "See you in 'Frisco."

"Peace."

As they hung up their phones, their minds wondered to thoughts of each other and they both began to smile.

CHAPTER

sixteen

She got his phone number from information. He had promised her it
would always be listed in the event she needed to reach him. She used her
last five dollars to purchase a calling card and was happy to hear the dial
tone since the last four public phones she tried to use were out of order. It
was a gloomy, night in New Orleans and had been raining most of the day.
She dialed the area code and seven digits. After the fifth ring the voice mail
picked up. A familiar voice:

"Hello this is Stenson and it should come as no surprise to you that
I'm not home. But I check my voice mail regularly so please leave a
message. Thanks for calling."

After the beep Gina said nothing. She just hung up the phone. She had
not felt well in some time and weighed a little more than one hundred
pounds. If she could just hear Stenson's voice everything would be fine. She
pulled the hood of her jacket over her head and stepped out into the night
rain onto a cobblestone street in the French Quarters.

CHAPTER

seventeen

"Let's make the rounds." Stenson motioned to his surgical team.

"How many patients must we see before surgery?" Stenson asked the senior medical student whose responsibility it was to keep a list of all the surgical patients with whom they needed to do follow-up visits.

"There are ten patients on our service," the medical student replied.

The surgical team consisted of three medical students, one surgical intern, Mark and Stenson. There was also an attending surgeon who rounded with the team. Dr. Odellious Brown was rounding with them this morning.

Their first stop was a Nurses' Station, which was almost like Grand Central Station. Medical students were retrieving charts, the nursing staff was reporting to the oncoming shift team and the unit secretary was busy removing physicians' orders from charts.

"Listen up everyone, the first patient is in Room 362."

The senior medical student was about to give a report. Odellious said, "Give us the history, current condition, medical plan and let's move on. I have a 7:30am gallbladder to do."

"Yes sir," said the senior medical student.

The entire trauma surgery team was dressed in long white coats except for the medical students who wore short coats. They had gathered close outside Room 362, as if in a football huddle, in order to hear the medical student's description of the patient.

He said, "Mr. Jones is a twenty-three year old male on Day 102 of hospitalization."

Dr. Odellious Brown asked, "Day 102 of hospitalization?"

"Yes sir." The medical student responded, "Mr. Jones has a known history of crack cocaine abuse. In order to pay for his drug addiction, he routinely beat his mother to make her give him her paycheck. During their last altercation his mother refused to turn over her check and when the beating began, she stabbed Mr. Jones in the chest with a large kitchen knife. Mr. Jones arrived in the Trauma Unit with a large knife in his right ventricle. He underwent emergency open heart surgery and received more than twenty-five units of packed red blood cells, multiple units of platelets, and fresh frozen plasma."

"How long was he on the ventilator after surgery?" asked Dr. Brown.

"Three weeks sir," said the medical student, "He ultimately required a tracheotomy."

"I'm surprised he didn't develop ARDS," said Dr. Brown.

"AIDS?" inquired the student.

"No, ARDS," said Stenson, "ARDS refers to Adult Respiratory Distress Syndrome. It is primarily a pulmonary complication which can occur after massive blood transfusions. In essence, the ARDS patient's lungs fail to exchange oxygen and carbon dioxide."

Mark continued, "It's life threatening and such patients almost always die. Some doctors believe if they don't die, they never had ARDS."

"The patient spent over two months in intensive care and required multiple surgical procedures." added the resident.

A first-year student asked, "Were charges pressed against his mother?"

"None. Strangely, this incident has brought them closer. His mother has visited him everyday during his hospitalization. Social services had him in therapy for his crack cocaine addiction and the Chaplain informed me that he attends noon Bible Study everyday."

"Let's go in and say hello," suggested Odellious.

In sets of two, they moved into the room, with Dr. Odellious Brown and Stenson leading the way. The others entered in order of seniority.

Juwan Jones was standing at the window looking out at the morning sunrise. He felt he had been given a second chance at life and he wasn't going to blow it this time.

"Mr. Jones?" said Dr. Brown, "Good morning young man."

"Good morning doc, call me JJ, that's what my friends call me." His demeanor was soft, in contrast to his hard appearance.

"I understand that you will be leaving us today," said Dr. Brown.

"Yes sir, I think I already wore out my welcome," answered Juwan.

"JJ we need to take a look at your wounds and your tracheotomy site," said Stenson.

"Sho' doc," said Juwan.

Juwan lay on the bed and pulled up his hospital gown. An incision down the middle of his chest and a large wound on the left chest reflected the knife injury. Also, he had a large abdominal incision from surgery for a bleeding stress ulcer that occurred during his intensive care stay. The wounds had healed quite well, including the tracheotomy site.

"Well JJ," said Odellious, "it appears that you have survived a close brush with death. I hope you have reflected on this experience and will make the appropriate changes in your lifestyle."

"Doc, I done lived hard and fast in my short life. I done done things dat only Jesus and a mother could fo'give. When I leave here today, I sho ain't the same man dat come to you wit a kitchen knife in his ches'."

"JJ, I wish I could get a dollar for every time I heard someone...."

"I know, I know," interrupted Juwan, "Let's see, let's jes' wait and see what de' future hold."

"Fair enough," said Odellious.

He took an ink pen from his lab coat pocket and began to write on the notepad next to Juwan's nightstand. He tore off the paper and handed it to Juwan.

Then said, "JJ, I have a program called Touch One where we help young men like you get their lives turned around. Call me, I'd like to get you connected with some of the guys and girls in our program. If you really want things to get better for you, we can help."

Juwan folded the paper and held it in his hand as if to prevent someone from taking it.

"Dr. Brown, I will sho' nuff call you. I want to be straight, I need someone to touch my life."

"Cool," Odellious said as he extended his hand and gave Juwan a firm grip, pulling him close so their chests met and their free arms were encircling each other.

"Take care JJ, I'll sign your discharge papers and look for you at our next Touch One meeting." said Odellious.

"I'll be there," said Juwan.

"Well it looks like we may have done a complete life save, body and soul," said one of the students.

"As Mr. Jones so eloquently put it, let's see what the future holds," Stenson said.

Upon completion of their rounds, Odellius conducted the mid-week M&M conference. When he called for the final case of the day, Stenson turned to Mark and asked, "Have you heard about the case Lee Chang is about to present?"

"No I haven't, is it good?"

"Just listen."

Lee Chang had strong Asian features but spoke perfect English. He was a native Californian who chose Memphis for one of his rotations to expand his knowledge of regional diversity in America.

"Dr. Chang is scheduled to make the final presentation for this session." said Dr. Odellious Brown. Dr. Chang approached the podium for his presentation and said, "My patient is a twenty-five-year-old man who visited the Emergency Room with rectal pain and abdominal fullness, resulting from his placement of a clawless gerbil into his rectum. After the patient made multiple unsuccessful attempts to rectally remove the gerbil, he came to the Emergency Room and underwent exploratory abdominal surgery where a single dead gerbil was removed from his colon. Apparently it crawled up from his rectum and died in the colon from a lack of oxygen."

He motioned to the projector, which was turned on by a medical student. A drawing of a gerbil in a running motion inside the colon of a bending male brought a uproar from the audience. Odellious just shook his head, Lee Chang with an impish smile motioned for the projector to be turned off. Stenson and Mark guffawed.

"Okay Dr. Chang, thank you for your presentation," said Odellious. "This ends our mid-week conference."

eighteen

Melanie led the way as she, Jim and Frank sprinted through the Memphis International Airport to catch their KLM flight to Amsterdam. When they arrived at Gate 18 Jim and Frank were both winded and flushed red in the face.

"You guys should take aerobics or something," said Melanie.

"Okay Ms. Fitness America," replied Jim, "if I were your age I could run it too."

"Let's get on board guys before we miss our flight. And for your information I was never able to run that fast at any age," said Frank.

They settled themselves in the first class section rows one and three. As the plane taxied down the runway Melanie again thought of how blessed she had been. As she peered out the window watching the City of Memphis get smaller and smaller Melanie reflected on the new business territory she had entered. She was glad to be seated next to Frank.

"Frank I'm glad I'm sitting with you on this flight. I couldn't take an eight hour flight next to Jim," Melanie said to Frank in a whisper.

"It is my wish that you can use this trip as an opportunity to improve your relationship with Jim. He really isn't as bad as you think."

First class seating made the eight-hour flight more tolerable. The in-flight movies were good but Melanie spent the majority of the trip enjoying "easy-listening" music, which included the Best of Bert Baccarat playing on satellite radio. As they approached Amsterdam, the runway glistened from the rain earlier that morning. It made the landing look like a natural fantasy. The runway lights embraced the KLM flight as it landed at The Netherlands International Airport.

Frank said, "Let's go guys, this is our first challenge."

"What is that?" Asked Melanie.

"That's where we make our way through customs," Frank answered.

They finally began making their way to Baggage Claim , and through customs, weaving in and out of other travelers like a Chicago driver on the Dan Ryan Expressway, skilled, yet dangerously aggressive. The Amsterdam Airport was spacious with décor reminiscent of a suburban shopping Mall. There was an abundance of retail stores, from high-end apparel to "duty free" liquor stores; and the travelers represented every part of the globe and seemed to speak every living language.

Melanie turned to Frank and said, "Do you speak a second language?"

"My wife says I do, usually it's mostly four-letter words spoken when the bills arrive each month."

"I wish I were multilingual," revealed Melanie.

"It would be interesting to have a conversation with some of these travelers."

"I'm sure that most of them speak English." Frank said.

"Sure, but that's not the same as speaking to someone in their native language."

"I've always enjoyed flying through Amsterdam's airport. It's better than shopping in a mall," Jim said.

"I've noticed that airport security is very tight here," said Melanie as she motioned to a pair of paramilitary soldiers in full gear with Uzis.

"Security has always been tight here, and in most major airports in Europe, even before America's 9/11," said Jim.

He continued, "You guys meet me at the entrance area. I'm going to see if there is a shuttle to the hotel. Melanie do you remember the name of the hotel?"

"It's the Amstel Inter-Continental."

"The Amstel Inter-Continental, great," Jim answered. He then turned and disappeared into the sea of travelers. Melanie loved European fashion which was represented extremely well on travelers and in the Amsterdam shops. Her first trip to Amsterdam was during her sophomore year at Spelman when she traveled with her parents to France. She was first introduced to the square-toed, wedged heel shoes in Amsterdam and learned to appreciate the seamless appearance provided by thongs. On first impression she thought they would be uncomfortable, but found them to be her favorite undergarment.

As Melanie and Frank made their way to the front entrance of the international airport, Jim called out to them, "Hey guys, come on the shuttle is boarding already."

Looking at Jim's flushed face Frank suggested, "Guys you know we should start doing lunch aerobics when we get back."

Melanie responded, "I already go to the sessions on most days."

"It's not going to happen with me," said Jim.

An attendant loaded their luggage as the driver opened the taxi shuttle for them to enter.

"This is the other thing I like about traveling in Europe." Melanie said while lowering her head to enter the taxi.

"And what is 'this other thing' you like about traveling in Europe my dear Melanie?" Frank asked.

"Europeans travel in style when possible. American taxis are Fords and Chevrolets; European taxis are Mercedes Benzes and BMWs. This I like."

The car door was closed after they all were seated and the driver headed towards the Amstel Inter-Continental Hotel, which overlooked the Amstel River. It had an impressive mansard roof and wrought iron window guards.

"Welcome to the Amstel Inter-Continental Hotel," was the greeting of the doorman, in an English-wrapped-in-Dutch accent. Melanie was impressed with the stately beauty of the graceful Grand Hall. The Amstel was the Rolls Royce of Amsterdam Hotels. It had hosted such guests as the late Princes Diana, Mick Jagger, Bill Gates and Sean "P Diddy" Combs.

Frank said to Melanie and Jim, "Let's get unpacked and meet in the La Rive restaurant for dinner. I've already reserved a private dining area so we can make our last minute run through before our presentation in the morning."

"Is that when we'll meet with the CORE team?" asked Jim.

Melanie answered, "They should be flying in by private jet this evening. Adam said he'd call us when they arrive."

When Melanie entered her room, she was awe-struck with its beauty. It boasted all the elegance of a country manor, complete with antiques and genuine Delft blue porcelain. The room was quite large and had a fax machine, personal answering machine, VCR, stereo sound system and CD player complete with some of her favorite CDs. The Italian marble bathroom was magnificent with separate areas for the toilet and shower.

Adam and his associates, Karen Cohen and Archer Garrett accompanied by Senator Daniels, were headed towards Amsterdam. The Gulfstream had experienced some head wind, which delayed the transatlantic trip by one hour. Adam said to Senator Daniels, "Senator, I believe we've covered all the details of our stock offering. It is very important that the pension fund for State employees make a significant investment into our opening stock."

"Adam, as you know, I have a great relationship with the mutual fund broker to which the State has assigned the pension plan. It has a value of approximately three hundred million dollars."

Archer Garrett, then asked the Senator, "How much of that amount do you think could comfortably be shifted to our public offering without drawing much attention?"

"It's important that this deal is advertised as being 'in the best interest' of the State employees and our local business community," responded Senator Daniels.

"So what's the bottom line?" asked Archer.

"The bottom line is, it depends on how much CORE is willing to spend to make this happen. I believe I can give you something you can feel. What's most important at this point is that you make a legitimate effort to get investors during your European and American tours," replied the Senator, and he continued, "If you do that, I will be able to solicit the kind of support you'll need to get the State pension investment. We are talking hundreds of millions of dollars."

Adam looked the senator straight in the eyes and with his Boston accent said, almost in a whisper, "Senator we will give you all the credibility you'll need to take this to the brokerage company. We must raise significant capital. Hundreds of millions of dollars will not be enough. We have high expectations in your ability as a politician and legislator." Then Adam continued in a louder and more jovial voice, "Enjoy your stay here in Amsterdam. Our jet will be at your disposal whenever you are ready to return to the States." Adam extended his hand and the Senator shook it.

"I won't disappoint you," said the Senator.

"You never have," Adam responded.

With permission to land, the plane finally touched the tarmac at The Netherlands International Airport. The seven-hour trip had allowed sufficient time for Adam, Senator Daniels and Archer Garrett to discuss tomorrow's presentations.

The three deplaned and entered separate limousines that were awaiting them. Each had a different destination but similar objectives: to score big.

Senator Daniels anticipated enjoying one of a series of all expense paid trips to Amsterdam. This was a gift from CORE for his loyal support in the Senate on a number of legislative votes. His support had allowed CORE to have a monopoly on healthcare for the Medicare and Medicaid population of the entire State of Tennessee. The Senator loved Amsterdam; he enjoyed the coffeehouses with their abundant selection of marijuana and hashish, the purchase and consumption of which was legal. He also cherished the anonymity Amsterdam provided. It enabled him to casually stroll the Red Light District and carefully inspect the prostitutes that offered themselves in the store windows of the Amsterdam brothels. The Senator shook his head when he thought about how much potential tax revenue the State could generate if it took the same approach as The Netherlands regarding the legalization of drugs. Maybe that should be his next bill proposal.

nineteen

"Well Dad, I dialed the number that showed up on my caller ID, but it was a pay phone."

"And you believe Gina had telephoned you from that phone?" asked his father.

"I can't think of anyone else who would call me from a New Orleans payphone."

"Okay son, don't tell your mother, I don't want her to get her hopes up. Okay?"

"Okay. Let's change the topic for a minute."

"Okay son, what's on your mind?"

There was a short pause. Then Stenson asked, "How's your political career looking?"

"I look at it more as a service than a career. I have no plans for being a career politician. But, I do have a committee currently investigating my chances for becoming a United States Senator from Alabama and I actually think my chances for winning are quite good."

"So Dad would we call you Senator Doctor Hawk, Doctor Senator Hawk or just Senator Hawk."

They both laughed the same laugh.

"How is Melanie?" Dr. Abraham Hawk asked as he changed the subject.

"I received an email from her this morning. She's in Amsterdam on the European leg of a trip with McKenzie, Ward and Lawrence, the company for which she works. They are getting investors for a healthcare company called CORE which plans to go public on the New York Stock Exchange."

"CORE?" asked Dr. Hawk.

"Yeah, CORE."

"Is that the Nashville-based, CORE Healthcare Enterprises that handles state and private contracts to provide healthcare coverage?"

"Yes, I'm pretty sure Dad. Why?"

"That's interesting." said Dr. Abraham Hawk

"Dad,why?"

"Well Stenson, I was approached by a representative of CORE just over a month ago."

"Really?"

Stenson asked with great surprise. Dr. Hawk continued, "Apparently, CORE identifies either current or potential legislators and provides them financial support, marketing and advisors at reduced fees. In some cases I've been told, they actually provide these services for no fees."

"How do their candidates do?"

"They actually do quite well."

"Great, are you going to use them?"

"I wouldn't touch that group with a hundred-foot pole." responded Stenson's father.

"I don't understand Dad."

"Stenson, always remember nothing in life is free, especially in politics. What CORE does after supporting these guys is tell them on which senate committees they must become members. And if they are successful in chairing one of these committees they receive gifts such as travel with all expenses paid, cars for their mistresses and other perks."

"And what does CORE get?"

"Please understand Stenson, this is all rumor, but it is claimed that they get to use the political influence. This occurs both in the form of votes and, or the legislature's ability to influence outcomes. That's how they've become the largest providers of covered Medicaid care in all the states where they are affiliated. They also provide healthcare coverage for a number of those states' employees."

"Shit! Oh, sorry Dad, I meant wow!" said Stenson.

"Really 'shit' may have been the more appropriate word because as a result of their domination in the markets they serve their payments to doctors, hospitals, pharmacies, and others is always much lower than in states where CORE has no control of the market. By making these rates so low, a number of physicians cannot afford to provide adequate services and as a result, adequate healthcare in some areas has declined. Consequently, the patients aren't being cared for so CORE doesn't have to pay out any money; which results in even greater profits for them."

"But Dad, has no one complained about this? Isn't this illegal?"

"It may be unethical but it's not illegal. Also, I'm sure that due to the amount of money involved the players keep their mouths shut and keep their hands open. Now, you understand why I want no parts of CORE, even if they are clean, I want to stay away from anything that could have a potential for controversy. As an African American politician, here in Alabama, a scandal could have me swinging from a corrupt political tree."

"I understand Dad."

"Tell Melanie I wish her well, she should make a lot of money getting these guys on the New York Stock Exchange."

"I will and telephone me with an update if you get any more information about Gina."

"Okay son."

Stenson placed the phone on its stand with feelings of despair. Ever since he could remember his father had instilled in him the responsibility to care for his younger sister. He remembered when Gina encountered her first school bully. She was six and he was ten. An older boy came up to Gina demanding her tennis racket; when she refused he punched her twice in the stomach. Stenson's father said to him when they arrived home, "Now Stenson, you must protect your sister, especially if some boy is going to fight her."

Stenson remembered what his father had said.

"What do you want me to do Dad?" Stenson asked.

"Son, you give the kid one warning, tell him if he hits your sister again, you will hit him twice as hard and twice as many times. You understand?"

Stenson looked into his father's stern dark brown eyes, which for him represented wisdom, strength and love. His father continued, "Son I don't want you to pick fights but I want you to defend yourself and your sister."

Stenson nodded affirmatively, he understood the command and would not fail the mission.

A few days later Stenson was told by one of his friends that the same kid had punched his sister again. Stenson had already given the bully notice that he would receive an unadulterated ass whipping if he as much as looked at Gina too hard. Stenson cornered the bully while he was at the baseball diamond. Despite being out weighed by twenty pounds, he punished him severely. He reflected on that experience when he finally caught Peter Pan, Gina's assailant and drug dealing associate. Peter Pan was found in his apartment unconscious with a skull fracture secondary to blunt trauma. The list of potential suspects, which never included Stenson, was so long the assailant was never found.

The phone rang. Stenson reached over to pick up the receiver.

"Hello." He could hear the greeting from his answering machine.

"Hello this is Stenson....." He was so deep in thought he did not realize the phone had been ringing and the answering machine had kicked in.

"Hold one second so I can cut off the answering machine."

Stenson said, speaking to the unidentified caller as he pressed a button to disable the answering machine.

"Okay," Stenson said as if speaking to himself.

"Hello, this is not the recording."

There was a long pause; Stenson could hear faint breathing in the receiver. His heart began to pound in sequence with his rapid breathing. He could feel the vibrations from the person on the line. In a soft, almost trembling voice he said, "Gina?"

Her tears were audible between her labored breathing. More than a year had passed since they last spoke. So many things had transpired since then.

"Stenson, it is so good to hear your voice. Have you considered upgrading your answering machine? That way you won't have to rush to cut the doggone thing off."

Her voice evidenced a love for life. She always seemed in a hurry, having to do it all so fast. She valued the importance of time and the fact that it is irretrievable once it's gone. Her voice was clearly weakened by the advancing lymphoma which rested in her lungs.

"Gina, how are you? I haven't heard from you for much too long. What in the world have you been doing? How...."

"Stenson, easy up, you are bombarding me with questions. Let's take them one at a time."

"Okay, one at a time. How are you?"

"Well big brother I am doing fairly well. As you probably know I am here in New Orleans and I've been here for just about nine months."

"Are you working."

"Yep, you know how I enjoy music."

They both shared a deep love for music; something passed to them from their parents. There was always music in the house: Miles Davis, Wes Montgomery, Dionne Warrick, every musician and type of music.

"Yep, I have two music jobs."

"Two?"

"I have one job selling pianos at a place called The Piano Store on Canal Street. The second job is at Tower Records. You know Stenson, this stuff about people not hiring you because you may be over qualified is bull. Immediately after reviewing my application, they hopped on me at both places."

"I guess when you can get a college graduate at a reduced hourly rate, hey, what can you say?"

"That it's a good deal," said Gina.

"So how's your health?"

"Mental or physical?"

"Both."

"Lets not talk about me just yet. How're Mom and Dad doing these days?"

"You really should call them Gina. You know Mom is worried sick and Dad has spent an arm and a leg on private investigators looking for you."

"Stenson, I'm so sorry. But I really needed this time to try and find myself. It's been so hard."

Stenson could hear her voice began to crack.

"Gina, don't cry," said Stenson, "I didn't mean to upset you. But we have all been so worried you just don't..."

She interrupted, "Stenson I know. I'll call them in a few days. Just let me run a few more things through my head."

"Look, I have a few days off. I'm meeting Melanie in San Francisco." Gina perked up;

"Melanie, really? How is she?" Gina began to speak slowly as if cross-examining a witness.

"Why are you meeting her in 'Frisco? Are you two finally a couple?" Stenson laughed.

"That's a bit of a stretch, a couple, but I'm going to meet her there and hang out for a few days."

"I think that's great. You know I love Melanie. She's really a good woman, Stenson."

"I agree. But look, why don't I fly into New Orleans overnight on my way to Birmingham?"

"Birmingham?"

"Yeah, I have an interview with UAB's Pediatric Surgery Program."

"Ooh big brother, that has made my day. Have I ever told you how proud you make me?"

"You stopped when you turned thirteen." They both laughed.

"I'd like to see my big brother, but no lectures."

Stenson said in agreement:

"No lectures. But do call Mom and Dad."

"Tell them that you spoke with me. I will call them within the next two days."

"Why are you waiting?"

Gina lied, "That's when I'll have my phone turned back on." They both laughed again.

"Well, I see that some things never change. You couldn't remember to pay the phone bill in college."

"And I still can't remember to pay the damn thing now."

Again they laughed. Their hearts were warm, and beginning to feel whole because they were happy to touch after so long. Stenson scrambled for a pen and paper and said, "Give me your address and will-be phone number when it gets connected."

"I'm living down in the French Quarters on Toulouse off St. Peters, about three blocks from Jackson Square." Gina lied again. She began to cough.

"Are you alright?" Stenson asked.

The coughing became more forceful.

"Gina, are you alright?"

Her coughing was almost rhythmic. Stenson was familiar with that sound, he had heard it often in patients struggling with terminal disease.

"Gina, Gina, are you alright?"

His heart was beating rapidly. Now he was yelling into the receiver.

"Stenson," Gina said, the coughing now interfering with her ability to speak, "I need to be a little better before I see you." The phone was silent.

"Gina, Gina, Gina!"

He could only hear the dial tone. Stenson set the pen and paper on his desk and walked slowly over to the large bay window, with its view of the Mississippi River. The lights on the tug boats were sparkling on the river like tiny dancers. It was good to hear Gina's voice, but he knew she wasn't well. He knew he would have to go New Orleans right away, he knew he must find her now.

twenty

"What time is it?"

The excitement could be heard in Adam's voice.

"It's eight thirty-five. Are you nervous?"

Melanie asked as if to tease.

"I shouldn't be, we have covered everything," Adam responded. There was a pause, and then he asked, "Haven't we?"

Frank, Jim and Melanie had been briefing the CORE presentation team for their first Investor's Meeting since 5:00 that morning. In addition to Archer Garrett, Karen Cohen and Ron Spencer their senior vice president of Marketing were present.

"Of course. Now let's do our final run through. I will do the introductions."

"What investment entities do you anticipate?" asked Adam.

"Hold on Adam," Melanie said as she raised her palm, sounding somewhat agitated.

"When I complete my introductions you will then give a history of CORE." Pointing to a laptop computer she continued, "Your entire presentation is on the hard drive. I do trust that each of you reviewed the Powerpoint presentation which was emailed to you prior to your departure from Nashville."

Everyone nodded affirmatively except Adam. Speaking in a tone reminiscent of a child explaining a broken window he said, "Melanie, I haven't reviewed the slides. So I won't do my part with the laptop presentation but I am the company's history and can present it well. I don't need visual aids."

"If you wish," said Melanie.

Turning to Archer and Ron, both appearing uncomfortable but stylish in the oversized chairs that almost seemed to swallow them, Melanie said, "After Adam, Archer you become the reason everybody is here. You will give them the bottom line numbers."

"How detailed should I be?" asked Archer.

"As you remember," said Melanie, "we discussed your presentation in detail. With all the concerns surrounding corporate financial misadventures, your financial projections and current cost, profits and earnings before taxes will be scrutinized. Therefore, all of these topics, including the impact of our current economic environment must be discussed in detail, give them everything, let there be no room for assumptions."

"You may also want to remind everyone that we have already sent a complete five-year evaluation of CORE's financial statements to all potential investors," Frank added.

"Thanks Frank," Melanie said.

"Frank will also give us a run down of all the investing institutions that responded to our announcement."

"I guess I will pull up the rear," Ron commented.

"You got it my friend," Melanie said.

"You will give the current lay of the land: competitors, strengths, weaknesses and future growth."

"I've reviewed everything and I'm ready," Ron said.

"Good. Frank, give us the run down on who will be present this morning."

Frank spoke as he passed out a list of potential investors.

"We are expecting three institutional investors and a representative from one bank. Two European venture capital groups who are aggressively trying to get into the United States healthcare market will also be present."

"Do we really want to wed ourselves to venture capitalists at this stage of the game?" asked Adam.

"No, we really don't," answered Frank, "What could happen is that the VCs would want to drive the company for its maximum value. Then four or five years down the road they would likely force us to sell or merge with some larger competitor. They would push up the stock price, sell and ride off into the sunset. They usually look for a thirty to forty percent return on their investment."

"So we really want the institutional investor guys. Generally they bring much more to the table financially and can provide more long-term stability," said Melanie.

After giving everyone a minute to review their lists, Melanie continued, "Okay, so please note the three institutional investors on your list. But pay particularly close attention to Francoise Baptiste, his company represents pension funds for more than five hundred European-based companies including European divisions of Federal Express, Dorchel International of Paris and America On Line. They manage over $850 million in pensions and mutual funds and a number of investment companies follow their lead. If we get significant investments from them, others will follow. Francoise Baptiste is their CFO and will be here representing them."

The room was silent, each introspective about the long, arduous preparation which was necessary to get to this moment. Melanie thought about her desire for financial independence and the notoriety associated with wealth. There was always the possibility of celebrity status associated with television appearances on financial programs like 'Financial', 'Bloomberg Report' or 'CNN's Lou Dobbs Tonight'. She was keenly aware that her career success had been supported by others. She stood on the shoulders of many to reach this space in time. Melanie wondered if Stenson was okay and smiled when she thought of seeing him in San Francisco.

"Okay team, you have all done extraordinary preparation," Adam's voice appeared distant, slowly coming into focus, gently pulling Melanie from her thoughts.

"It is approaching the working hour," He continued with great energy, as he glanced at his platinum Ebel.

Adam was standing in the center of the small but elegant conference room where the dome-shaped ceiling and gold plated crown molding cast a regal atmosphere. The potential investors, most with the attentiveness of a cat watching fish in a pond, waited to hear his words. Adam's gray-streaked hair highlighted his thick black eyebrows, along with his sculptured chin and uncharacteristically full lips, gave him the appearance of a mature Adonis.

He said, "This is something much larger than I could have ever dreamed. This is our opportunity to share with the healthcare and financial communities of the world. It is a benchmark for future corporate healthcare entities that are truly committed to supporting quality healthcare for patients and competitive reimbursement to healthcare providers that share our vision. And there will certainly be a solid financial return to those shareholders who support us."

Francoise Baptiste appeared tanned and energetic after a recent Mediterranean vacation. He nodded with signs of satisfaction as he listened to Adam speak.

"I will keep the promise I made at the onset of this meeting; to be brief. You will hear from Archer Garrett our Chief Financial Officer followed by Ron Spencer our Senior Vice-President of Marketing."

Archer and Ron moved through their presentations, laying the information out as artists painting on canvas. They answered a variety of questions which ranged from corporate ethics to projected earnings per share over the next five years. The mood was festive when the presentation ended, with Melanie moving from guest to guest confirming the benefits of investing in CORE's upcoming public offering on the New York Stock Exchange.

"Madame Walker."

Melanie turned to look in the direction of the French-accented voice.

"I am quite impressed with what I see," said Francoise.

"Well thank you, we believe this public offering has the potential to be the largest on the NYSE this year."

Melanie spoke in her business tone, which her girlfriends describe as her "white girl voice."

"Yes Madame, I agree that Mr. Wellington's company does look quite attractive, but I was referring to my appreciation of an intelligent, beautiful American investment banker."

He extended his slender hand, which seemed to belong to a pianist.

"My name is..."

But before he could finish Melanie said, "I know who you are," she smiled, "you are Monsieur Francoise Baptiste, the internationally known financier. I hope you strongly consider investing with CORE, we...."

"Madame Walker, I believe the presentation speaks for itself, as I understand it, your team will be making a presentation in San Francisco following your London meeting."

And before Melanie could respond a familiar voice intervened, "Francoise," Adam walked over with outstretched arms, "How are you my friend and how is your boss?"

"Adam, I am quite well and my boss who is equally well sends you best wishes," said Francoise.

They greeted each other with the two-sided face kiss, a fashion acceptable in Europe. Then, turning to Melanie, Adam said, "Francoise, I see you've met Ms. Walker our shining star."

"Adam I had no idea that you and Monsieur Baptiste know each other."

"Indeed we do, at one point we shared the same boss," said Francoise.

"And what a boss!" Adam added.

They both laughed like two schoolboys telling a dirty joke.

"Indeed, indeed," said Francoise speaking to both of them, "As I was about to discuss with Madame Walker, I should be arriving in San Francisco at the same time as your presentation and I thought it would be quite nice if she and I could discuss more details over dinner while in San Francisco."

"I believe that we should be able to...." Adam began,

"I'm sorry Adam," Francoise said as he turned and placed his hand gently on Melanie's shoulder, "I believe Madame Walker is more than capable of handling my questions concerning the public offering of CORE Healthcare."

"Francoise, I sincerely appreciate your offer but I have already planned..."

Adam, looking directly at Melanie with a slight frown on his forehead, said, "Francoise, CORE has paid Ms. Walker's company handsomely for her time and I'm sure she'll look at dinner with you as an extension of this project. She will be delighted to dine with you. Isn't that correct, Melanie?"

Adam's blue eyes confirmed his position but Melanie started to speak, "Adam I really must..."

Adam interrupted, speaking in a tone reminiscent of her father when she was a child.

"Melanie, isn't that right?"

The brain waves went into action. If she were able to secure the investment of Dorchel International she would be on a level that could not be easily paralleled. Not to mention Francoise was extremely rich, powerful and as she would later tell the girls, smooth.

"I'm sure that I will be able to rearrange some of my plans for dinner," said Melanie.

"Excellent, Madame Walker."

"Please call me Melanie."

"Melanie, do you favor a particular restaurant in San Francisco?"

"No, not at all. Your choice of restaurants will be just fine."

"Wonderful, I have an excellent place for you. Where will you be staying?

"The Park Fifty-Five Hotel," said Melanie.

"I usually stay at the Ritz Carlton, so let me call you when my flight arrives."

Adam inquired, "On which airline will you arrive? We can have someone pick you up."

"I appreciate the offer, my friend, but we travel via corporate jet and have ground service waiting when we arrive."

Softly stroking Melanie's shoulder Francoise gazed deeply into her eyes as if to pierce her soul. He then said, "But I can assure you Adam, I will call Madame Walker before I land."

"So your overall impression is that things went well?" Phoenix asked, seated at the rear of the sixty-foot yacht cursing the King Mackerel lost after a twenty-minute fight. The waves of the Gulf of Mexico gently tossed the vessel back and forth.

"I should have bought that new fishing rod."

"What did you say?"

The voice at the other end of Phoenix's cell phone asked with a tone of confusion.

"Damn, I'm sorry. Did the meeting in Amsterdam go according to my plans?"

"Phoenix, it could not have gone any better."

"She did fine?"

"She was superb!" He said with much excitement.

"When will you approach her?"

"The offer will be made in San Francisco."

"Now remember, don't lose sight."

"Yes, I know, I know."

"Don't cut me off!"

"Pardon, pardon! But I do understand your desires."

"And never forget that my friend, never forget." Phoenix turned off the cell phone and motioned to the first mate to add poggies to the hook. Phoenix placed the burning cigar in a gold-plated ashtray and, with a single thrust, cast the baited rod in another attempt to snare the elusive King Mackerel.

"When I get you on my hook this time, you scaly son-of-a-bitch, you will be my dinner before sundown," said Phoenix.

CHAPTER

twenty-one

It had been a long day; Melanie sat at the foot of her bed rubbing her aching feet. She loved the look of Manolo Blahnik shoes but by the end of the day her feet felt as if a morbidly obese four-year old had been standing on them. She walked slowly across her suite to the bathroom and added her favorite bubble bath to the running water in the large pear-shaped, marble bathtub. She undressed in front of the full-length mirror positioned on the center wall in the bathroom. With such a busy schedule over the last few weeks, her exercise regimen had been completely interrupted. She admired the fullness of her almond shaped breasts, but cringed at the thought of the changes that childbearing and gravity would bring. She slowly submerged her right foot into the water. The temperature reminded her of the hot springs she had visited in Arkansas during a business retreat. A bird-like chirp caught her attention and speaking aloud, she asked herself, "What is that?"

She looked around the bathroom trying to determine the direction of the sound. The chirping was rhythmic and continuous.

"Why is it that whenever I'm trying to relax or I'm submerged in a wonderful bath I get interrupted; even when I'm in Amsterdam?"

Melanie finally zeroed in on the source of the chirping. The sound was coming from a telephone setting on a small table next to the bathtub.

"Hello," she said, but it was too late. Whoever it was had already hung up.

"That's a weird sound for a telephone!"

It was probably Adam calling to make sure she kept her date in San Francisco.

"Okay, no more interruptions. It's time to relax and enjoy my bath," she said to herself.

The chirping started again and she looked at the receiver, hoping to identify the caller and avoid the interruption in this rare moment of solitude. But since the phone had no Caller ID, she felt obliged to answer it.

"Hello, no one is available right now. At the sound of the beep pl..."

"Girl, cut the drama. What's happening?"

Melanie screamed. It was Kathy.

"Girlfriend, it's so good to hear your voice! How did you get my number?"

"Girl you know if I want to find you, I can find your behind."

"Okay Colombo, how did you locate me?"

"I called your secretary."

"She knows not to give out my telephone number."

"Yeah, she said that. But she knows me and I told her it was urgent. I also promised her you wouldn't be upset. So please don't give her grief."

"I'm not going to give her grief, I'm just going to fire her."

"Melanie."

"No girl, I'm just kidding. She knows for whom to break the rules and when she shouldn't."

"Girl, I have been praying for you big time. How's it looking? Were the investors receptive to the presentation?"

"Things couldn't have gone better. The trip over was good; and we had a good attendance where some of the largest investment firms in Europe made commitments to invest in CORE. I believe this segment of the trip should raise somewhere between one hundred twenty to one hundred thirty million dollars in investments."

"Melanie that's great but you really don't sound very excited."

"It's been a long day. I'm also confused about one of the investors."

"Is there some kind of problem?"

"I believe one of the potential investors has taken an interest in me."

"An interest in you?" Kathy's tone reflected a degree of puzzlement.

"A Frenchman, Francoise Baptiste, who is with an international investment group was at the CORE presentation today."

Kathy listened as if she was receiving the combination to a secret vault.

"After our presentation he asked if I would meet him for dinner in San Francisco."

"San Francisco?"

"Yes, his company is having a meeting of their American division there."

"What's the problem?"

"Well, I'm supposed to meet Stenson there."

"Is he rich?"

"Yes."

"If he's rich, then looks really don't matter that much. But does he look okay?"

"He looks okay, but..."

"But what? If he's rich and he looks okay then what's the problem?"

"He's European. He's not Black and you know how I feel about dating men who are not African American."

"No I don't. I'm white and I date men who are not Caucasian."

"Yes, Kathy but..."

"But what, is he asking to marry you or sleep with you?"

"No, but...."

"Isn't his company a potential large investor?"

"Yes, but..."

"But what, go out to dinner with the man. If nothing else you will get a good meal, possibly increase your bonus and maybe, just maybe enjoy yourself."

"But what about Stenson?"

"What about him? Stenson is still a resident making a little more than minimum wages. He can't invest more than five bucks in this project. He's not your man, as a matter of fact I'm not sure if you know what he is to you."

"You're right, I'm not sure what he is to me but I am sure that he is important to me. I'm only going to be there a short time, I would rather spend that time with Stenson."

"Melanie, get a grip..."

"Kathy, hold on for a minute, there's a call coming in on the other line."

"Hello."

"Hello, Melanie this is Adam. I called to commend you on the wonderful presentation. I was..."

"Adam, thank you very much."

She hoped he wasn't calling to twist her arm about this date thing. Plus, she was a little pissed that he had not told her he knew Francoise Baptiste and had failed to be considerate of her previously made plans.

"Would it be okay if I call you back, I have someone on the phone calling from the States."

"Why yes of course. I'm sure you want to share our early success. Please don't let me detain you only let me acknowledge our appreciation for your agreeing to dine with Francoise in San Francisco. It could prove to be extremely helpful."

"Adam, I'm a good solider. But why would you send me out without all the information?"

"What do you mean?"

"Why didn't you tell me that you knew Francoise Baptiste?"

"Melanie that's not important to where we are now. Call me when you finish. Thanks again."

The line was dead.

"I'm sorry Kathy that was Adam."

"So what did you tell him?"

"I told him that I was a good solider but I didn't like surprises."

"What was the surprise?"

"It's not important."

"Well Melanie, that means dinner, free I might add,"

"I'm not attracted by a free meal. I can certainly afford to dine at any restaurant on my own. Besides I asked Stenson to join me here."

"Okay, okay please spare me the 'I got my own money' stuff. Okay? As I was saying before being interrupted by an independent, educated, high salaried, manless, but full-time friend."

They both laughed freely into the telephone.

"But what shall I say to Stenson?"

"Tell him the truth, that you have a business obligation which must take precedence for a couple of hours."

"But Kathy, Stenson is going through a lot now and this was going to be a getaway for him to relax and sort some things out."

"And it still can be. Look Melanie, I like Stenson, he's intelligent, fine and funny but he's not your man and it isn't your responsibility to provide recreational activities for him."

"You are really being hard. You almost sound like a sister. I think you should stop your subscription to *Essence*."

"I'm not sure if that's a good thing. Maybe I should stop dating African American men and move on to Chinese."

Again, they both laughed in unison.

"I'll tell him the truth and make it up to him later."

"Melanie, please. Don't tell him you'll make it up. Men think there's only one way to make things up."

"He knows that I'm not going..."

"Men, all men, even educated doctor men, think there's only one way to make things up."

"And I don't make up that way."

Then Kathy changed the subject by asking, "When will you be home?"

"We leave for London in a day and will fly to San Francisco after we finish our business there. Then we'll go to Chicago, Atlanta and back to Memphis."

"I am so excited for you. I can't wait for you to get home."

"I'll call you when I get settled in San Francisco."

"I'm very proud of you Melanie, stay safe and enjoy yourself, I'll see you soon."

"Thanks Kathy, you're a good friend."

"I know. And Melanie, Stenson is a good man."

"I know."

Melanie replaced the receiver and sank back into what was now a cold tub of water. She reached over to turn on the hot water and looked at the clock. Since the time in Amsterdam was substantially ahead of Memphis she decided not to email Stenson on the change of plans. She needed to hear his voice.

As soon as the water was just the right temperature, the phone started its chirping sound again. The person calling was really interfering with her greatly deserved intimate encounter with this bath. It was probably Adam calling to stress the importance of that dinner meeting in 'Frisco.

"Damn!" Melanie said aloud as she reached over to answer the phone. Ever since she was a little girl she could not stand to let a phone ring without answering it. The excitement of anticipating who was on the other end had turned into a habit that in this case, was detrimental to her leisure time.

"Hello."

Melanie's voice was less than cheerful.

"Melanie, Frank. We'll meet you in the lobby in thirty minutes."

"Frank, I'm not hungry. I was trying to relax."

"We're not going to eat. We just want to tour the Red Light District."

"Frank, I..."

"See you in thirty minutes."

The receiver was dead. At least that conversation was short and her water still warm. The chirping immediately started again.

"Ahhh!" Melanie screamed as she reached over and grabbed the phone.

"Frank, Adam, now what? I'm exhausted and trying to take a relaxing bath. So please let me finish if you want me to be civil for the remainder of this trip," pleaded an exasperated Melanie.

There was a long pause and then a sudden burst of laughter. Her favorite laugh, it was Stenson.

"Stenson!" Her tone was soft with passion.

"Well, I certainly don't want to be the guy who comes between you and a bar of soap. But I really need to speak with you."

"I was just thinking about emailing you. How did you get my number?"

"I called your office and ..."

"And my secretary gave it to you."

"Yep. She was quite cooperative. I guaranteed her that you wouldn't mind."

"And I don't. So, what's up?"

"Before I move into my thing, tell me how your trip is going."

"Stenson, it has gone quite well. I'm glad you asked. But tell me what's on your mind."

"Melanie, I spoke with Gina recently."

"Great! How is she, Stenson, and where is she? I know it has been quite a while since you've spoken with her. Is she okay, is she working, how is her health?"

"Well, I don't have any answers but I think I told you that my father has hired a private investigator."

"Yes, you told me something about thinking Gina was in New Orleans."

"Yeah, well that's where she is. But before I could find out exactly where she hung up."

"Hung up?"

"I have my own ideas about that. Anyway, I know we were planning to meet in San Francisco, and please understand I was really looking forward to seeing you in the City by the Bay."

"But?"

"But, I really need to go to New Orleans. I plan to meet the private investigator Dad hired and see if we can track down Gina. I have an interview scheduled at UAB next week. So it's essential to get this out of the way now."

Melanie had gotten her exit. She truly understood Stenson's position and felt somewhat guilty that she would use this as the opportunity to have dinner with a client.

"Stenson, I understand, it's really not a problem. You just have to make it up to me later. Or should I say, we'll just plan another trip later."

She didn't mean to mislead him and have him think she would have sex with him to make up the missed opportunity to hook up in San Francisco.

"When you get to San Francisco I should still be in New Orleans. I'll call you."

"I pray that all goes well. Give Gina my love."

"I will, be careful and get a load of investors."

Her emotions were reeling like a leaf in a wind tunnel. The tone of Stenson's voice was haunting her. It was as if he was not prepared for an unwelcome encounter with destiny. Unsure if this encounter was the final destiny for him or his sister.

Since Frank, Jim and Melanie had an early flight the next day, they agreed it was best to tour the Red Light District and other noted Amsterdam landmarks from the comfort of the hotel limousine. It was late afternoon and the sun was beaming like a yellowish orange spotlight in a cloudless, mint-colored sky. The Dutch limo driver was their unofficial tour guide. Speaking English with a heavy Dutch accent he said, "I will show you the best things here in my land."

"And what will that be?" Jim asked.

"Please enjoy your ride. The rest you will see, you will see."

They left the hotel and traveled west on Prindengracht to Anne Frankhuis.

"My friends, please look," said the driver.

The limousine slowed and they rolled down their tinted windows to view a building that almost had the appearance of a warehouse.

"My friends, this was once the home of Anne and Otto Frank. Do you know their story?"

"Really?" Melanie's voice reflected surprise.

"I completed a research report on Anne Frank my freshman year in high school. Her diary gave an account of her family's hiding from the Nazi army during World War II."

"Unfortunately they were found towards the end of the War and deported to concentration camps." Frank added.

"Life's a bitch," said Jim.

The driver then took them to Paulus Potterstraat to view the Van Gogh Museum and down De Rosse Buurt to the infamous Red Light District. The Red Light District was a warren of streets and old canals and was reflective of tolerance for all people in Amsterdam.

"Here," said the driver, "unlike most of America, prostitution is legal. The ladies in the storefront windows, in their leather and lace, are waiting for work. Unlike America, instead of spending money and crowding jails to stop the oldest profession, we try to control it."

The three stared in amazement as men entered and left the storefront and the women stopped their knitting or turned off their TVs to disappear from the store window. Jim motioned to a figure standing in front of one of the store-front windows and said, "That guy must be really trying hard to get the most bang for his buck."

The man looked familiar as he stood facing two windows. Each with a female sitting perched on a stool, void of enough clothing to dress a Barbie doll.

"That guy looks familiar," said Melanie.

Directing her voice to the driver, she said, "Will you drive a little closer please?"

The driver moved closer and parked directly across the street from the man who had attracted all their attention. It appeared that he had settled for an Asian looking Barbie doll. When she disappeared from the window the man gave a 'thumbs up' sign and started up the steps. Before opening the paint-stripped wooden door he turned and looked across the street as if trying to see into the tinted window of the parked limousine.

"Shit," Frank said.

"It's a small world," added Melanie.

"That's what I call an international fucker," laughed Jim.

Senator Colin Daniels was unmistakable, even with a hat pulled down partially over his face. He turned, leaned forward as he opened the door and disappeared inside the store front.

The presentation in London was equally as successful as the Amsterdam meeting. It resulted in two major institutional investors who guaranteed additional millions of dollars in investments. Tired and exhausted, Melanie, Frank and Jim left London traveling to the first leg of the American tour.

CHAPTER

twenty-two

The flight from Memphis to New Orleans took a little less than two hours. Stenson wasn't hungry, but found it impossible to resist an order of beignets and coffee as he waited for the investigator. Café du Monde, located on the southeastern edge of the French Quarters near Jackson Square on the bank of the Mississippi River, is a century-old, quaint, open café, which is a throwback to an earlier era. Stenson sat at one of the small café tables, crowded in so close together that patrons had to huddle closely in order to avoid hampering the movement of the waiters and other customers. Every scent, sound and sight unique to New Orleans could be absorbed while sitting at Café du Monde. The aroma of fresh breads, heavy Cajun seasoning, the rhythm of New Orleans music, the gallop of horses and carriages taking visitors on local sightseeing adventures, awakened all five senses to the excitement of New Orleans.

Some of the passers-by caught Stenson's attention. One guy, with bleached blond hair and multiple body piercing, sashayed as he walked down St. Louis Street, in wedged flip-flops, as if on a fashion runway. Stenson thought it must be so nice to have little concern about how one is viewed by the rest of the world. The bleached blond noticed Stenson staring at him as he walked by, so he smiled, winked and blew Stenson a kiss.

The open café welcomed pigeons as they mingled with the patrons without inhibition. The waiters sat on small mushroom shaped chairs, smoked cigarettes and waited for customers to beckon their services.

Meanwhile, other waiters rushed back and forth through the kitchen double doors providing the powdered sugar treats, usually with something to drink.

"May I help you?" asked the petite, middle-aged woman with the enduring smile. She was wearing a chef's apron and the smell of fresh cigarette smoke.

"Yes please, may I have a single order of beignets and a bottle of water?" requested Stenson.

"Coming right up."

She turned and headed towards the double doors and returned shortly there after with his order. The ceiling fans created a light breeze that eased but did not remove the smothering summer heat and humidity that engulfed him.

"Stenson?"

He looked up from his beignets, the white powder encircling his lips.

"Stenson Hawk?"

Stenson thought he would see a tall, suave, and physically intimidating man. One who was well dressed and possessed an air of sophistication; with a mature face to match his experience. He immediately realized he had imagined the private investigator to be like those he'd seen in movies.

"Yes?"

"Doctor Stenson Hawk?"

"Yes, I'm Doctor Stenson Hawk."

He extended his thick, muscular hand, with finely manicured nails and a diamond ring on the first finger. He was casually well dressed in tailored slacks with cuffs and pleats, square toed bulked shoes, and a short sleeve silk shirt with an open collar. In his left hand was a small black leather case.

"My name is Michael Stone, but my friends call me Mick or Mickey. Your father sent me here to meet you."

"Yes, I was expecting you. Please sit down." Stenson motioned to the seat across from him.

"Would you like an order of beignets?"

"No thank you, I've been here for three days and have eaten them everyday. I can skip today."

"So you're the private investigator who will help me find my sister?"

Stenson's surprise when meeting Mickey must have shown on his face.

"You're a little surprised, huh?"

Stenson remembered the conversation he had with his father the day before arriving in New Orleans.

"You're going to meet the private investigator who has tracked Gina to New Orleans," Dr. Abraham Hawk had said.

"Did you tell him about my conversation with Gina?" Stenson asked his father.

"Yes, but he doesn't think she's working or living in the area she mentioned to you. He thinks she may actually be living on the outskirts of the City. She may live either on the West Bank or in Slidell."

"Dad, what is this guy's name?"

"His name is Michael Stone."

"How did you find him and what are his qualifications and experience as a private investigator?"

"I don't know much about him except he's quite expensive. Apparently he's reluctant to share much information about himself. He won't even allow himself to be photographed. He doesn't have an address and you can only reach him via an email address. He sends a courier to receive his payments in cash. But he comes highly recommended by the Chief of Police here in Selma. Mr. Stone was used to solve a murder case here in Selma two years ago," said Dr. Hawk.

"I see."

"You are to meet him at Café du Monde on St. Louis Street. Your Mom and I carried you and Gina there while visiting New Orleans when you guys were still school-aged."

"I remember, Gina got a bad batch of oysters on that trip and was sick for days."

"I thought we were going to have to place an IV in her to keep her hydrated because she couldn't stop throwing up," said Dr. Hawk. They both laughed.

"How will I know him?" asked Stenson.

"You won't, but he'll know you," said Dr. Hawk.

"You seem puzzled or perhaps surprised by my appearance," said Mickey.

"Somewhat."

"Most of my clients are surprised, but never judge a book by its cover. My youthful appearance gives the impression of inexperience. But I've investigated almost two hundred cases and solved over ninety-five percent of them. The ones I did not solve, have not been solved. My clients live throughout the world."

Stenson was impressed by this articulate and confident young man with the slight "street" edge in his demeanor. His maturity seemed far greater than his twenty something appearance. His hair was short and slightly balding and his skin was a smooth chocolate brown. His build was standard, long and lean. Making his tailored apparel fit like a glove.

"Mick, I really didn't know what to expect but if you meet my father's standards you certainly meet mine." Stenson said almost apologetically.

"Cool, now let's get down to business."

Mickey placed his black leather case on the table, opened it and pulled out a small digital camera.

"I've been here for the past three days. I have here pictures of your sister that I've taken since my arrival."

"Oh my God," said Stenson, "she really doesn't look well at all."

"I thought she looked small too but when I made comparisons to previous photos there really wasn't much difference."

"Why is she wearing a wig?"

"The reason for the wig can be anything from fashion or occupation, to medical."

"You mean chemotherapy?" asked Stenson.

"Yeah, chemotherapy," replied Mickey.

"Look at these other photos, you see, her hair is different in each of them."

"You're right. And who is this guy in all the pictures?"

"He's the problem," Mickey said, "I'm not real sure what their relationship is. But he always seems to be around."

There were several photos of Gina in different settings. In one photo Gina and her mysterious companion were leaving a French Quarters breakfast spot called Petunia's. The guy towered over Gina in a protective fashion, shielding her with a large umbrella from the morning showers. He was in almost half the photos, looming over her as if daring others to approach. He wore dark sunglasses which made him appear menacing, as did the small but prominent scar under his left cheek. He looked battle tested and tough.

"What has Gina gotten herself into this time?" Stenson wondered.

"I'm not sure if I yet have the full picture of their relationship. But I have a plan."

"When can I see her? Are you aware of her medical condition?" Stenson questioned.

"I am," said Mickey.

"So you can understand why it's imperative that I get her back to Memphis for evaluation and treatment."

"If this guy is who I think he his, we could have a small bump in the road. If not, we can get her to Memphis without problems."

"Well, who do you think he is?" asked Stenson.

"I'm pretty sure who he is."

Stenson looked into Mickey's eyes searching for the answer.

"Shit man, cut the suspense," said Stenson.

"His name is James Beaudoure. He is from an old New Orleans family and is the lead detective in the Narcotics/Gang Division for the New Orleans Police Department."

"Why is she hanging out with a cop?" asked Stenson.

"He's not just a cop. He's been indicted twice by Federal Investigators on drug and racketeering charges. He's been associated with prostitution kickbacks and the murder of a high profile Baton Rouge drug kingpin. Four years ago someone put out a $100,000.00 contract on him. Supposedly, that's why the drug kingpin plus the assassin got smoked," Mickey continued.

"So Mick, he's not just a cop, he's a bad cop."

"Perhaps Stenson, but the brother hasn't been convicted of anything and he works in a tough world. He's not going to be a choir boy."

"Where is Gina staying in the French Quarters? She told me she's staying three blocks from Jackson Square."

"I've tracked her residence to the same place as Beaudoure. They are living together in East New Orleans in one of those stately mansions with a great view of Lake Pontchartrain."

"Gina has always believed in living large. Daddy spoiled her that way. What's the next step?"

"The next step must be very cautious, because I'm not sure if Gina's involved in prostitution, drugs or something else. Also, since he can be such a difficult dude, I think what I'm going to do is a straight up snatch and run."

"Snatch and run?" Stenson asked with some confusion.

"Yeah, snatch and run; kidnap her."

"When will we do it?" Stenson asked.

"We aren't going to do anything. I'm going to do it, but 'we'," Mickey said as he pointed a finger back and forth between the two of them, "aren't going to do shit."

"Look, she's my sister and things would likely go without incident if she sees a familiar face."

"First of all Stenson, it could get nasty and secondly, I work alone. Ever so often I use friends, which may be the case on this one."

"I'm not trying to be a tough guy, but it would be a lot easier if I were there when you approached Gina. She has had some bad experiences and it could be more than traumatic for her if some stranger takes her away even if her current situation is one that is less than ideal."

"That's the problem," said Mickey, "I'm not sure of the status of her current situation. I don't think she's prostituting but, she could be, I'm just not sure. With this guy she could be into almost anything but most of it is illegal. Your father wouldn't want me to allow your involvement in something that could impact your career in a negative fashion."

"Mick, I'm a grown man. I love and respect my father's opinion and concern, but Gina is my only sister and there's no way I'm going to come here to New Orleans and sit around doing nothing under these circumstances. It'll be easier for you if I'm there."

"I agree, your presence may well make it easier."

"Fine." Stenson said, "What's the next step?"

"We're going to get her in the morning, she'll be in Selma before nightfall," said Mickey.

"Selma?" questioned Stenson.

"Your father wants her brought to Selma. His idea is that if there are any emergency medical issues they will be closer to her at UAB. Especially since you plan to do your pediatric surgery fellowship at UAB. Meet me in the parking garage of the Ritz Carlton Hotel on Canal Street at four o'clock in the morning."

"What should I wear?" asked Stenson.

"Dark colors that won't easily show blood stains, something comfortable, disposable, and shoes that you can fight in or run in. Understand?"

"You don't expect any violence do you?" Stenson appeared concerned.

"You must be prepared for anything," answered Mickey.

"Don't worry about me, I can handle myself, I'll be prepared for anything," Stenson said with true grit and determination.

CHAPTER

twenty-three

Melanie kicked her shoes off as she entered the room.

"Thank you Ms. Walker," The bellman said as he dropped her bags in the suite and closed his hand around the very generous tip. The trip from London had taken a toll on her. There was a major delay in getting through the San Francisco customs because of a false bomb threat; now all Melanie wanted was to shower and sleep. Her suite presented a "reach out and touch" view of the Golden Gate Bridge which illuminated the night sky.

Responding to the soft but firm tap on the door, Melanie moved across the room to find the view of her peephole blocked by a person carrying something.

"Who is it?" She asked.

"Ms. Walker this is room service. I have a gift for you."

Melanie opened the door and was greeted by two bellmen who held a dozen roses of various colors interspersed with lavender, in each of their two hands.

"Ms. Walker, if you like, we can place these flowers throughout the living area, bathroom and bedroom."

"Fine, thank you. Who sent these beautiful flowers?" she asked.

Melanie hoped they were from Stenson but she knew he had too much occupying his time to be so thoughtful. He had never been this thoughtful when he had nothing to do.

"They were sent to you by Mr. Baptiste. He has also requested us to inform you that a driver will arrive tomorrow evening at seven o'clock to transport you to dinner. The dress attire is casual," said one of the bellmen.

After closing the door behind them Melanie looked around the suite to appreciate the beauty of the floral arrangements. As with most things that she enjoyed, her thoughts began on focus on Stenson. Then the telephone rang.

"I am so happy to get away from that dumb-ass chirping sound," she said while reaching for the telephone.

"Hello," she said.

"Wassup? How does it feel to back on United States soil, you international money magnet?"

"Kathy, you always have the best timing!"

"I know, just one of my many finer qualities. So tell me, tell me how it went."

"Better than we expected. We should do extremely well when CORE goes public on the Exchange. If things go as well on the Stateside of the tour, I think we can easily have the largest public offering of the year."

"Are you pumped up about your upcoming date?"

"Actually, I'm a little uncomfortable about a conflict of interest here since this is a business associate who just happens to represent a potential investor for my client. I just think it could be misinterpreted."

"Girl, you never know what your future needs may be and how Francoise Baptiste may be able to help you."

"Or not help. He's more of a liability if we shift the roles here. Let's say we hook up or not, either way if it's even suspected that I have something going with him, I'd be viewed as a woman who uses her womanly charms to persuade this man to play ball and close the deal. This is my future here, my career could be on the line."

"It's what men expect of us. They hire us to charm other men. And even if you don't, they'll think it's your back and booty that got you wherever you end up. You know how the old boys say, tits and ass are all they're looking at."

"Exactly. That's why I have to be careful and calculating here. I'm trying to make partner in a few years. Everything's got to be above board. I don't care what they think. As you know, I offer much more than tits and ass. Kathy, let's talk again tomorrow, I need to get settled in."

"Alright girl," said Kathy, "just follow your own mind on this one."

The next day as expected was long and intense, but Melanie knew the typical questions that came from the potential investors. Furthermore, the presenting team had fine-tuned their answers so they were short and specific. Adam, as usual, was the consumate sales person. It was obvious that he was committed to and believed in CORE's success which, most importantly, resulted in investor confidence.

The morning presentation was the last meeting of their grueling investment tour. Things had gone so well, all agreed to bypass the Chicago and Atlanta legs of the trip and simply invite those investors to Memphis.

After the morning presentation Melanie returned to her hotel and spent time talking to the Memphis office reporting their progress and informing them of the decision to bypass Chicago and Atlanta. The remainder of the day was spent doing some heavy shopping in Sausalito, then pampering herself with a hot rock massage, manicure and pedicure. Now the only thing between her and Memphis was this dinner meeting with Franciose.

That evening, as she stood in the lobby of the Park-Fifty Five Hotel, she felt as if this dinner with Mr. Baptiste was a betrayal to Stenson. She'd left a message on Stenson's voice mail in Memphis and had paged him several times with no response. She had no idea where he was staying in New Orleans. But she was also concerned about Gina. Melanie always liked her, but while friendly enough Gina was never really close with any of the girls at Spelman. She was a loner. In fact, although they exchanged letters and a few phone calls right after graduation, Melanie completely lost contact with her.

"Ms. Walker your driver has arrived," the doorman said as he motioned towards the front door.

"Thank you," said Melanie as she moved through the open doors towards the waiting limousine. She was sped off to dine with CORE's largest potential investor.

CHAPTER
twenty-four

The heat and humidity were high for ten o'clock in the morning, even in New Orleans. A white delivery van was moving slightly above the speed limit as it traveled down Canal Street towards the Ritz Carlton Hotel. The driver stopped at the traffic light as riders on a trolley car exited and crossed Canal Street. The driver paid constant attention to the cargo, neatly wrapped in blankets in the back of the van. He directed his voice to the van's cargo, and said, "We won't be much longer."

He made a quick U-turn on Canal Street into the Ritz Carlton Hotel parking garage. He drove past valet parking and maneuvered the van towards the lower level. Stenson was standing, holding a duffel bag, near the entrance. He wore a Nike baseball cap turned backwards that complemented his oversized, dark-colored T-shirt, jeans and sneakers.

Stenson had slept poorly throughout the night, unsure of what to expect; knowing this situation could possibly affect his entire future. His pediatric surgery future had already taken a backseat to his family and he knew these issues with Gina had to be resolved before anything could move forward in his life.

As the van neared Stenson he could see an unfamiliar driver sitting alone. The van stopped so suddenly in front of Stenson that the wheels made a squishing sound. The door flung open and the driver, a balding man with salt and pepper hair, got out of the van. He had a trickle of blood from a small cut on his neck and less obvious blood on his navy blue water delivery uniform.

"Dr. Hawk?"

Stenson noticed the flashing gold teeth which were highlighted by the man's dark skin complexion. Stenson did not move. He did not move and was unsure of what would be an appropriate response.

"Dr. Hawk please get in."

"Who are you and where is Mickey?"

Stenson asked in a curt voice which evidenced his irritation and concern.

"Dr. Hawk, quit shitting around and get your ass in the damn van!"

The voice coming from the grey-haired, balding, old man with the gold grill and foul mouth sounded familiar. It was Mick Stenson finally concluded. He leaped into the van and pulled the door shut just as the van sped towards the service entrance of the Ritz.

"Mick, it is you isn't it?" Stenson asked while looking for some other signs of the man's identity.

"Yeah, it's me Doc, just trust the voice 'cause looks can be deceiving." Mickey said flashing a broad, gold-toothed smile with satisfaction.

"Where are we going, why are you dressed in that getup, and who kicked your ass?"

Stenson had noticed the abrasions on Mickey's hands as they held the steering wheel.

"Doc, I'll answer all your questions in a minute and if you think I got my ass kicked you should see the other son of a bitch. He really took a good old fashion, nigga ass whipping."

Mickey stopped the van in front of the service entrance door. Almost immediately the door swung open as if someone was expecting them. Mickey opened the van door and said, "Doc get out, I need some help."

Stenson looked puzzled but stepped out and followed Mickey towards the rear of the van. He asked, "What the hell is going on?" Anger and confusion resonated in his voice.

"You've had me waiting for you since four o'clock this morning. You know we are suppose to get Gina, but you show up late in a goddamn masquerade outfit and won't give me a single straight answer. Goddam Mick, you're fucking with my sister's life, my time and my father's money."

Mickey, by this time had the rear door of the van almost open and looked directly at Stenson, who for the first time noticed the black contact lenses that had replaced the color of Mick's naturally light brown eyes. Flashing a smile that revealed the row of fake gold teeth, Mickey asked, "Okay, Doc what is it that you want to know?"

"Where is Gina and when will we get her?"

Mick had opened the van door by now and motioned for Stenson to look inside. There were several large bottles of commercial water stacked one on the other.

"Help me move these." Mickey said as he started to unload the water bottles.

"Mick cut the shit. I want..."

Stenson stopped in mid sentence. As Mickey removed the bottles Stenson noticed a figure covered by a large moth-eaten blanket.

"Well, are you going to help me or not? I'm trying to give you the answer to your last two questions," Mickey said.

Stenson leaped into the van and moved quickly towards the motionless figure under the blanket. He turned to Mickey as if to get his approval, because he really did not know what to expect.

"It's okay Doc, it's okay." Mickey said with a broad smile, gold teeth shining.

Stenson kneeled and slowly removed the blanket. Gina was lying there in a robe with a scarf around her head. But she was resting comfortably as if in the middle of a peaceful dream.

"She's fine Doc. She got a little combative so I had to sedate her pretty heavily, but she should wake up fine in a little while."

Two big men with small semi-automatic weapons moved quickly towards the van. One was wearing the same water distributor uniform as Mickey, the other was dressed in a Ritz Carlton doorman's uniform. They kept their eyes on Stenson as he took an offensive stance.

"Relax Doc," Mickey said placing his hand on Stenson's shoulder, "these are a couple of my boys, it's all good. We're down like four flat tires."

The Ritz Carlton guy entered the back of the van and lifted Gina over his shoulder. He moved swiftly through the service entrance and into a waiting elevator. Stenson and Mickey followed closely. The water distribution guy got in the driver's seat of the van as Mickey stopped in the doorway to give him a 'thumbs up'. He nodded, returned the thumbs up sign and slowly pulled off as if going to make another water delivery.

twenty-five

Mickey inserted a key card in the door slot and a red light appeared. He flipped the card and inserted it again and the door clicked open as a green light flashed. They entered a large suite of the Ritz Carlton Hotel overlooking Canal Street.

"Yo! Man," Mickey said, as he looked at his muscular associate who had Gina cradled like an infant in his arms.

"Place her in the king-size bed in the room to the right."

"What happened Mick?" Stenson asked, "I thought I was suppose to be in on this thing. And what gives with this outfit you're wearing?"

"Doc, I never put a client in harm's way. Anything could have happened back there. You're a doctor, that's what you do for a living. I'm a hunter, in this case on the hunt for your sister. As a hunter I can do whatever it takes to get the job done. Your father would not want you involved in what just happened. I wouldn't want you involved in what just happened."

"Well Mick, tell me what happened?"

Mickey strolled over to the bar and poured some orange juice and Champagne into a flute. He pulled off the wooly afro wig and took out the gold grill. Then he reclined on a large, pastel-colored sofa which blended perfectly with the wallpaper and other décor in the elegantly appointed room. He lifted the glass to his lips and tasted the refreshing drink, and said, "I love drinking a coupla Mimosas in the morning. They help me get my day going."

"Mick, why is it always so goddam hard getting information from you?"

"Well Doc, we've already discussed the company Gina was keeping, so I thought it best to get her first thing this morning. I can't give you the details of how we operate, the number of people involved and all that stuff. But when Beaudoure left we did a snatch and run. There were only two other guys in the house with Gina."

"Why did they let you guys in?" asked Stenson.

"That's why we have these water delivery uniforms, water delivery is a common service in New Orleans."

Stenson walked over and sat on a chaise lounge facing Mickey. He leaned forward and questioned Mickey as if he were listening to a murder mystery around a midnight campfire.

"What happened next?" he asked.

"Doc, the less you know the better but to answer some of your questions suffice it to say we met major resistance from the two wise guys. They put up a pretty good fight but were neutralized in quick order. Gina was in the bathroom brushing her teeth and never knew we were in the house until we had thrown a blanket over her. But we didn't anticipate the two in-house guard dogs. We had to kill both dogs and during the confusion Gina got away and tried to get out the back door. She put up such a fight the second time we had to sedate her. We made a quick exit but remembered to change out the water bottles before leaving."

"What about James Beaudoure?" Stenson inquired.

"We just waited until he left. I'm sure his two guys should be conscious by now. So he probably knows Gina has been snatched, but he has no idea by whom. So the hunt is probably on."

Stenson walked into the bedroom and stood over Gina who was sleeping comfortably. He then sat on the bed beside her, admiring the peacefulness of her rest. He wondered what her dreams involved and what the last couple of years of her life had been like. He was also concerned about her response to the orchestrated kidnapping. Quietly moving the hair from her face he gently placed a soft kiss on her forehead. She opened her eyes and smiled as if in a dreamlike state and said, "Stenson, I'm not sure what happened but I knew you would come and get me, I'm so happy that you watch over me."

She closed her eyes again, smiled and returned to her dreams.

"**M**ick, honestly, I had no idea who you were." Stenson said with some degree of admiration. "You looked completely different."

"Thanks Doc, I told you I'm good at what I do. But now that we have Gina I've made arrangements for you to take her back to Selma. Your father wants her under his care."

"I understand and have no problem with that idea. The pace of Selma will be good for Gina."

"I'm not going to Selma."

Stenson and Mickey quickly turned to see Gina standing in the bedroom doorway. She wore a long Mickey Mouse nightshirt under her robe and her hair was in disarray. With wandering eyes, Gina tried to discern her surroundings, including Stenson's companions.

"Stenson, where am I and why are we here?"

Gina was walking towards Stenson as she spoke, then fell almost as if in slow motion and her head made a slight thud as she landed on the floor.

"Are you alright?"

Stenson asked while trying to break the impact of her fall.

"Be careful baby girl, you have not completely slept off the medication in you," Stenson said.

"I'm fine, but Stenson what's going on? I was kidnapped."

She sat on the sofa next to Stenson and put her arms around him with a tight embrace. The morning traffic on Canal Street had reached the rush hour peak. Sounds from trolley cars and city buses were audible. The bright rays of the sunbeams that streaked through the sheer window treatments seemed to cement their embrace.

"You really weren't kidnapped Gina, Mick here," Stenson nodded in Mickey's direction, "was hired by Dad to find you. He's been on your trail for at least two months and finally traced you here to New Orleans."

"Tracking me?" she asked with disdain.

"Yeah, he's the one who saved you this morning." Stenson said.

"Saved me?" Gina asked.

"Yeah, saved you from James Beaudoure, the police officer," Stenson said.

"Well Stenson, the last time I checked it wasn't required by law for me to notify my family of my every move. And you must remember I'm an adult now."

"Okay Gina, hold on and let me explain," Stenson pleaded.

"No you hold on," Gina shouted, "the guy who snatched me earlier was much older, taller, with gold teeth."

"Ms. Hawk, we did look a little different but, as your brother has told you, we are responsible for removing you from your home."

Mickey spoke as if answering a direct question.

"So let me get this straight," Gina focused all her attention at Mickey, "You are responsible for coming into my home, uninvited I might add, kicking the shit out of two of my friends and killing my dogs at the request of my father and with the support of my brother?"

Gina's voice was controlled rage.

"Gina, it's not really like that," Stenson intervened as peacemaker.

"Well, tell me if you're the shithead who came into my home."

"Yes, but it wasn't like you think," said Mickey.

"But my ass!"

Before he could continue, Gina leaped across the room and attempted to grab Mickey by his shirt collar. He protected himself well, as Gina's early barrage of punches did not find their mark. Before Stenson could reach Gina, Mickey had gently secured her arms and wrapped his legs around hers to stop her from kicking him. Gina began coughing violently; each cough seemed to radiate through her small frame.

"Mick let her go, she's trying to cough."

Stenson now sounded more like a physician than a brother. Mickey followed his request. He released Gina and she leaned forward as if trying to clear her throat of some large object. But with one motion she turned on her heel and landed a right fist across Mickey's lower jaw, sending him backwards.

"You son of a bitch! I can't believe you killed my dogs."

Before she could land her left fist, Mickey had her pinned to the floor.

"Gina I'm really sorry about the dogs but they would have eaten us alive," Mickey said.

"That's what they're supposed to do to uninvited guests. Stenson I don't understand. I really, really don't understand."

She began crying uncontrollably. Stenson moved towards her and Mickey released her into Stenson's outstretched arms.

The limousine slowed to a stop in the quiet commercial district of San Francisco. The driver lowered the partition to ask his passenger, "Young lady have you previously dined at Crustacean?"

"No," said Melanie, "but I have heard great things about the food."

"You are certainly in for a treat."

Pointing to an unimpressive building on the opposite side of the street, the driver continued, "The entrance to the restaurant is somewhat unusual. Do you see the elevator door at street level to your left?"

Melanie looked at the series of small shops and noticed, between two of the shops, an inconspicuous black elevator door.

"Okay, yes. I see it," Melanie said.

"Fine, take that elevator to the second floor, which is the only floor it stops on, turn left and you'll see the entrance to Crustacean. The Maitre 'd will be expecting you."

The driver stepped out of the limousine and opened Melanie's door.

"I will wait here for you Ms. Walker."

"Thank you," Melanie said.

"And remember to order the Dungeness crabs in pepper garlic sauce or the tiger prawns on garlic noodles. You can't go wrong," he said almost as if offering fatherly advice.

"I will and I thank you for the suggestions," she responded.

Melanie stopped midway across the street to avoid an oncoming motorcyclist who was traveling at a high rate of speed. Hurrying on to the sidewalk she made her way to the elevator. On the second floor she followed the instructions given by the driver.

Crustacean had a beveled and stained glass front entrance to the dimly lit main dining room. Track lighting focused on the beautiful floral arrangements, Mediterranean décor and patron dining areas. The background music of soft contemporary jazz created a mood conducive to romantic conversation. The delightful aroma of the food whetted the appetite for a wonderful meal yet to come.

"Ms. Walker, welcome to Crustacean."

Melanie was greeted by the Maitre d, a strikingly attractive young Asian-American woman.

"Thank you," Melanie said, "I'm impressed that you know my name."

"Yes, Ms. Walker, we know you are the guest of Mr. Baptiste. He is waiting for you in our private dining area. Please follow me."

The Maitre d' led Melanie through the crowded restaurant, filled with laughter and whispers, large groups and couples who were enjoying the food, music and conversation. The atmosphere was festive yet elegant, Francoise had selected a good place; it was her kind of place. When they reached the rear of the restaurant, the Maitre d' stopped at a set of double doors, knocked, then parted the doors.

"Melanie, it is so wonderful that we are able to meet here," Francoise said, with a broad smile and opened arms, while walking towards Melanie.

"It is so good to see you also," Melanie said as she leaned in his arms for the friendly embrace.

"Your waiter will be here shortly to serve you, may I bring you the wine list or would you like to order drinks?" The Maitre d' asked while standing very poised in the doorway.

"Melanie." Francoise motioned to her for a response to the question.

"Water please and Mr. Baptiste will select from the wine list," Melanie said.

"Water for me as well and we'll have a bottle of Pinot Noir, preferably a Napa Valley."

"Yes sir, I'll have your water and wine shortly."

The Maitre d' stepped back and closed the double doors.

"So Melanie, did you find great success in your remaining European investment tour?"

"The trip was extremely successful, but I'm sure you're aware, we had no single European investor with the financial strength of Dorchel European International."

"We know and because of that I hope you will find interest in the offer I have for you," Francoise said.

Here we go, Melanie thought. I guess this is the part where he tells me how much money they will spend based on how freaky I can be tonight.

"Francoise, look let's cut to the chase. What is it that you want from CORE and what are the expectations of me? I don't cut business deals in the back seat of cars, on office sofas or in hotel rooms," Melanie said with a tone of annoyance. Francoise uttered a soft laugh, staring at Melanie with warm eyes.

"Melanie, I find you extremely attractive and would be dishonest if I told you I wouldn't love you in any one of the three previously mentioned locations. But I have a beautiful wife and a creative mistress. At this time, I have no romantic or sexual needs of you."

Francoise spoke as if he had been insulted by the suggestion in Melanie's comment. He continued, "And if I were looking, I'm not sure you would be selected since I'm not convinced you would meet my standards for wife or mistress."

Melanie felt so small, she realized she should have handled the situation with greater finesse and perhaps listened better before jumping to conclusions that were valid only in her head. She wished she had the magic to make herself disappear. Any escape from the embarrassment of misinterpreting Mr. Baptiste's intentions would be welcomed. But more importantly she hoped she had not blown the possibility of a done deal. She had just been politely told by an extremely wealthy European gentleman that she may not be up to his standards.

"Francoise I'm sorry if I misunderstood your intentions. And I apologize for my less than sophisticated conclusions. I only hope that you will forgive me and excuse my actions as those of a starving, over worked, fatigued business woman," and Melanie smiled as a prelude to her judge's sentence.

Francoise held up a hand with his palm facing her.

"Please Melanie, there is no need to be apologetic. I'm sure men on a regular basis first judge you by your beauty and assume your success is a result of that. I watched you conduct business in Amsterdam and it was quite apparent to me that you are quite a professional woman. Hence my offer to you is based on that and nothing more."

Francoise pulled the handkerchief from the pocket of his sports jacket and handed it to Melanie.

"Thank you."

The conversation had turned her face beet red with embarrassment and she had begun to perspire on her forehead with the thought of pissing off Francoise such that he would not invest in CORE at all. Wiping her hairline she continued, "I think it's always good to have a clear understanding."

There was a soft knock as the double doors parted. Melanie thought, saved by the waiter.

They shared a bottle of Pinot Noir, the meal was delicious, the atmosphere was pleasingly seductive and the driver had not overstated the Dungeness crabs. Francoise's conversation was both stimulating and entertaining. At times she laughed so hard she had to wipe her tears. Francoise was truly world traveled, good humored with many stories about his travels, the early days of Dorchel European International, life in France, London and New York during his wild and youthful days. It was as if they were old friends who had not talked in years.

"Melanie I have truly enjoyed your company but as you said earlier, let's cut to the chase."

"Good, that should answer my questions of intent since I grossly erred earlier."

"As you know, Dorchel International has great interest in the United States healthcare market."

"Isn't that your reason for investing in CORE?" asked Melanie.

"Yes, of course. American healthcare is a trillion dollar industry and you probably also know that Dorchel International is an acquisition-based company. We have grown and entered into a number of different markets and product lines through acquisitions."

"That is very interesting," said Melanie, "I read in your corporate biography that you've had a large number and variety of corporate takeovers in the previous eleven years, a number of them were hostile takeovers."

"You are observant," said Francoise.

"I'm not sure of the direction this conversation is taking," said Melanie.

"If I may continue, we believe that with selective marketing from our marketing division, CORE will open at around fifteen to eighteen dollars a share."

"That's pretty low. My assessment of the value of CORE stock is closer to the twenty to twenty five dollars a share range."

"But what Dorchel International wants is to be the majority shareholder with an opening price at fifteen dollars a share. This will come as a result of your report that will discuss poor management issues and possible slowed future growth in the healthcare arena. For this you will be paid handsomely. Next, with the low stock market price and our majority shareholder position, we will orchestrate a buyout of CORE that you will represent for us."

"Just a minute," said Melanie, "you are being quite presumptuous in this proposal you're describing."

By this time Francoise had gotten her complete attention. Melanie was quite aware of the commission and bonus dollars she could potentially generate. It was staggering. But she knew such an offer would have strings attached. Her first impulse was to end the conversation immediately, but since she had previously jumped to an erroneous conclusion she said nothing.

Francoise continued, "With the merger completed we could easily push the stock price up."

"Easily into the thirty-five to forty-dollar a share range." Melanie said.

"I see you understand quite well."

Melanie then added, "That means, the company that you took over with an initial value of fifteen dollars a share would, in a short time after takeover, become valued at thirty five to forty dollars a share. You would have more than doubled your investment."

"And we believe that could happen in less than six-months," said Francoise.

Melanie was speechless. She was curious as to why Francoise would come to her with such a financially attractive offer.

"Now, for your assistance to insure the opening price stays in our preset range," he continued, "you will receive one million dollars. You will receive another million after the acquisition deal with CORE is final. Of course this will be independent of the commission bonus from Smith Henderson Enterprises, the subsidiary of Dorchel International that will purchase CORE. Finally, with the good news you will provide about the merger when the stock hits the forty dollars a share value, you will receive one percent of the corporate stock value. The value should be around three hundred and fifty million dollars, of which you would receive a guaranteed minimum of three and a half million dollars. The total value of your deal will be between six and one half to seven million dollars."

Melanie was intrigued by the offer. She thought this to be an incredible proposition and asked, "So you believe I have the ability to drive the stock price that much?"

"At this point very few people have credibility in the market. But we believe the knowledge, insightful presentation, presence, and freshness that you can bring to this deal will easily drive the market on this stock."

"What about financial security issues?" asked Melanie.

"The money will be placed in an off shore bank of your choice. It does not matter to us; it can be European, Caribbean, whatever you choose."

"Franciose, you and I both know that what you're asking me to do could have major legal repercussions. The Security and Exchange Commission would be all over me if this became public. I could be disgraced and lose my job, my license, I could even go to jail for this."

"In our research and discussion with legal council, both in-house and consulting lawyers, jail time should not exceed eight months with proper legal representation, which you would have. We believe your representation of two minority groups will work in your legal favor. We will also place an additional fifteen million dollars in the off shore bank account of your choice. This money will be available for you to access within thirty days after being indicted of any criminal charges. It will be a war chest for an adequate legal defense, plus any inconvenience."

"Okay, is this the point where someone comes out and tells me to smile for the camera, that this is only a big joke?"

"Melanie, we didn't become the largest European investment company by joking."

Francoise reached into the brief case that had gone unnoticed next to his chair. He took out a thick, confidential-labeled envelope that was the size of a small town phone book.

"Please open this and review it. It may help you understand how serious we really are."

Melanie tore away the heavy tape that provided security on the package envelope and removed a bound black notebook. There was a sense of fear when she saw her name on the cover with a picture of her on the inside.

"You see Melanie, we are aware of your entire background. We know everything about you from your birth until now. Your friends, family, virginity and even Dr. Stenson Hawk's desire for a pediatric surgery residency."

Maintaining her composure Melanie said, "I'm impressed and I must admit," she paused because everything was happening so fast she couldn't fully get her arms around the enormity of the offer Francoise had placed before her. Her voice remained steady and her words calm.

"I really am impressed and, I must admit, concerned about your research efforts. You have certainly made quite an offer to me."

"But of course, success is better when you have someone to share it with. We are aware of you desire to be close to the young Dr. Hawk."

"That true. What does that have to do with this deal?"

"This is the closure. We know of your desire to be close to your family in San Diego as well; we have the influence to guarantee the good young doctor a pediatric surgical spot at the University of San Diego. The chairman of the department and I are actually old friends. If you would like to relocate to San Diego we can offer you a spot with our international currency exchange firm. As you Americans say, that should be the icing on the cake."

"Are you serious?" Melanie asked the question slowly and pointedly.

"Quite serious," said Francoise his response equally slow and pointed.

This time he produced another smaller envelop and handed it to Melanie.

"This is a small indication of our good faith intentions and our interest in working with you."

Melanie's hands were visibly moist and shaking as she accepted the thick business envelop. The flap was not closed and she could see the contents.

"You'll find inside one hundred fifty thousand dollars of good faith money. It's yours to keep regardless of your decision to work with us on this project."

Melanie said, "No, I can't accept this. I'm flattered but extremely uncomfortable with the way this works."

"Most newcomers are, but I assure you while this may be new to you it is quite the way business is transacted at this level. If you want to be in this league, this is how we play. Please, take the money and buy your mother that new car she's never had."

"I'm sure your research has revealed my ambition for financial success and recognition."

"And this offer provides that." said Francoise.

"This offer provides that," repeated Melanie, then she paused before asking what was probably the most important question, "Are you sure you can help Stenson?"

"You have my word on all that we have discussed."

"What about Adam and the shareholders of CORE, how will this impact them?"

"This should truly be a winning situation for everyone. CORE will get the fair market value for its company and offered the same positions under our new ownership."

She reflected on Francoise's offer for a moment, than extended her hand, which was embraced by both of his outstretched hands.

"Okay Francoise, perhaps I should think about this for a few days, but I know a good deal when I see one. Who will know about our arrangement?"

"Three people will know; the corporate owner, who likes to go unnoticed, you and I."

"It's important that you never tell Stenson."

"He will never know, I assure you. If you handle your part of the deal we will handle ours."

"To say that Stenson would be very upset if he had any idea I was intervening in his fellowship program would be an understatement. I believe he can get into a program on his own merit but I like the idea of having him in San Diego."

"Rest assured Melanie that we are not novices at this. We will guard your interest as well as our own. Now for a more important topic, do you smoke?"

"Smoke?"

"Yes, do you smoke?"

Francoise retrieved a small metal case from his briefcase.

"After each business deal I like to share a cigar with my new partner."

"My friend, I shall not be the one to break that tradition."

Melanie had actually developed a taste for cigars. She and Kathy often met in one of the cigar bars on Beale Street to smoke and drank cognac at the end of a trying week. Francoise extended the open cigar case to Melanie and gave her a cigar cutter. She placed the cigar to her nose, having learned to appreciate the effect a cigar has on all the senses. The touch and sight of the paper wrapping, the scent of the fine tobacco and the taste of the smoke as it danced against her palate were all exhilarating. She clipped the end, placed the cigar to her lips and Francoise provided the blue flame. He moved the flame to his cigar and in a short time the room was filled with the aroma of Cohiba tobacco. She looked at Francoise with a broad smile and said, "I'm not sure if it gets much better than this."

"Melanie, I assure you, this is only the start. It does get better, in fact, the best is yet to be."

Melanie was quite curious about another topic which she thought Francoise could offer some clarification.

"Francoise," she said in a soft but inquisitive voice.

"Yes, my dear Melanie," Francoise responded, with his head leaned back and his lips puckered in an oval as he exhaled smoke rings.

"What is the connection between you and Adam? I was surprised to observe that you guys clearly have a personal history."

"Melanie," the corners of Francoise's mouth were arched in a smile and his eyes were distant as he continued, "You should be reminded of the level at which you are currently operating." He paused in search of the most appropriate words, then said, "you will find the players to be few and the circle small.

"Really Francoise, have you previously done business together?"

He moved into his response as if he had expected the question.

"I studied in Montreal and it was there that I met Adam Wellington. I have been Chief Financial Officer for Dorchel International for quite some time. During the early years, when we had recently gone public, Adam was chairman of the board for an American company that aggressively tried to take over Dorchel."

Melanie's eyes widened. She placed her cigar in the ashtray before saying, "The company was Atlanta-based. I can't remember its name right off," she was holding the sides of her head with both hands.

"You're right, it was Atlanta-based, the name is unimportant. Adam served as chairman of their board during that period and was the architect of the acquisition effort."

"We reviewed that case in one of my business courses. The chairman of Dorchel prevented the acquisition by following an old Asian approach..."

"Suicide."

"Did that really happen Francoise?"

"The CEO of Dorchel International died, but was it really suicide?" He reached for an ashtray as he picked up his cigar, using the cutter to remove the previously lit end. The blue flame from his lighter produced a red glow of the tobacco which generated the pleasant aroma that circulated about the room. He continued, "Was it suicide? Maybe." He tilted his head, exhaling as the rings of smoke slowly floated about the room. Francoise held his cigar at a right angle as his eyes locked with Melanie's. He then said, "Or how do you say it? Maybe not."

twenty-seven

The extra leg space in the first class cabin made the four-hour flight from San Francisco to Memphis tolerable. Melanie had taken an earlier flight so she would not have to travel with Jim and Frank. She needed time to think about the deal she had made with Francoise Baptiste since she was uneasy with all aspects of it. She didn't like the idea of having Francoise orchestrate Stenson's acquisition of a pediatric surgery fellowship, she should never have accepted the money from Francoise, nor should she have agreed to accept money for betraying Adam. The pieces did not fit. There was more to this deal than she had been privy to. She was sure Francoise had already decided to make this offer to her when they met in Amsterdam. But why her? Did her youth, ambition and inexperience make her the best choice? Better than Jim Little or Frank Bailey? Things didn't feel right, they just didn't feel right.

Melanie was standing on the sidewalk of the departure terminal waiting for Kathy when she was aroused from her thoughts.

"Hey girl!"

"Kathy!"

Melanie's voice showed delight in seeing her friend, although she was double-parked, standing outside her car with the trunk open.

"How long have you been here?" Melanie asked as she maneuvered through others who were busily trying to load their bags and leave before the airport security hassle started.

"Not long, but this airport security guy kept sweating me to move until I gave him my phone number," said Kathy.

"I can't believe you still give out that fake phone number."

"Melanie, this guy didn't seem too bright but he was as fine as hell," Kathy said.

"So you gave him your real number?" asked Melanie.

After placing the luggage in the trunk they gave each other a warm hug. The drivers behind them started honking their horns.

"Let's get out of here before your airport cop comes back," Melanie suggested.

Kathy turned on to I-240 and traveled East.

"How was it, Melanie? Did you make a lot of money? Are the European men as sexy as people say? I'm told all this freaky stuff we do here comes from over there. And what about that guy you had dinner with in San Francisco, did he offer you a couch promotion? Oh yeah, and what about Stenson, have you heard from him yet?" Kathy was more inquisitive than a research scientist.

"I have so much on my mind right now, Kathy. I'm concerned about Stenson because I haven't spoken with him since I returned to the States."

"But what about everything else?"

Kathy's car swerved into an adjacent lane, causing the driver to scream obscenities while giving a middle finger gesture as he drove by.

"Kathy please, if you don't keep your eyes on the road we'll either end up in a ditch or someone is going to act out their road rage."

"Okay, okay. But what about everything else?" Kathy asked again.

"Everything went fine but I need to speak with Stenson, I really feel a need to talk to him. I'm certain now that I have agreed to something I could never do."

Melanie walked into the house with Kathy trailing on her heels and moving her mouth like a bell's clapper. They each sat in one of the over-sized chairs Melanie had in the center of her media room. They were trying to catch their breath after hauling the luggage from the garage into the kitchen.

"Melanie I'm going to leave this stuff in the kitchen. I'm not going to take it upstairs. You really should have your master bedroom downstairs."

"It doesn't matter, I'm going to do some house hunting soon," said Melanie.

"Really, that's great. What part of town are you considering?"

"Honestly, after this deal is finalized I'm not sure if I won't consider relocating."

The phone rang and Melanie reached for the portable phone on the table next to her.

"Hello."

"Madame Walker?" The voice had the tonal quality that accentuated his French accent.

"Yes."

"Monsieur Baptiste instructed to call and inform you of a package which will be delivered to you this afternoon at three o'clock. You must be available to receive it. The instructions are clear and an email address will be enclosed for contact purposes in addition to a verification for completion of the initial financial agreement. Goodbye."

The line went silent.

"Hello, hello. Hello?" Melanie repeated.

"Melanie, who was that?" Kathy asked.

The room suddenly felt unusually cold for such a bright Indian Summer day and Melanie began to shiver as she replaced the phone.

"Melanie you look like someone just scared the shit out of you," said Kathy with a concerned look.

Melanie noticed the clock on the table near the telephone showed the time as 12:30 pm. She knew Kathy would ask a hundred questions if the package arrived while she was there. So she replied, "No girl, I guess I'm just tired from the trip and I was thinking about what Stenson must be going through."

"Well, who was that?" Kathy asked as she motioned her head towards the telephone.

"Kathy please, you're worse than my mother. Look, I need to shower, unpack and have a little time to myself. I'm sure you understand."

Melanie rose from her chair, lifted Kathy gently by the arm and walked her towards the door.

"I really appreciate your picking me up. I'll give you a call later, okay?"

"But I thought you wanted me to bring you up to speed on everything that's been going on while you've were away."

"I'll call you later and we'll go over everything then."

Melanie opened the door and Kathy was still talking as Melanie said "goodbye" and shut the door.

twenty-eight

Gina cried uncontrollably, it reminded Stenson of her high school graduation where during her commencement speech she broke into tears while speaking of the unconditional love of her family.

"Gina I'm sorry we had to go this route but we were really worried about you," said Stenson.

"You obviously were able to find out where I lived. Why wouldn't you just walk up and ring the damn door bell?" she asked, while looking at Mickey. Her eyes were menacing when she closed them into narrow slits to make them barely visible.

"But I guess in the future I won't be answering many door bells because that's how this worthless piece of shit came into my home and ..."

"Gina stop!" interrupted Stenson.

She stopped herself and turned again to Stenson.

"Stenson have you and Daddy lost your fucking minds?

Why would you do this to me? I'm completely in the dark on this one!" said Gina.

"Gina, Mick has done a surveillance of you and a background check on your friend. James Beaudoure is a pretty shady character and we didn't know if your life was in danger."

Gina held up her hands with one palm turned towards Stenson and the other covering her ear as if trying to shut out a terrible sound.

"No, no, please don't tell me you came all the way to New Orleans to kidnap me from my boyfriend. Please don't tell me that." Gina continued, "Yes, Captain James Beaudoure is my best friend and my boyfriend. I met him over a year ago when I was living in New York. He was in town attending a police conference. And yes, he does have enemies. That's why we have the dogs and the guards. But Stenson you must meet him, he is the smartest, kindest, most loyal and funniest man I've ever known. He's good to me in ways that I haven't experienced in quite some time. And you know that's saying a lot, because you and Daddy spoiled me rotten."

Stenson loved it when she smiled and remembered how he, after the incident in Atlanta, never saw her smile again after she heard of the comatose state of Peter Pan, her rapist and batterer. She always felt responsible for that, even though she and Stenson had never discussed what really happened.

"But Gina, why would you get involved with someone who works on both sides of the law?"

"Stenson, I know him, you don't. You can't believe everything you read. Listen, James is no choirboy but he isn't a sadist either. He works around bad people and sometimes he has to use nontraditional means of convincing them that he is determined to do his job and get the desired results."

"Gina, no one needs to remind you that he's been accused of being responsible for the murder of people."

"Yes, Stenson you're right. He has been accused of killing people. But I gave him the benefit of the doubt just like I did you."

Mickey was sitting in the kitchen area of the suite drinking orange juice, eating a leftover beignet and reading the *Times Picayune*.

"Mick," said Stenson.

Mickey turned, with beignet in mouth, to look in Stenson's direction.

"Will you give us a few moments alone please?"

"Sure Doc, no problem. When you guys finish, call me on my cell phone. The number is on the nightstand and I'll be at Petunia's having breakfast. I'll leave one of my guys in the area just in case he's needed."

Mickey nodded towards Gina then turned and closed the door behind him as he left the suite. Stenson said to Gina, "Let me tell you about that night in Atlanta."

"Stenson, I'm not sure I need to hear it. I just know that if it weren't for me you wouldn't have been over there with Peter Pan in the first place."

"You really don't need to know the details but I did go to his place with bad intentions. When I confronted him about what happened to you he began to mock me, 'Oh, so baby sister got too high and big brother is here to take up for her.' When he said that I lost my cool and grabbed him, threw him against the wall and roughed him up a little. But when I left he was still alive, talking, walking and promising me an ass whipping next time we met."

"Stenson, Peter Pan had so many enemies, even his mother could have left him in that comatose state. That's all behind me now, I really only care about my life and those who are in it."

"How's your health? That has been our big concern. We were worried that you were not receiving the proper medical follow up."

"I've been fine, of course I lost some weight and hair with chemo but now my hair has grown back. As a matter of fact I have a medical appointment tomorrow. The lymphoma has not grown over the last six months but the doctor still says it's inoperable."

"Does James know?"

"Now he does. At first I tried to keep my illness from him. I didn't want him to feel sorry for me. But when I started losing weight he thought I had some kind of eating disorder."

"You, an eating disorder? The way you can put away a good meal, that's a joke!"

They giggled like two small kids.

"But as we grew closer, I couldn't keep secrets from him. So I told him I had lymphoma, I told him about Atlanta, the time I spent in the hospital and how I felt dirty and worthless and just wanted to die; but was too chicken to kill myself. I told him everything."

"Every thing?"

"Every thing." Gina appeared thoughtful, as if she was searching for what to say next. Then she continued, "Except that I come from a family of doctors and educators who would not accept my relationship with a New Orleans cop who most people considered dirty. Stenson, you would really, really like him."

"Gina, Mom and Dad want you back in Selma. Dad has made arrangements for you to be treated at UAB."

"Stenson only God knows how much longer I will live, so what ever time I have left I will live with James. I appreciate the effort you took to find me, but I won't leave him. I won't, not for anything or anybody. I love him desperately and I feel his commitment to me is equally measured. Stenson you just gotta meet him, you've just got to."

Her eyes were beginning to tear again.

"I am not asking you to leave him Gina. But I will have to meet him before I leave New Orleans."

"You bet! I'll call him now."

She jumped up lifting the cordless phone from the coffee table then said, "Stenson, I'm sure by now James knows I'm missing and he probably thinks someone is trying to get to him by kidnapping me."

"Well, call him before he kicks the shit out of the wrong person," Stenson said with a smile.

Gina dialed the number.

"Hello," said James.

"Hey baby."

"Gina, are you alright, where are you? If anyone harms one hair on your head, their ass belongs to me!"

"Baby, hold up, hold up. I'm fine, my brother Stenson is in town from Memphis and we had a little misunderstanding. I'd like you to meet him."

"Where are you?" Gina placed her hand over the receiver and asked, "Stenson, where are we?"

"You're at the Ritz Carlton Hotel on Canal Street. Suite 506"

"Baby, I'm at the Ritz Carlton on Canal Street. We're in Suite 506."

"I'll be there in twenty minutes."

twenty-nine

When the doorbell rang, Melanie looked at the clock on the fireplace mantle, it was 3:00 pm. She thought, "At least the anticipation is over," as she moved across the room to the front door. Melanie stopped to peer through the stained glass door prior to opening it. Her heart was racing at a pace of its own. When she finally opened the door the only sign of life was the squirrels playing between the trees in her yard. The package at her feet almost went unnoticed. She picked up the surprisingly small envelope and stepped back into the foyer where she quickly closed and locked the door.

Melanie had become melancholy since her return from San Francisco. While she usually enjoyed hip-hop and some rap, now she listened to the old masters and thought about her father. The music of John Coltrane's "Love Supreme" played in the background as she took the compact disc from the black and silver envelope.

Her computer was located inside a mahogany armoire in her sunroom facing her rose garden. She briefly reminisced about her father's saying that "God was in an extremely good mood when He made San Diego and red roses." She knew her father wouldn't approve of her current business agreement to earn money by deceit.

Melanie took a seat and placed the CD in the computer drive. When the disc started the moving images instantly disturbed her. There appeared to be Adam Wellington with Senator Daniels in a small, dimly lit room. Large pillows were strewn about the floor and other men were standing around. The gathering of men appeared quite social as most of them were drinking and smoking, while others appeared to be inhaling a white powder. Each appeared to have one or two undressed young boys next to him. Melanie switched the computer off as she was unable to continue watching the disturbing scenes. She noticed a small note inside the envelope, which she opened and read.

"I will call you now," was the message. The ringing of the telephone at that moment startled her.

"Oh my God," she said just above a whisper, "what have I gotten myself into?"

She walked over to her caller ID, the display showed: PRIVATE INCOMING CALL, "Damn," she thought. She had forgotten to set her phone so all unidentified calls were rejected.

Melanie took a deep breath and picked up the receiver.

"Hello," she said.

"Hello, I see you've made it back."

"Oh, I'm so happy to hear your voice," it was Stenson.

"So much happened during my travels that I need to share with you," her voice reflected quiet desperation.

The phone line beeped to indicate another call. Melanie didn't want to answer it, partly in fear of who it might be and, because she had not heard from Stenson in so long that she wanted nothing to interfere with their conversation.

"Stenson where are you?"

"I'm in New Orleans at the Ritz Carlton. Don't you want to catch the other call?"

"No, not really, but hold on for one minute. I'm expecting a phone call."

"Hello," said Melanie.

"Madame Walker?"

It was the same voice with the thick French accent.

"Yes."

"Monsieur Baptiste requested that I call you."

"Hold one minute please," said Melanie, "I have a long distance call on the line."

"I will call back in four minutes."

The line went silent. She returned to Stenson's call.

"Stenson, I'm sorry I've got so much going on. How's Gina and when are you coming home?"

"Gina looks fine under the circumstances. She's taking a shower now and her boyfriend is on his way over."

"Her boyfriend ?"

"Yeah, it's a long story that will blow your mind. This has been a trip like something you read in a novel."

"So when are you coming home?"

"Well, I must interview at UAB soon and I hope Gina will go home to Selma."

"Is she considering that?"

"Well, not exactly. We'll see what happens after I meet her boyfriend and she speaks with our parents."

"So, again, when will you be home?"

"I'll call my parents after I get some idea of what Gina's plans are and hopefully get back to Memphis late tomorrow and then to Birmingham for the interview."

They continued to chat until Melanie's phone beeped again.

"Stenson, hold one minute."

She hoped the incoming call was not business. She clicked over.

"Hello."

"You are still on the other line."

It was the French accent.

"Yes, would you..."

"Listen to me swiftly." The voice interrupted, "The images are to be used to discourage Monsieur Wellington's resistance to our acquisition. Dr. Hawk's pediatric surgery fellowship is done and your funding has been completed. You should begin by lowering the initial stock price. There should be no further questions; we have fulfilled our end of the deal. You have one week to do your part. I shall monitor your progress. Goodbye."

The receiver went dead. Melanie's fingers were numb. Her thoughts were running rapidly without control to images of the disc, the men, the nudity, the encounters, the young boys. Images about New York,

Amsterdam, the dinner in San Francisco, Stenson and her parents bombarded her mind. She wondered how she would be able to confront Adam when he discovered her betrayal. She imagined her thoughts to be similar to one's life flashing before them prior to death. Melanie knew she wasn't dying but felt death would be kinder than the damage she was about to inflict on Adam Wellington and CORE.

The phone began to ring. Stenson! She forgot Stenson was on the other line.

"Stenson, I am so sorry. My thoughts had just taken me away and I forgot you were still on the line."

"That's okay Melanie , I need to go now because someone is at the door. I'll call you when I get back home. I'll be in Memphis for only one day before traveling to the Birmingham interview."

"Have you received an invitation to interview at UCFS?"

"No. I've been gone for the last few days, but I do expect some kind of correspondence when I check my mail."

"I'll look forward to hearing all the good news when you get back to Memphis. Stay safe."

"I will and how was the tour? I don't think we've spoken since you were in Amsterdam."

"Stenson, I'm not sure but I may have gotten into something much bigger than me."

"What?" Stenson's voice reflected his concern.

"When you get in call me; let's meet and talk. We need to talk, it doesn't matter what time."

"That sounds good. I'll hit you back as soon as I get in. We do need to talk. I really miss your face."

"And I miss yours. Bye."

"Bye."

Melanie placed the phone back on the armoire and looked out at the rose garden because the beautiful flowers always brought her joy and comfort. Now everything fits, she thought, she understood everything; but whether or not Stenson would understand was her immediate concern.

thirty

Their images didn't seem imposing when viewing them through the peephole. But when Stenson opened the door the three men standing in front of him were quite imposing. One was dressed in an ocean blue pinstriped suit, the other two were in uniforms of the New Orleans Police Department.

"My name is Captain James Beaudoure of the NOPD and I'm looking for Ms. Gina Hawk." Mr. Beaudoure removed a badge from his inside coat pocket and held it for Stenson's inspection.

"Sir, who are you?" James Beaudoure asked in a heavy Cajun accent. He looked more like a banker than a New Orleans police officer.

"I'm Dr. Stenson Hawk. Gina's brother."

"May we come in sir?"

"Sure."

Stenson moved away from the door to allow the trio to enter. The two uniformed officers immediately drew their guns and began to move through the suite. One opened closet doors while the other moved into the back rooms. Then James drew a gun from his jacket. Speaking to Stenson he said, "Turn around please sir, put your hands on the door and spread you legs."

He was polite but quite police-like. He began to frisk Stenson with one hand while holding his gun in the other.

"Do you have any ID? Who else is here with you?"

"There's ID in my back pocket, and Gina and I are alone."

"James!"

Gina had come from the rear bedroom with her hair wrapped in a towel and wearing a white Ritz Carlton robe.

"Gina?" James responded.

"James! Put that gun away before you shoot somebody." James ignored her command and continued to frisk Stenson.

"Now tell me why you're treating my brother like a New Orleans criminal? Although I must admit he's been acting like one," she said while looking at Stenson.

"Kidnapping is a Federal crime Dr. Hawk and killing my two dogs should be a capital offense punishable by death."

"Trust me, I've given them all kinds of shit about those dogs."

The phone began to ring. Gina answered it.

"Hello."

"Gina is everything okay?" It was Mickey calling.

"One of my boys spotted two NOPDs and a third guy entering your suite. We are right outside the door, cough twice if you need us to come in."

"Mickey, everything is fine. It's my boyfriend and a couple of his officers. We're okay."

"Are you sure?"

"I'm sure."

"Chief, everything looks clean in here." One of the uniformed officers reported.

"Good, will you guys please wait for us outside?" asked James.

"Sure Captain."

Then James looked at Gina standing in the middle of the room and walked over to embrace her. She appeared to disappear in his large arms, her feet dangling as he lifted her from the floor.

"Gina what in the world is going on, I've had my guys all over the City looking for you. They even roughed up a few people. Now I'm going to have some serious apologizing to do."

"Baby, I'm sorry. We had some family issues here that we needed to talk about."

"Since Gina is obviously not dressed to go out, I'll call room service and get us some food up here." said Stenson.

"That'll work," Gina said as James lowered her to a standing position.

"Now, let me formally introduce you two, for the record. Dr. Stenson Hawk, this is the light of my life Captain James Beaudoure of the New Orleans Police Department. Captain Beaudoure, this is the future Pediatric Surgeon extraordinaire, Dr. Stenson Hawk, my big brother."

"Hi Stenson, I've heard good things about you. But I don't think Gina ever mentioned you were a doctor," James extended his hand to greet Stenson in the traditional manly grip with eye contact.

"Well, my sister is very sold on you and I'm not surprised she didn't tell you I am a doctor. She tries to down play the family's dark side." They all laughed.

"Look, I'm totally confused. Let's sit and talk about what the hell's been going on this morning," said James.

After their food arrived they ate and talked for several hours. Each of them revealed something new; each shared something that had never been shared. James spoke of his experience being one of five children, his parents working two jobs to move them from the Lower Ninth Ward of New Orleans to East New Orleans. And how the untimely death of his father, led to his involvement with the criminal element of the city and then law enforcement. Gina spoke of her emotional as well as physical struggles since she'd last seen her brother and how James was instrumental in getting her to this point in time. Stenson shared funny and tragic stories of his experiences in medicine. He told them about the unintended suicide of Caroline Lewis and how it still haunted him. There was much laughter, some tears and great concern as to what the future offered. Gina's health was of concern to all of them.

"I feel fine and have one more round of chemotherapy and that's it," said Gina.

"She really has done well. We had a few tough times with the nausea and her loss of energy because she's accustomed to doing a dozen things at one time. But we got her on a great diet and started using one of the trainers from the New Orleans Hornets basketball team three days a week. Now she's pretty much her old self as I'm sure you can tell," James said with the compassion of a loving caregiver.

"But Stenson, would you believe the crap I thought would bother me the most didn't." Gina said.

"What was that?" asked Stenson.

"You know, I really thought that hair loss was going to throw me. But it really didn't. A bald head can be quite a fashion statement," Gina said with a smile.

"And what was your fashion statement with a baldhead?" Stenson asked.

"I wore the neatest hats, scarves, wigs and earrings. I must show you some pictures of me with a bald head. I think you'll like the style."

Her face blushed with a sense of wholeness. She was at peace and it wasn't just a matter of love, she seemed comfortable yet unresolved with her place in life. Stenson knew that she was fine and that James shared her love and would care for and protect her with his life.

"I tell you what, let's call Mom and Dad. They will be so happy to hear your voice."

Gina and James were on the love seat next to a window that overlooked Canal Street. Stenson walked over to the window and looked at the people who were strolling, window shopping, entering and leaving the trolley cars. He wondered if their lives were fulfilled and if they were happy. He also wondered if love or companionship had much value to them. Then he said, "Okay, let's give Mom and Dad a call."

"Would you like to speak to my parents?" Gina seemed really interested in having James speak to them more than Stenson did. James' response was like great sarcasm wrapped in a warm day.

"I could think of nothing better." He picked up the phone and passed it to Gina.

thirty-one

The next afternoon James turned onto I-10 West heading towards the New Orleans International Airport.

"We may be cutting it close but I think you'll make your flight," said Gina.

"Yeah, the traffic isn't too bad in the evening so we should be able to get you there," James added.

"Look guys," Stenson said, speaking from the back seat of the truck. "I'm really sorry about your dogs. I have a good friend in L.A...."

"Now when you say 'L.A.' you don't mean Lower Alabama do you?" James asked.

"No, L.A. is truly Los Angeles. At any rate, he breeds and trains Rottweilers. Let me have him send you two pups." Stenson offered.

"I really appreciate that Stenson, maybe that will help reduce the grief." Gina's tone reflected her realization of her loss.

"Thanks Doc," James said as he slowly brought the black utility vehicle to a stop.

"Northwest Airlines departure terminal," James said in a hip-hop, subservient tone with a splash of Creole flavor.

"Okay man, take care of my sister," Stenson said while placing a firm hand on James shoulder from the rear seat.

"Your sister is covered dude," replied James.

"Hopefully she's covered better than she was on yesterday when

Mickey 'jacked her," Stenson said with a sarcastic giggle.

"He better be glad I wasn't there," retorted James.

"By the way James, my father has a friend in Mississippi who lives right outside of Memphis. He once worked for the FBI," said Stenson.

"Fleetwood ?" Gina asked with a bit of surprise and excitement.

"Yeah, Dad left a message for me to contact him when I get back to Memphis," said Stenson.

"I haven't seen him in years. When you speak with him give him my love," said Gina.

"I will. James, this guy is a technology security expert. He may be able to give you some free tips on how to improve your home security."

"Baby, you should talk to him," Gina said, "nowadays technology is much more effective than people and dogs."

"Cool, thanks Stenson, I appreciate that information," said James.

Stenson lowered his head and balanced himself as he descended to the sidewalk from the utility vehicle. Gina lowered her window as Stenson approached.

"Okay baby sister, I'll see you at Mom's and Dad's in a couple of weeks."

"Stenson, next time you need to see me just call, okay."

"If you promise me you won't disappear again."

"I promise."

"Then I promise also."

"Love you, and tell Melanie's executive ass to call a sister sometimes."

"I will little sister and I love you too."

He placed a warm kiss to her forehead, nodded his head to James, then turned and disappeared among the flow of travelers through the electronic doors and into the airport terminal.

thirty-two

"Mark, I tell you, I really feel good about my interviews." Stenson and Mark were in the Trauma Holding Area waiting for the arrival of their other team members.

"Do you really?"

"I really do. I like UAB because it's close to home, but I really think I'd take the San Francisco spot if I get the offer."

"Well bro, I'll say a prayer for you. I hope you get the San Francisco gig, then the wife, kids and I can stay with you when we visit."

"Mark, I really don't know about that, I've heard your kids still aren't house broken."

"They aren't, that's why we need to stay with you. The word is out so we can't stay in any hotels in San Francisco, in fact, the kids' pictures are posted in the lobby."

They both laughed.

"Code Blue trauma level one, Code Blue trauma level one, Code Blue trauma level one." The operator could be heard over the intercom throughout the hospital. A patient was being transported by ambulance to Trauma Area One in full cardiac arrest secondary to a gunshot wound. Mark grabbed his still unwashed lab coat. Stenson removed his stethoscope from a nearby table and placed it into his lab coat pocket and said, "Let's go and join the rest of the team."

They began running at a speed slowed only by their negotiations with the freshly mopped hallways.

"Oh shit!"

The loud profanity echoed in the hall. Mark had failed to fully negotiate a turn and lay sprawled on the floor.

Stenson slowed to assess Mark's injury while still in sprinting form. Mark had cursed but there was no sign of blood so, after sliding into a wall, all extremities were still in motion.

"I'll meet you there," said Stenson as he continued to run.

Mark threw up his hands and motioned Stenson forward. Stenson made a sharp left that led him into the short hallway feeding into the major trauma treatment area. Several white coats surrounded a stretcher where their movement, speed and intensity were much the same as worker bees attending to their queen.

"What's the story on this guy?" Stenson directed his question to the lead nurse who was documenting the resuscitation efforts.

"Do you guys need any help?" asked Stenson.

"No," the nurse responded, "I think Trauma Team Blue is handling this one."

Stenson looked over the shoulder of one of the residents who was working franticly to regain a blood pressure. The patient's face looked familiar but Stenson couldn't quite put it together. He appeared to have gunshot wounds in the head and chest.

"That guy looks familiar," he said, again directing his conversation to the lead nurse.

"Don't all trauma patients with gunshot wounds?" the nurse answered.

"Not really. Do you know his name?" asked Stenson.

"Sure, let me see," she stumbled through her papers until she found the Patient Information Card.

"Okay, his name is Jones, Mr. Jawun Jones."

Stenson's mind flashed back to a young man standing in the window of a hospital room. He remembered entering the hospital room to change Jawun's dressing for an injury received from a knife wound inflicted by his mother. Jawun's voice was haunting, as he had told them, "Doc, I got things together."

"Who is this guy?" Mark had managed to hobble to the excitement.

"Man, how're you doing, that was a nasty fall. Will you do it again so I can videotape it?" Stenson asked.

"I busted my ass, but I'm fine. Who is this guy?" Mark asked again.

"You remember the guy whose mom stabbed him?"

"Yeah, I remember. We thought he would die in ICU. Didn't he change his life around, started reading the Bible and all that stuff?" asked Mark.

"Same guy. Well, that's him with gunshot wounds in his head and chest," said Stenson.

"He probably pissed off some drug dealer and the guy decided to bust a cap in him," Mark speculated.

"It was more like helping instead of walking away," a police officer said. They had not noticed him standing next to them, also observing the resuscitation efforts. He continued speaking but addressing the two physicians more directly.

"Apparently he was pumping gas and noticed a woman being pulled from her car by two young punks trying to carjack her. He intervened, knocking one of the guys to the ground. Giving the mother time to remove her daughter from the backseat of the car and run away. He didn't notice the second punk, who walked up to him from behind and shot him twice, until it was too late. When we got to the crime scene he was breathing but unresponsive."

"Did you get the shooters?" Stenson asked.

"No, but we have a good description of them both. They won't be free very long," said the Policeman.

There was no sign of life in Jawun's body; the table and floor were covered with the blood that had previously maintained his life. The resuscitation efforts had ceased and the hospital attendants were unfolding a body bag for Jawun. The hospital Chaplain walked into the family waiting area to inform the mother of Jawun's departure. The initial silence was short lived and exploded with the screams of his mother's palpable cry.

CHAPTER

thirty-three

Melanie had not slept well and had not been into her office since returning from San Francisco a week earlier. Her friend Kathy stopped by to check on her because she was concerned. When Melanie opened the door Kathy stood speechless at the sight of her. Melanie's eyes were streaked like Christmas candy canes, her eyelids were puffy and her hair looked like she was trying to make a poor fashion statement. Melanie looked like a losing contestant on Survival. As she entered the kitchen Kathy noticed shoes in the middle of the floor, dishes in both sinks and she smelled a stench of old garbage.

"Kathy I think I'm in over my head with this thing," Melanie was frantic.

"Well isn't Stenson back in town?" was all Kathy could say.

"Yes, but I really haven't had a chance to talk with him. I saw him briefly for lunch when he returned from New Orleans but he flew out the next day for his interview in Birmingham."

"But he's back in Memphis now, right?" asked Kathy.

"I told you yes." Melanie's voice was stressed and she was beginning to let the tension show.

"Melanie, calm yourself."

"I'm sorry, I just feel overwhelmed. Stenson got in from Birmingham last night, we talked briefly but he was on call."

"Are you going to tell him?" Kathy asked after they spent the

Ambition | 199

better part of the morning with Melanie's confessions. She needed someone to confide in and Kathy got the job. Melanie unleashed everything like water flowing over a dam including the initial meeting with Adam Wellington, the meeting in San Francisco with Francis Baptiste and the CD containing the activities of the Senator and Adam. The more she spoke the more she cried. It had all happened so fast and the more she spoke it became obvious that her seducers—power and greed —had blinded her.

"I can't tell Stenson that I had a hand in his Pediatric Surgery interview in San Diego. I can't tell him I cut a deal that will screw my client. Kathy you do understand, don't you?"

Her comments were really pleas. Kathy embraced her as they both cried.

"Hello, Melanie? Frank and I have been quite concerned about your absence. What kind of symptoms have you been experiencing?"

That was exactly what Melanie needed. A call from Adam concerned about her absence and at the same time trying to make a medical diagnosis of her.

"Really Adam, I should be fine in a couple of days."

"I'll have my assistant send a wonderful fruit basket to our number one investment banker," Adam continued.

"Adam that really isn't necessary, but I do appreciate your phone call and thoughtful concern."

Talking with him, she still found it incomprehensible, a relationship between Adam and the Senator with underage boys.

"That's the very least I can do at this point. I have suggested to Frank that you receive a significant bonus reflecting your hard work and dedication to our success," Adam said.

"That's kind of you Adam," Melanie was beginning to feel like Judas.

"Melanie, I've heard a few rumors that there might be some efforts to interfere with our stock market opening."

Melanie's heart began to race, her hands moistened and small droplets of water formed on her brow. For a moment she was speechless.

"Melanie?"

"I'm sorry Adam. I haven't rested well for the last few nights. Would you repeat your question?"

"Oh Melanie, I'm sorry for bothering you with rumors. I'll talk to you about things when you get up to speed."

"Sure, be good and I'll see you soon."

Replacing the phone to the receiver, Melanie knew it was impossible to keep her end of the deal. Her greatest concern at this time was what the cost would be for backing out.

"I am sending someone to Memphis tonight to secure our deal for the upcoming public offering on the New York Stock Exchange. Madame Walker has only forty-eight hours to close this deal."

The Lear jet was flying over the Atlantic, on its way from Amsterdam to New York against a backdrop of rain and turbulent winds. Francoise had to stop in New York to make final arrangements for Dorchel International's immediate acquisition of CORE after its opening on the New York Stock Exchange.

"Are you concerned that she may become unwilling to complete the deal on our behalf?" Phoenix asked.

"There is always such a concern. That is why I am sending someone to Memphis to monitor and motivate her progress," Francoise said.

"I see, if the news is not good, notify me immediately."

It was an atypical, cold and rainy evening uncommon for the Gulf of Mexico. Phoenix thought it wouldn't be a bad idea to consider setting up in the Caribbean. With the profits from the acquisition of CORE perhaps it would be wise to buy a place there because unlike life rainy days are few.

thirty-four

Stenson was bouncing off the walls. He was running through his apartment leaping and touching the recessed lighting during his springboard elevations. The certified envelope, addressed from the University of San Diego, was in one hand and his telephone in the other.

"Hello."

"Dad!" Stenson yelled into the receiver as if trying to warn his father of an oncoming train.

"Son, are you alright?" The senior Dr. Hawk questioned.

"Dad, I did it, we did it, I got it Dad, they took me, I'm in, I'm in!" exclaimed Stenson.

"Son, calm down so we can talk about whatever it is that you've done, got, or that took you."

Stenson stopped in the living room area where huge windows faced the Mississippi river. He sounded out of breath.

"Dad, I got accepted into the Pediatric Surgery Program at the University of Alabama Birmingham and to top that off, I've been accepted into the University of San Diego without having an interview and I really don't remember applying! Can you believe it? I got both of them!"

"Well, well, well. My son the Pediatric Surgeon, your mother is going to be so excited to hear that you plan to attend UAB for your training."

Stenson sat in one of his oversized chairs.

"Well Dad," his father could sense the hesitation in his voice.

"I'm not one hundred percent sure I'll take the UAB offer. I've done most of my training in the Southeast and it may be nice to study in a different part of the country."

"You know what Stenson, I think you will find that your mother and I both agree with you in principle. Plus you are a man now; I like your thought processes and decision-making ability. Just think about it and let us know what you decide."

"Thanks Dad, you guys did a great job preparing me."

"We think so. Have you told your sister yet?"

"No Dad, I'm going to call her when we finish talking."

"Good, I'm sure she'll want to share in the good news. I'll be glad when you two come to visit and, if her schedule permits, bring Melanie. Your mother would love having her and Gina in the house at the same time. And I can spend time with you and James."

"You know Dad, that's a great idea. I'm seeing Melanie later and it may actually be a good time for her to visit Selma. Now that she has finished with that CORE Healthcare project she can probably schedule a weekend."

"How did it go?"

"I'm not quite sure. She sounded excited during the tour but when I spoke with her since she's been back she sounds a little flat."

"Well give her my best and extend the invitation for her to join us."

"Great, oh yeah, Dad I almost forgot. How is the election campaign going?"

"Quite well son. I've been endorsed by the Alabama Education Association, a teachers' union, and have a fundraiser coming up this week."

"I am really proud of you Dad."

"And I you, son."

thirty-five

"*Madame Walker, I understand* your reluctance but you must remember that we have a deal."

The phone call had caught Melanie by surprise and she found the tone of the conversation disturbing.

"Look. I'm not going to do this. You can take your money and we can call it a day."

"Madame Walker."

His French accent adopted a more menacing tone.

"Your associate, Dr. Hawk should have already received his acceptance to the University of San Diego, funds have been transferred to off shore bank accounts as we agreed. There are no options."

"Mr. Wellington called me today to ask had I heard about a plan to interfere with the initial stock offering. He already has a sense that something is up."

"No Madame, he understands that he has a valuable company, many enemies and how do you Americans say it, skeletons in his closet. These should bring cause for his concern."

"Who are you, I want to speak with Francoise about this, I'm not going to do this and I don't care who you tell."

"You truly do not want to know me. If I speak my name to you it will be in person and that would mean you have not done what was expected of you. At that point my meeting will be to persuade or punish you."

"Listen, don't threaten me."

Melanie said trying to control the trembling of her voice.

"I'm not going to do this and I plan to let Mr. Wellington know what's going on."

"In that case Madame Walker, you will shortly know my name."

"Hello, hello." The line was dead.

The phone rang again. She jumped, startled by the sound, but did not pick up the receiver. A few minutes later it rang again. Melanie looked at the caller ID that only showed "Out of Area." She was not going to be intimidated to do something that she thought would be unforgivable. She picked up the receiver.

"Hello," her strong voice belied her nervousness.

"Melanie."

The male voice was quite familiar.

"Dr. Hawk?"

"Yes, how are you?" His tone was low and his speech not as brisk as she was accustomed to hearing.

"I'm okay, but you don't sound so good."

"Have you seen or spoke with Stenson? I've been trying to reach him without success."

Melanie could hear the tension in his voice, something uncharacteristic for the senior Dr. Hawk.

"Actually he should be on his way here. Is something wrong?"

"We just received a call from James, Gina's boyfriend. Gina's missing, apparently she went shopping and never returned home."

"What does he think happened to her?"

"I'm not sure how much Stenson told you about New Orleans but Gina's boyfriend thinks this could be the result of him roughing up a few guys when he thought Gina had been kidnapped to retaliate against him."

"Stenson gave me some background on that trip," said Melanie.

Dr. Hawk continued, "I feel directly responsible. Had I not taken my approach to getting Gina the circumstances for this event would not have been set."

"Dr. Hawk, don't beat yourself up about this, I'll try to reach Stenson and have him call you ASAP."

"Thank you Melanie, I haven't told my wife yet. I don't want her to know until I have more information. James has asked me not to call the police, he wants eighteen to twenty-four hours to check his sources."

"Dr. Hawk I am sincerely sorry, I'll find Stenson."

"I've already attempted to reach him at home, without success." said Dr. Hawk.

"Have you tried reaching him on his cell phone or paging him?"

"I've tried all means and have not been able to reach him."

"I'm expecting him anytime now. When he gets here I'll have him call."

The sun had set several hours earlier without any word from Stenson. Their dinner reservations were for seven and it was now past ten o'clock. This was extremely unusual for Stenson. He was always on time or would phone to say that he was running late. Melanie decided to call his father, so she placed a call to Selma.

"Dr. Hawk I've paged Stenson and called the hospital but he's not there; and he's not answering his cell phone. But let's not worry."

"Melanie, I'm sure he's fine. Perhaps we'll hear from him by morning."

Melanie decided to go to bed at eleven o'clock. The house was quite and made the chimes of her doorbell take on a mystical quality. Melanie rolled over to view the clock on her nightstand. The doorbell rang a second time before her eyes could focus on the clock, which she could barely see. Even with the luminated numbers she needed her contacts to see that it was after midnight. Then her phone rang, she looked at her Caller ID. It was Stenson's cell phone.

"Hello."

"Melanie, I'm at your front door let me in," said Stenson.

"Where have you been, I've been trying to reach you all evening and so has your father."

"Will you please let me in and I'll tell you what happened. It's been a bad enough day." Stenson said.

"Okay."

She wrapped herself in her robe and slid her feet into her slippers. As she moved towards the door she thought of all there was to share with Stenson. Where could she begin, where had he been, and why did he show up on her doorsteps after twelve o'clock in the morning? Not to mention he had missed their dinner date.

"And where have you been?" Melanie asked when she opened the door; leaving the chain latch hooked.

"Why are you looking at me as if I'm fresh off a bootie call? I just got out of jail," said Stenson.

"You just got out of jail. What happened?"

She unhooked the chain latch, allowing Stenson to enter. His jacket and pants looked as if they had been slept in but his eyes were without sleep.

"Stenson, what happened to you? Why were you arrested and why didn't you call me?"

"I got arrested on a DWB."

"What's a DWB?" Melanie asked.

"A DWB is Driving While Black."

"Driving while Black!"

"I got pulled over downtown for a U-turn and sometimes shit happens. Specifically, I was driving my car without any identification. When I realized it, I made a U-turn to go home and get my wallet and a policeman pulled me over."

"Stop right there," said Melanie, "it appears to me that you were stopped for making an illegal U-turn."

"Perhaps so, but anyway I tried twice to reach you. Your line was busy the first time and when I called later, no one answered. I didn't want to call anyone else. But I finally decided to call Mark at the hospital and he came and bailed me out of jail."

"The phone rang earlier but I didn't get to it in time. It must have been your call."

"What's going on? You said my father is trying to reach me."

"Stenson, Gina is miss..."

"Do you hear that?" Stenson interrupted.

"What? I didn't hear anything."

"Sounds like someone is trying to get in the kitchen door."

They both heard the noise coming from the back door. As they quietly made their way into the kitchen they saw the doorknob turning.

"Melanie, are you expecting anybody? Or does Kathy or some dude have a key to your house?"

"No to both questions."

"Where's your gun?" whispered Stenson.

"I don't have a gun."

"You told me your father bought you a gun and showed you how to use it and that you went to the shooting range and all that stuff."

"I lied, I was trying to impress you."

"Damn, Melanie!"

The intruder had bypassed the lock and the kitchen door was slowly opening.

"Melanie, dial 911!"

Then Stenson moved quickly behind the kitchen door waiting for the intruder to enter and Melanie picked up the phone, placing it to her ear.

"Stenson the phone is dead!" Melanie whispered.

She did not realize the intruder was making his way through the doorway. The tall muscular man was bent slightly forward to enter without bumping his head. Before he could stand up straight, Stenson leaped from behind the door landing on his back. He placed his left arm around the intruder's neck and, applying pressure with his right arm, administered a chokehold. The intruder stood upright revealing his six-foot-plus frame and began to spin around, trying to throw Stenson from his back. He grabbed Stenson's arms while leaning forward and pulled them so that Stenson flipped forward and landed on the floor in a fashion usually seen in professional wrestling. In the same motion he removed a metal pipe from his jacket and raised it over his head.

"You should not have been here," the intruder said as he swung the metal pipe towards Stenson's head. Melanie heard a loud crack and the intruder just stood still with the metal pipe in a midair swing position. There was initially a look of satisfaction on his face but in a split second it was replaced by an empty stare. He dropped the metal pipe and fell forward like a tree cut down in a forest.

Melanie began screaming when she saw the second intruder standing in the doorway with an object in his hand.

thirty-six

He was much smaller than the first intruder. He was a well dressed African American who held an object that appeared to be a small, weighted, leather bat in his hand.

"That's a big ass boy, but he's not worth a shit when it comes to taking a hit. I really thought I'd have to slam his ass a coupla more times to make him fall."

Stenson slowly got up from the floor and looked at the lean, but muscular, figure in the doorway.

"Mick, what in hell are you doing here?" Stenson asked with a big smile.

"You know this guy?"

Melaine asked Stenson, surprised and frightened by the events of the past few minutes.

"Your father sent me, apparently he was concerned that you couldn't be reached." Mickey walked into the kitchen and closed the back door.

"Who is this guy?" Mickey asked as he began searching the intruder's pockets.

"You don't see cat burglars in twelve hundred dollar Brioni suits and six hundred dollar Ferragamo shoes," Mickey said. The search revealed a German passport, a cell phone, cash, a Glock handgun and a small sack of equipment used to pick locks. Mickey also removed two sets of handcuffs from his jacket pocket which he used to lock the intruder's left hand to his left foot and his right hand to his right foot.

This gave the intruder an arched, hamstrung appearance.

"Melanie, this is Mick." They both nodded. "He is the private investigator Dad hired to find Gina," Stenson explained.

Melanie fell to her knees and began to cry. Stenson moved to her side and lifted her to a large sofa.

"Melanie what's happening, what is going on?"

"It is so bad Stenson, things are all wrong and everything in my life is falling apart. It's bad Stenson, it's really really bad."

"What's happened, is something wrong with my family, is something wrong with you? Melanie, come on."

"Stenson, it's everything. Gina is missing, that's what your father was trying to reach you about. I think that burglar was here to harm me because I cut a bad deal, I cut a really bad deal."

"Gina is missing?" Stenson asked as he removed his hands from Melanie's shoulder and stared forward expressionless.

"Your father said James called and told him Gina never returned home from shopping yesterday. He's not sure if it's some kind of retaliation for his roughing up a few guys when you were in New Orleans."

"Shit!" Stenson yelled.

"I know, I know, it's bad Stenson. It's really, really bad. The deal is bad, it's all no good," Melanie was beginning to ramble.

"And what's this stuff about you cutting a bad deal?" Stenson frowned his brow as if nothing made sense to him.

"Stenson, the CORE Healthcare deal, Adam Wellington and the Senator are having what appears to be illegal homosexual liaisons involving young boys," Melanie blurted out.

"What, Melanie are you out of your mind?" asked Stenson.

"You're not talking about Senator Colin Daniels are you?" Mickey's interest in the conversation was now stimulated.

"Yes, and I've been asked to convince Wellington to make some concessions prior to the stock offering."

"What're they planning to give you for the job?" asked Mickey.

"They've given me some money already and are offering me lots more. They've also promised to get you a Pediatric surgery fellowship spot in San Diego. When I told them I had changed my mind about helping them, I got this phone call saying they would send someone over," Melanie said, as she pointed to the figure laying on the kitchen floor. Mickey asked, "So they sent this guy?"

"I think so."

"Are you telling me the letter I received from the University of San Diego was a result of this deal?" Stenson appeared completely confused.

"Stenson, I know it sounds bad but I know how much you wanted to be on the West Coast and I wanted to be there with you."

"What?" he asked, still in a state of confusion.

"Stenson, you may think I'm not ready for anything between you and me, but I saw this as an opportunity to have it all; to get the financial security and power that I want and to have the man I want. We would be in the same place and doing the things that make us happy."

"Well what's the problem?" Mickey injected, "It sounds like you cut a pretty good deal for everybody and these guys are coming through."

"I can't do this to Adam. He gave me an opportunity that others would not have even considered. I can't turn on him like that, I just can't, I just can't. If what I saw on the CD is true, something needs to happen to him but not like this."

"And if you could deceive Adam, you certainly wouldn't be the woman I know, so we'll have to work through this. But this situation with Gina, I just don't understand it and I don't know what to think. I've got to call James," said Stenson.

The cell phone on the waist of the fallen intruder began ringing and Mickey removed it. Stenson said, "Let me have it."

He walked over and extended his hand to receive the phone from Mickey.

"Hello," Stenson said. There was no response, but he could hear someone's breathing becoming faster and faster.

"Hello," Stenson said again. The rapid breathing continued to interrupt the silence on the phone.

"You can keep quiet but we just fucked up your boy." Stenson said while looking at Mickey standing over his large victim, who was now moaning. Mickey opened the door adjacent to the kitchen, which led to the garage.

"Ms. Walker please," The voice on the phone spoke just above a whisper.

"Who's calling?" Stenson demanded.

"Sir, to delay me from speaking with Ms. Walker is in no one's best interest."

Stenson walked over to Melanie, who at this point was regaining her composure, less fearful of the unknown person on the other end of the phone. Stenson switched the cell phone to speaker and handed it to Melanie.

"This is Melanie Walker," she said in a business-like tone.

"The gentleman that your associate professes to have "fucked up" was sent to get the CD. We are quite disappointed in your lack of loyalty. If you do not cooperate and return the CD, there will be serious repercussions."

Mickey moved his car into the second empty slot in Melanie's garage. But he was listening carefully to the conversation that was taking place as he returned to the kitchen. He stopped and parted the large wooden kitchen blinds to look through the window facing the front of the house.

"Look, its not like you think. I'm not...," Melanie said as Stenson walked over and whispered to her, "Melanie, you really don't know who you're talking to. Don't say too much."

A black utility vehicle with its lights off stopped across the street from Melanie's house. Mickey noticed two men getting out of the back seat as one man exited the rear door. The driver and a front-seat passenger remained inside. As the three men crossed the street towards Melanie's house the utility vehicle, with its lights still off, slowly drove away.

"Stenson, Melanie, I think we have some more company," Mickey's voice was calm but concerned.

"What's going on Mick?" Stenson asked as he walked to the window and looked over Mickey's shoulder.

Mickey turned the lights off in the kitchen and said, "We have three bad guys, Melanie hang up the phone."

Melanie continued talking on the phone so Stenson walked over, took the cell phone and disconnected the call.

"Why did you do that Stenson? I think I know who sent this guy."

"Melanie, slip on some shoes and jeans," Mickey ordered with a sense of urgency, as she stood in her pajamas, "and let's get the hell out of here!" Mickey continued, "I'll go into the garage and start the car while you guys grab a few things. We need to be out of here in sixty seconds."

Stenson turned to the intruder who was lying face down on the floor moaning and smelling of urine and grabbed his shoulder. He rolled the large man over so the handcuff position arched him on his side like a bow. Stenson straddled him and placed his thumb on his right eye.

"Who sent you?" Stenson asked as he began applying pressure to the intruder's right eye.

"If you don't tell me in two seconds I plan to blind you and I'll do the same to your left eye. Furthermore, if being blind doesn't bother you, I'll cut out your fucking tongue and ram it up your ass."

As Stenson suspected, the big guy had a low threshold for pain. It took less than two seconds for him to say, "I was sent by Phoenix."

"Oh my God, that means the three guys outside must have been sent by Adam to get the CD!" Melanie said. Then, almost as an afterthought, she and Stenson spoke in unison.

"Who is Phoenix?"

Things began to happen very fast but the action seemed like slow motion. The sound of the front door being kicked in was simultaneous with the sound of footsteps moving, in a brisk pace, on the hardwood floors down the hallway. Stenson stood quickly from his straddled position over the intruder. He looked at Melanie and said, "Lets get the fuck out of here!"

He grabbed her hand and quickly moved through the kitchen, into the garage, and jumped into the car where Mickey was already behind the wheel. The toxic scent of the engine exhaust branded his urgency to leave.

"Get in the back seat and lie down." Mickey instructed. The garage door was opening slowly, but when it did they would be ready to go. He was driving a CL 55 Mercedes Benz with a backseat roomy enough for a midget or a bilateral amputee.

As the garage door slowly opened two pairs of shoes, then legs, then bodies and arms could be seen. Stenson could also see the third man who was in the kitchen headed towards the open door that led to the garage.

"Ms. Walker, you have something for us. Get out of the car and everything will be fine." They were unable to tell which of the two men was talking.

"Hold on guys, it may get a little bumpy." Mickey said. But as he placed the car in reverse, the third man made his way through the kitchen and was attempting to open the car door. He snatched Mickey's hand from the steering wheel.

"You should never touch anybody without asking permission, so don't touch me!" said Mickey in a firm voice.

The assailant quickly released Mickey's arm as the car speed from the garage. He did notice, however, that blood covered his entire hand and forearm which was initially numb but quickly overcome with the sharp pain associated with the amputation of his first three fingers. The assailant never saw the razor sharp surgical knife Mickey always carried.

When the other two men attempted to side step the speeding car, one wasn't swift enough. The sound and sensation of the tires rolling over his body was similar to the popping of plastic bubble wrap used to pack boxes. The guns must have had silencers because only the sound of the bullets bouncing off the cement could be heard.

"They must be shooting at the tires," Mickey observed.

"Mick! You may have killed that guy!" Stenson exclaimed.

"Maybe, but I prefer that to having him kill us."

A black utility vehicle blocked the long driveway, so Mickey made a sharp turn and cut across Melanie's front yard.

"They'll never catch us," he said. In his rear view mirror Mickey saw the second figure jump into the utility vehicle as they began to follow. Mickey quickly drove to I-240 and headed West. By this time he was traveling well above one hundred miles an hour and saw no signs of anyone following.

"Well team I think we lost them," Mickey said as he slowed his speed. "What's next?" he asked as if this was all in a day's work.

"We need help, I think we should go to the police," said Melanie.

"Not the cops. Not right now or we would sound crazy," said Stenson.

"It seems like Adam is after me but I have absolutely no idea about the identity of Phoenix," Melanie said.

"You have absolutely no idea about who Phoenix is?" asked Mickey, looking over his shoulder as Melanie and Stenson sat up on the back seat.

thirty-seven

"Do you think we should head to Nashville?" asked Melanie.

"Isn't that the headquarters for CORE," Mickey inquired.

"Yeah, and it might not be too late to speak with Adam about this," Melanie added.

"Noooo, nooooo." Stenson shook his head from left to right as he spoke. "Dad said if I ever had any trouble I should go to Fleetwood's."

"Yeah he did," Mickey was reminded of the conversation.

"I've heard his name before but I don't think I've ever met him," added Melanie.

"You've never met him because if you ever did you wouldn't forget Fleetwood."

"Okay, I have his address which your father gave to me. So let's head to Coldwater, Mississippi," Mickey said.

"Well, maybe after those goons search the house and get the CD, things might cool off," said Mick.

"I don't think so," Melanie said as she reached into her jacket pocket and held the CD for Stenson and Mickey to see.

"I still have it," she said.

"I'm not sure that's a good thing," Mickey commented.

There was a brief period of silence.

"So Gina is missing?" Stenson asked looking at Melanie.

"Yes."

"I need to call my parents."

"Not now, let's get to Coldwater. Stenson, didn't you say Fleetwood was ex-FBI?" Mickey asked.

"Yeah, he has a technology background so he might be able to help us sort things out. Maybe he can help us discover who this Phoenix person is and find out what kind of shit Adam Wellington is into besides the Senator and little boys," commented Stenson.

"I wish I had thought this through better, I'm sorry Stenson, I am so sorry," pleaded Melanie.

"I know Melanie, I know you were just trying to help me and get some of the things you want. We'll work this thing out. But remember, you must be careful what you ask for."

Mickey merged from I-240 onto I-55 South to Coldwater, Mississippi. The early morning sky was so dark it looked like a black velvet curtain draped down onto the highway. It was nearly two o'clock in the morning when the trio exited on to I-55 South and they expected to arrive in Coldwater before daybreak.

Meanwhile Phoenix was outraged about the turn of events with Melanie.

"Francoise! Why would you try and pressure her that way?"

"I thought he would just intimidate her a little and then she would be more cooperative," said Francoise.

"You must find her within twenty-four hours, alive. CORE Healthcare is coming to the New York Stock Exchange and we desperately need her to complete this deal," said Phoenix.

"I understand."

"Then get on with it Francoise!"

"I will."

"I'll fly to Memphis as soon as the pilot prepares the plane. Find where she has gone and let me know in-flight. At this juncture no harm must come to her. She is still of much value to our project. Do you understand?"

"I do Phoenix, I do understand."

"Please don't continue to disappoint me, such is not in your short or long term best interest."

The phone line went silent.

Phoenix lit a cigar and looked out over Cinnamon Bay. St. John Island was always a favorite place where peace and order could be found. But now there was no order or peace. The price Melanie was willing to pay to achieve her business aspirations had been grossly overestimated. Her sense of loyalty and right were much stronger. Phoenix inhaled softly, creating a bright red glow of the cigar's tip. Exhaling slowly, the cigar smoke floated like a cloud overhead.

There are pressure points for everyone and everything. For people with morals like Melanie the suffering of others was a point of change, a pressure point. So Phoenix decided it was time to create some pressure points. Pressing the intercom a voice quickly responded, "Yes, what would you like of my services?" the male voice was quite attentive.

"Call New Orleans, I want James Beaudoire on the line, it's time to let him play hardball."

thirty-·eight

"You couldn't find a safe house that was on a paved street?" Stenson asked. The light rain only made the potholes much more difficult to avoid.

"We need a four-wheel drive out here." Stenson added.

"Well Doc, this is where your father told me to bring you if there was any trouble."

"Why would his father think there would be trouble?"

"Apparently he received two strange phone calls, one asking for Stenson and the other for you Melanie, both callers had foreign accents. Anyway, we shouldn't have much further to go," said Mickey.

They were headed to the home of Dr. Edward Fleetwood, a retired FBI recluse who had claimed Stenson's father as one of his few friends for many years. Dr. Fleetwood and the senior Dr. Hawk were classmates when both were medical students at the Medical College of Wisconsin. Although Dr. Fleetwood became disenchanted with medicine after his sophomore year and dropped out of medical school he decided to pursue a career in software engineering. He continued to live in Milwaukee and his studies in software engineering earned him a Ph.D. from Marquette University. He and the senior Dr. Hawk were able to continue their friendship, each depending on the other for moral support.

When Fleetwood finished his academic studies, he did free lance software design for computer companies from Microsoft to IBM. Then he was brought to the attention of the Federal Bureau of Investigation because of his development of some of the first successful antiviral software and firewall protectors. He later helped the FBI in the apprehension of a number of computer hackers and ultimately joined the FBI on a permanent basis. But that was short lived. After five years he found the rigid structure of the FBI quite similar to the structured world of medicine, so he resigned his position and continued his freelance ventures to develop new ideas for computer surveillance and software security.

In truth, Fleetwood was equally brilliant and unpolished. His speech, style and demeanor were much too eccentric for the FBI or any institution. He never married because marriage was another institution he found too rigid. The idea of answering to one person for the rest of his life was unthinkable. Except for an equally intelligent but toothless female he shared time with while on assignment in Mexico City for the FBI, Stenson's father was one of the few people who understood and accepted his eccentric ways.

"Are we there yet?" Melanie asked from the back seat where she had fallen asleep shortly after crossing the Mississippi State line.

"We have about one mile of this gravel road left and then we should be there," said Mickey.

"Where is 'there'?" asked Melanie.

"We're about eighty miles south of Memphis just below Como, Mississippi," Stenson said. He continued, "Fleetwood has a home here on the Coldwater River."

"Is he expecting us, Stenson?" asked Melanie.

"I gave Stenson the number," Mickey said, looking at Stenson for confirmation.

"No, I didn't call him. I hope he's home."

"Me too," said Mickey.

The gravel road was lined with trees so close together they brushed the car doors and made the potholes more difficult to avoid.

"Wow!" Melanie exclaimed.

"No shit!" Stenson responded in kind.

The beauty of this location was evident. There was a small home, almost like a European cottage, nestled against a large river backdrop.

"I haven't been here in years, since Gina and I were kids, but I do remember it being quiet and peaceful," Stenson said, as he reminisced about the fun they had enjoyed in this rural area. They parked in the open carport next to an old red pickup truck with a shotgun rack and rebel flag in the rear window. The lights of their car allowed full view of the river.

"Okay guys this is it," said Mickey.

Stenson stepped out of the passenger side and instantly a pain, the likes of which he'd never experienced, forced him to the floor of the oil stained, concrete carport. A painful, inaudible sound pierced his ears. Melanie and Mickey where equally stricken. Mickey fell next to Stenson and used both of his hands to cover his ears and prevent the invasion of additional pain. Melanie was pinned to the back seat of the car by the discomfort and confusion of the bright lights and the horrible sound. As quickly as the onset of pain started, the carport became illuminated in a blinding light. Closing their eyes did not prevent the intrusion of the brightness. Melanie assumed a fetal position while Stenson and Mickey were both pinned to the floor of the carport. Lights in the interior of the house were now on but there was no sign of movement.

"Who are you?" The voice was menacing and mechanical, almost like the voice behind the curtain in the Wizard of Oz."

"Who are you? If you don't answer in ten seconds you will never see or hear again."

"Dr. Fleetwood, it's Stenson Hawk and two of my friends," Stenson yelled.

"Stenson Hawk, Abraham Hawk's son?" The voice was still mechanical and menacing.

"Tell me something that only Abraham Hawk or his family knows." The menacing tone became more inquisitive.

"Stenson, I thought this guy was a family friend," Mickey said. He was lying close enough to hear Stenson's rapid but controlled breathing.

"Shit Mick, I always heard that he was a little different."

Stenson rolled from his side to his back in order to project his voice upwards towards the mechanical voice.

"There is a picture of you and my father in the gross anatomy lab at the Medical College of Wisconsin from when you were first-year medical students. My father told me that you threw up all over a cadaver and that..."

"Stop, okay, okay, I don't need to hear that story again."

The mechanical voice had been replaced by a pleading yet expressionless human sound. The blinding white light was replaced by the starless darkness of the night and the noisy sounds created by the chirping crickets. A door adjacent to the carport opened and the silhouette of a small, rounded man with large ears could be seen behind a screened door. He just stood there wearing a baseball cap and rocking side to side, as if to the beat of music. Then he opened the screen door and yelled, "Please, ya'll come in, I done spoke wit' yo' daddy. He said it would be two and when I seen three folks, I thought maybe it be some not welcomed company."

Stenson stood and extended his hand to assist Melanie who had bent forward to get out of the back seat. They moved towards the screened door, maneuvering around the fishing tackle boxes and riding lawn-mower. They entered through a side door into a small hallway with wood paneled walls. As they went into the kitchen a washer and dryer could be heard behind a closed door. The area was quite compact with a small cherry wood table, set for one, in the middle of the room. The aroma of fresh coffee and the sound of a window unit air conditioner filled the room.

"Come on in folks and make yerselves at home, I'll bring up a few mo' chairs here in the kitchen. I was 'bout to make a lit'le breakfast for me and Kitty."

He motioned to an object in the corner of the room where a small dog of undetermined pedigree, and not much larger than a wood rat, stood in an attack position, growling.

"Relax Kitty," Fleetwood said in a paternal tone and continued, "she's not use to company since we don't get a lot of visitors. I'm still working wid' 'er on some house manners." He extended both arms openly and said, "That's aside anyway Stenson, sho' gud to see yer. Ain't seen yer in quite some time! Yer done got quite big like yer daddy, but good lookin' like yer ma."

Fleetwood was slightly taller than the back of a high chair and his moon-like face was seamless. He wore an Ole Miss baseball cap with the Confederate mascot positioned above its brim. His ears were so large that his looks reminded Stenson of Dumbo the elephant. His faded overalls obviously had not made the washing pile in some time and his worn cowboy boots had certainly seen better days. Fleetwood enjoyed the slower pace of the south and the anonymity rural life provided.

No one would have suspected that his software programs had recently been purchased by ten major Fortune 500 companies and five major government agencies for their antiviral capability. Much of his work dealt with such problems as the Worm computer virus. He also created an interactive web site for the senior Dr. Hawk's Senatorial Campaign.

His movements were swift and purposeful. He took several short steps to position himself in Stenson's arms and they embraced. Then he turned to the two bystanders and asked, "And who these here?"

"Melanie, this is Dr. Fleetwood," Stenson said.

"Is she why ya'll running?" asked Fleetwood.

"Yes, and this is Mick."

"And this is Mick. Your father told me he found Gina."

"Yes, he did a good job on that," said Stenson.

"Why do you suspect we're here because of me?"

"Well, it won't be the first time a buteeful lady got a man in trouble."

Fleetwood smiled and simultaneously extended his hands to Melanie and Mickey, warmly grasping them both.

"Um sorry fer the lights and stuff but I don't like guns and I hav'ta protec' mysef."

"Dr. Fleetwood," Melanie was interrupted.

"I'm simple, jes' call me Ed or Fleetwood. I don't like that docta stuff. Have a seat and how 'bout a cup a' coffee? I ain't sho' how much ya'll know 'bout me but tell me what yer trouble is and I will try to hep ya."

Fleetwood gathered three additional chairs and poured coffee for the four of them. The sun had begun rising and the dawn could be seen from a large window as rays from the sun danced on the river. Kitty settled down and slept comfortably in Fleetwood's lap as he listened to the full story of CORE Healthcare, Dorchel International and Melanie's deals with Francoise that involved Stenson and his fellowship program. They also described the CD of Adam and the Senator, the break-in that caused their exodus to Coldwater and the unknown player called Phoenix.

"Well Ms. Melanie, I think yer got quite a problem," Fleetwood said.

"Let's do this, you folks take a lit'le nap, ya'll seem to be a bit tide. Melanie you got the CD?" asked Fleetwood.

She reached into her pocket and passed it to him.

"Okay, while you folks res', I'll take this CD to my computer lab," said Fleetwood.

"Computer lab?" Melanie repeated with surprise.

"Yup, it's in the basement. When you wake up jes' come into the door off the den."

Fleetwood pointed to a small door the height of which only he and Kitty could enter in an upright position.

"Ya'll have to stand in front of the camera and call me to let you in."

He pointed to a small speaker located in the corner of the crown molding above the door's small entrance. It was the size and shape of a woman's lipstick tube.

"These the speakers that greeted you. I invented 'em myself to provide three major functions. Each got a'small digital camera, th' speakers' good fer music and to make th' sound you felt but couldn't hear and they gotta visual capacity too."

"All in that?" Melanie questioned as she pointed to the lipstick-size object in the corner.

"All in that," Fleetwood confirmed.

"Thanks, Fleetwood," they each said.

"Stenson, I'll call yer Dad and let'em know you're fine. But I don't think we oughta worry him wid' all this other stuff 'til I'm more clear on what's hap'ning. I think he got enouf' to worry wid' the senate race an' all," said Fleetwood.

They all agreed.

"I only got one bedroom and one bath," said Fleetwood, "I'll set some clean towels and clean linen on da' bed. Melanie you kin have th' bed and th' boys kin have th' floor. I got sleeping blankets that'll make it more comfey fer yer."

As they began their rest the sun was rising over the river. Fleetwood took the CD from its case and placed it into his computer. The scenes were disturbing and as the scanning started Fleetwood wondered why anyone would knowingly let such a film be created. But he was quite sure about the credibility and authenticity of the film.

CHAPTER
thirty-nine

She was excited about being in Memphis for Stenson's surprise party. Gina thought how sweet it was for James to pick up the cost for plane tickets with such short notice. He was so thoughtful to take time off from work to make the trip to Memphis with her just to see Stenson.

"So, sweetie is Melanie going to meet us at the airport?" Gina asked as they waited for their luggage at Baggage Claim, but they were in no hurry as their flight had arrived in Memphis a few minutes ahead of schedule.

"Melanie is taking Stenson out today to keep him occupied while things get set up. So we'll take a cab downtown, I've made reservations at the Madison Hotel. We can do a little shopping before the party," said James.

He grabbed the two small Hartmann cases when they arrived on the conveyer and Gina picked up her cosmetic bag. They left the terminal and took a waiting Yellow Cab. It was a sunny day and Gina was certain Stenson would be surprised to see her and James. On the one hand Gina was really excited about being in Memphis with Stenson and Melanie, while on the other she had a nagging concern that there was something untoward about it all. It did appear strange and unusual that Melanie would plan a party on such short notice.

The driver of the burgundy Ford Taurus which was following Gina and James had gone unnoticed. He had placed a call to Phoenix and was waiting for the call to connect.

Ambition | 231

"Hello."

"Phoenix, they have arrived."

"Very good, I will be staying at the Madison Hotel."

"I will continue to follow them."

"Well I hope so, isn't that what you're hired to do?" asked Phoenix.

"But of course!"

"Goodbye."

As Franciose suggested, Melanie's background check had been extremely thorough. The envelope he gave her in San Francisco did not include the information he had for Gina, which included the background on James. When Franciose initially approached James he thought it was a setup:

"Naw man, I'm a NOPD officer, I'm not taking no money to help you do nothing with Gina. Plus I don't even know her brother or this Melanie person," James said to Franciose, "and for all I know this could just be another set up for me."

"But Monsieur Beaudoire," Francoise said, "we are an international company which you can verify. My boss is willing to give you money for being available and should we choose to use your services the stock options that will be offered you will make you an extremely wealthy man. This offer is much more than you will ever have by just being the boyfriend of a Black American Princess."

"Well Mr. Baptiste, I'll take the stand by money in large unmarked bills. But if you need my services I'll take the cash value of the stock options and not the options themselves."

"So we have a deal?"

"We have a deal."

"I trust you understand that telling Gina means the deal is dead?"

"Don't worry, I don't mix business with pleasure. Women can be obtained easier than wealth."

CHAPTER

forty

She didn't hear them enter, but they had subdued Stenson and Mickey tying them to wooden chairs. Their feet and chests were bare and their bodies immobilized with rope and wide, clear duck tape. They both had dirty, blood-stained towels stuffed in their mouths and had been severely beaten. Open cuts covered their faces and heads. Fleetwood lay motionless at their feet, with a stream of blood running briskly from the back of his head.

The three men in the room looked familiar. Melanie had seen one of them at her home the previous night, the one whose fingers Mickey had cut off. His hand was wrapped in a bloody dressing. The other two men resembled Adam Wellington and Franciose Baptiste. They were all dressed in black, standing at the foot of the small bed were she huddled.

Sunlight from a small window appeared to create a halo around Stenson and Mickey; in one motion, without hesitation or stimulus, Adam turned and placed a gun to Mickey's head and pulled the trigger. Brain matter and body fluid covered the wall as the impact pushed Mickey's head back when his body fell to the floor. He lay motionless, but remained in the chair, the towel falling from his mouth his eyes empty.

Stenson sat upright in his chair, rigid but not shaking, his soft brown eyes connected to hers and closed as he fell backwards, his splattered brain matter created a similar pattern on the wall as Mickey's.

Melanie screamed but it was inaudible and her eyes were tightly shut. The persistent barking of Kitty filled her ears, but she could not see him in the room.

Her clothes were drenched with perspiration but the room was cold from the breeze of the window unit air conditionor. She continued to hear the barking dog and a voice calling her, which sounded like Stenson.

"Melanie, Melanie!"

She had to force her eyes open because her eyelids were very heavy; as if someone had tied them shut with a tight blindfold. Everything appeared blurred as her eyes began to focus on the eyes closest to her face. They were brown, bloodshot and squinted with concern. They were familiar eyes. They were Stenson's.

"Melanie! Baby, are you alright?"

"Yes Stenson. I'm sorry. I must have been dreaming," responded Melanie.

"You scared the shit out of me. You were screaming, yet in a deep sleep. Waking you was very difficult," Stenson said as he embraced her, placing her head to his shoulder and softly stroking her soft, beautiful hair.

"Could you please get that ornery mutt to stop barking," Melanie pleaded sofly.

Kitty was standing in the doorway going at it full throttle.

"I beg to differ with your assessment of Kitty's dog lineage."

Fleetwood was now in the door with Kitty standing between his legs and Mickey at his side. His southern dialect was noticeably gone.

"Stenson, is Melanie okay?" Mickey's concern was obvious.

"Just a bad dream Mick but I'm fine now," said Melanie.

"Well, while you folks were up here sleeping, I got a lot of work done and I think you'll be surprised," said Fleetwood.

"Why has your voice and demeanor changed?" asked Melanie. She was confused and somewhat skeptical about the character change.

"This is probably who he really is," Mickey said.

"Correct, sometimes you have to hide your hand until you know the full story," answered Fleetwood.

"What did you find?" Melanie asked.

"Follow me."

Fleetwood motioned his hand forward, turned and moved down the narrow hallway with Kitty at his heels. The walls were lined with pictures of music greats. Of course Elvis was there, but he also had pictures of Miles Davis, John Coltrane and Johnny Cash, all in similar wooden frames. Everyone walked in single file behind Fleetwood through the small living room to a small opening where immediately the stairway was lighted by sensors. Stenson lowered his head and followed, with Mickey and Melanie behind.

"Watch your step, 'cause these here steps be close together." Fleetwood chuckled at his momentary character change.

They each held on to the wooden banister as they descended to a small landing. Fleetwood moved near a large steel door where an illuminated panel was mounted on the wall. He placed his palm on the face of the panel that created an orange glow followed by a silent parting of the steel doors.

"This is my situation room, it helps me stay in touch with other folks in the world. I can also handle any situation from this location," Fleetwood said with pride.

The technology in the room was a surprise to all of them. Melanie, Stenson and Mickey all considered themselves on the cutting edge of technology for their respective professions. But what they saw here exceeded their wildest imagination. It was what one expected to see in a Pentagon War Room, but never in the basement of a home in Coldwater, Mississippi.

"Well, what do you think?" Fleetwood inquired.

"I'm speechless," Melanie answered, "truly speechless."

The room was dimly lit and slightly chilly. Eight computer terminals with apparent activity on large screen monitors lined three of the walls. Fleetwood moved to the central computer and slowly slid into a small leather chair in front of the keyboard.

"Okay Miss Melanie, let me share with you what I've found."

Fleetwood pressed a key and all three wall monitors began to show the CD of Adam, the Senator and the young boys.

"I evaluated this disc for image placement, two dimensional

changes and color and shadow alterations. I discovered it to be quite authentic. What you see is what it is."

The images on the screens were becoming more graphic. When it appeared the Senator was about to sodomize one of the young boys, Melanie reached over and turned the monitor off.

"Please, I can't watch anymore," she said.

"Well. Now I understand why it's so important to get this disc. If any of this information was leaked before CORE Healthcare went public the stock value wouldn't be worth ten cents," said Stenson.

"How do you think Adam knows I have this thing?" Melanie asked.

"That kind of information is always out there. It's the kind of misadventure clients pay me to keep them from getting side swiped with," Mickey said as he looked around at the unbelievable amount of technology in the tiny basement.

Fleetwood continued as if he was unaware of the ongoing conversation, he said, "Next, I have transferred your money to an account I set up in Barcelona."

"Wait. I was told it's location is a secret and I'd receive all necessary information about it after the stock transaction was complete," said Melanie.

"Well?" asked Fleetwood.

"Well," she said looking at Stenson and Mickey as she spoke, while thinking Fleetwood must have been mistaken.

"Well, how did you get the code?"

"It was easy. Remember, this is what I do. You told me what country the account was in and the FBI has a file of all banks and company affiliations throughout the world, which is the result of the President's efforts to freeze international bank accounts of terrorist organizations," said Fleetwood.

"You must be a Republican," concluded Mickey.

"Please. Anyhow, since I've had so much experience designing the FBI systems it was easy for me to get through their fire wall and find the banks with which Dorchel International is affiliated," Fleetwood explained.

"So once that was done, the next step was easy?" asked Stenson.

"Quite easy. I got through to both banks and Dorchel's firewall, accessed their account and transferred the funds to the Barcelona account. But the neat thing is that I left a ghost behind," Fleetwood giggled.

"Fleetwood what does 'leaving a ghost behind' mean?" asked Melanie.

"The ghost is something new that I created. I removed the money but the transaction doesn't show up for seventy-two hours. The money can be seen on the accounts but it's not there. That's the ghost. So congratulations Miss Melanie, you've just become a millionaire," Fleetwood then saluted her.

"Fleetwood, I know you meant well but when the transfer is discovered they're going to kill Melanie."

"Stenson, they may be planning to kill her anyway. I don't think Adam's guys were coming over so early in the morning for coffee," said Mickey.

"But you said the guy who actually entered the house said he was sent by Phoenix, correct?" asked Fleetwood.

"Yeah, he did say he was sent by Phoenix, not Adam," confirmed Melanie.

"Okay, so I searched FBI, CIA and Defense Department files and found several "Phoenix" code names, but nothing that I was able to cross-reference with Dorchel, your brokerage firm, Adam Wellington or CORE Healthcare. Nothing. Nothing at all that fits," Fleetwood continued, "however, when I checked both your emails," he looked at Stenson then Melanie, "I found something interesting for you Melanie."

"How did you get my email address?" asked Melanie.

Fleetwood's expression was that an unnecessary question had been asked. He did not respond but continued to scroll the touch pad on the computer.

"This is it. It was sent late last night," he said.

Hi Melanie,

James and I will be there tomorrow for Stenson'ssurprise party. Can't wait to see you.

Gina

There was dead silence in the room. Melanie looked at Stenson with total confusion and overtones of fear.

"I haven't planned a surprise party for you Stenson."

"And I thought Gina was missing," Stenson added.

"Something must be terribly wrong," she said.

Fleetwood continued.

"Next, I cross-matched Gina and this James guy and discovered he is with the New Orleans Police Department and is not such an upright citizen. I believe that..."

Mickey interrupted, "Fleetwood we know all about him, when I tracked Gina to New Orleans we snatched her from that guy's house."

"I'm totally confused with that email," Melanie said reflectively.

"As I was about to say before you and Mickey jumped in, I believe I can put some of this together for you. Just give me a few minutes."

Fleetwood pressed a key on the computer keyboard and several photos of individuals appeared spread between the three wall monitors. Most were familiar but some were not.

"Okay, I believe these are the players and I believe these are the connections," he said.

On one wall monitor there were three photos, one of Adam, one of Colin Daniels and the other of Francoise Baptiste. The second monitor had a photo of James and Gina and the last monitor on the center wall contained the photo of a female with a young boy.

"Okay here we go," Fleetwood directed everyone's attention to Colin, Adam and Francoise.

"Remember all of these are done by cross matching people, places, events, and so forth. The FBI and CIA have all kinds of files that can be tapped into and I created the software that allows this cross-referencing of people, places, events, social-political and economic similarities. So do you guys understand the basic concept?" All three nodded "Yes".

"Good, with that in mind, I think it is no secret that these three men," Fleetwood said as he pointed to the photos, speaking their names, "Adam, Senator Colin Daniels and Francoise with whom you," now looking directly at Melanie said, "closed your deal in San Francisco; all three met at McGill Institute in Montreal."

"Adam and Senator Daniels were sophomores and Francoise was a graduate student in Finance. But what is interesting is that they were actually a foursome."

Pressing a computer key, Fleetwood produced a third picture, a younger version of a woman holding the young boy.

"Fleetwood, I'm impressed with your research skills so please cut to the chase," Stenson pleaded.

"This young lady was Adam's love interest. At the time she had a young boy from a previous relationship. Her father was CEO of Dorchel International. Several years ago there was an aggressive attempt to take over the American Division of Dorchel by an Atlanta-based investment firm," said Fleetwood.

"Okay, Fleetwood, but what's the point?" queried Stenson.

"This is where the rubber meets the road. I think, in fact I'm sure you didn't know Adam Wellington was Chairman of the Board for the company that orchestrated the attempted takeover which ultimately led to the CEO's questionable suicide."

Melanie interjected, "Fleetwood, Francoise came clean when he and I spoke briefly about that suicide over dinner in San Francisco. I asked him about his acquaintance with Adam and he said they met years ago in Montreal. He also mentioned the attempted takeover and implied that the death may not have been a suicide."

Fleetwood continued to move the cursor and stopped on another screen. He said, "Read the title of this article from the *Wall Street Journal*: 'THE PRESCRIPTION DRUG BLACK MARKET'.

"Fleetwood, I don't believe it!" Melanie said with her mouth agape.

"I believe it. I believe one of the reasons for CORE's success has been its ability to secure foreign drugs at a significantly reduced price on the black market and sell them at a significant markup at their company-owned satellite pharmacies. This article actually identifies CORE as one of the companies deemed worthy of investigating," responded Fleetwood.

"How does that work?" asked Mickey.

"Let me help you understand it," Stenson added, "if you use a drug such as Paxil, which may cost only fifty cents per pill to produce in a country such as Ireland or Thailand..."

"Such countries also have no FDA regulations," added Melanie.

"Right. You then purchase the drug on the black market in bulk, which further reduces its price. Consequently, in the United States the price of each pill can be five dollars or more depending on the drug."

"Very good Stenson, I see you read the *Wall Street Journal* article," said Fleetwood.

"Actually my Dad told me all about the black market trade in prescription drugs."

Mickey said, "They are nothing but corporate drug dealers."

"You got it!" agreed Fleetwood. "The article notes that a federal investigation was being pushed by..."

Melanie interrupted to read aloud the words on the monitor: "By the CEO of Dorchel International American Division, Mr. C.W. Rousselle."

"He was found dead three days later of an apparent suicide. After his death, the issue of black marketing drugs was dropped. The federal investigation never happened and the police never explained the logic or rationale for a left-handed man to position a gun to his right temple and commit suicide," Fleetwood said.

"So you don't believe his death had anything to do with preventing a corporate takeover?" asked Stenson .

Melanie answered for Fleetwood. She said, "Stenson, think about it. Companies experience attempted takeovers all the time."

"It comes with the territory," added Fleetwood.

Melanie continued, with Stenson and Mickey listening closely.

"But if you have dirt on the CEO of the company that's pushing illegal prescription drugs, there's enough reason for someone to kill you."

"Good Melanie, very good. But it gets much deeper than that." Fleetwood again moved his cursor to open another window. The woman's face filled the screen and she was beautiful. He said, "The daughter became the silent CEO and named Francoise as CFO, the person who actually runs things. She has taken a leave of absence to mourn the two deaths." Fleetwood said.

"Who was the second death?" asked Mickey.

Fleetwood again touched his computer cursor, which brought up a gruesome photo.

"I got this from the *Crime Lab Photo Journal* in Nashville," he said.

The photo showed what appeared to be a teenage boy, floating in mid air, suspended by a rope around his neck.

His arms were hanging freely by his side and a fallen chair lay beneath his feet.

"The next connection is this young man's death, which was ruled an apparent suicide. Notice the similarity in facial features."

Pressing another key, the faces of the child sitting next to the woman and the suicide victim were side by side.

"Okay hold it for just one second."

Fleetwood brought up the image of the CD, which included Adam and the Senator.

"Okay, hold for just one more second."

He zoomed in on a face in the background that had gone unnoticed in the real time motion of the CD.

"Okay here we go."

He moved the enlarged face and placed it next to the three photos. The young boy, the teenage unclothed boy and the suicide victim. Side by side it was easy to see, the three were the same, they were all the same person.

"Oh my God," Melanie gasped.

"Fleetwood," Stenson could not finish the sentence and Mickey was speechless.

"I checked police reports in Canada and found that apparently during Adam's tenure in Montreal there was a closed case file where the boy had been sexually molested, but the name of the perpetrator was kept confidential. I'm not sure of what happened after that time, but if we return to the CD and our close-up..."

Moving to the touch pad of his computer they all looked at a still photo from the infamous CD.

"Okay, let's look at things a little closer."

Fleetwood focused on a small sofa table next to Senator Daniels.

The magnification became closer and closer until a small white powdery substance could be seen on a similarly small transparent dish.

"So are you going to tell us this is likely cocaine? Surprise, surprise," commented Mickey.

"No my friend, look through the glass dish to the table top on which it is setting," said Fleetwood.

The magnification increased until the print on the small napkin that was embossed with...

"The Hermitage Hotel," said Melanie.

"Yup!" responded Fleetwood.

"The Hermitage Hotel in Nashville? The one across from the Capital Building?" Stenson asked.

"The very one where Senator Daniels maintains a suite," answered Fleetwood.

"Get the fuck out of here, are you suggesting the Senator and Adam may have had something to do with this? And that this suicide is the same kid in the picture?" asked Mickey.

"Well, if he indeed had been molested as a child it would not have been unheard of for the victim to continue a relationship with the assailant. There's a psychological component to abuse that we don't understand completely," said Stenson.

"So if all this is true, I believe this woman is Phoenix," Fleetwood added.

He clicked to a newspaper headline, which read:

HEIR TO DORCHEL INTERNATIONAL MOURNS AGAIN

Even with the large dark sunglasses and black wide-brim hat with a sheer veil covering her face you could see the resemblance in the newspaper photo to the photo with her young son.

"Her name is Chloe Rousselle and she is head of Dorchel International. If you notice the caption below the picture when asked how she would deal with the deaths of her father and son, her response was..." said Fleetwood, but Stenson interrupted by slowly reading the caption aloud.

"I have grown numb to pain and loss, time will pass and I will rise from the ashes like the Phoenix."

"Phoenix is a woman?" Melanie's responded with surprise.

"Yes, Phoenix is a very emotionally wounded and powerful woman," said Fleetwood.

"They've arrived at the hotel." The voice seemed eager to deliver the news.

"Good!"

"I am also pleased to tell you the scouts have tracked Melanie and her cohorts to a Mississippi location and Mr. Wellington has also been informed of their location."

The voice then sounded even more upbeat, as reflected in her melodious French accent.

"You have done well. Let James know that Plan B will be initiated tonight and that he should be prepared because all options are on the table."

"Death?"

"I only wish death to those who bring death. Melanie and her friends have done me no harm."

Phoenix returned the cell phone to the table. The Madison Hotel was similar to the W Hotel in Chicago but the rooftop in Memphis had a much better view. It was very relaxing to watch the boats cruise the Mississippi River while smoking her cigar and thinking about this opportunity to make everything right. It was impossible to undue what had been done, but Adam Wellington would certainly feel the pain of his transgressions.

CHAPTER
forty-one

Two SUVs crept slowly down the gravel road towards the riverside cottage and found it difficult to maneuver the potholes.

"How much longer must we travel?" asked Phoenix who obviously had become impatient with the drive to Mississippi.

"Not much more than ten or fifteen minutes according to the map provided by our scout," Francoise said.

Directing her attention to James and Gina, both passengers in the backseat, Phoenix said while dumping cigar ashes into the ashtray, "My dear Gina, I'm sure your brother will be quite surprised to see you under these circumstances. I have no plans of harm to you, please do as you are told and things should be fine."

"I'm not sure what this is all about but when I get the chance I plan to put my stiletto-heel in somebody's ass if anything happens to my brother."

"Gina, don't be so rude, she has paid for our trip here and...," said James.

"You shut the fuck up, I trusted you, I loved you. I'm not sure what role you're playing in all this but I was all wrong about you, all wrong," Gina sobbed. "Stenson and Mickey were right about you. I should have listened."

Dusk had settled and the final rays of sunlight were fading. A welcomed coolness had emerged at the end of this late summer day.

"We have visitors," Fleetwood pointed to a monitor that showed the first SUV stopping at the edge of the front yard near the narrow walk-way lined with white, purple and red blooming zinnias, begonias and caladiums. The second SUV stopped on the passenger side of the first. Three men got out of the first vehicle. One of them moved to the front, one to the side and the other moved to the rear of the small cottage.

"Are they going to get the same welcome that we got?" asked Melanie.

"But of course, but of course," Fleetwood assured them.

As the trio reached the entrance of their respective areas they were all knocked down by lights and the piercing, inaudible sound.

"Gotcha!" Fleetwood said to the monitor.

"Turn that goddam shit off!" The voice came from a large figure standing next to the second van with a small female figure in front of him.

"It's Gina!" Stenson shouted.

"That son-of-a-bitch James has a gun to her head!" Mickey said.

"Turn that shit off or I'll put a bullet in the back of her fucking head." James was yelling at the top of his voice as he pushed the gun to the back of Gina's head forcing her forward.

Without warning the house returned to its pitch dark status and the noises were those of crickets, frogs and other night sounds. The occupants of the second vehicle moved towards the open door of Fleetwood's house. Fleetwood stood there, rocking side to side, with Kitty standing next to him barking wildly. Fleetwood opened the screen door and they all entered. The three muscle men separated and moved through the house with their guns drawn. James was holding Gina by the arm as he entered with Francoise and Phoenix behind him. Kitty kept up her incessant barking.

"If you don't stop that yapping dog I'm gonna put a bullet in him," James said pointing the .38 revolver at the dog.

Fleetwood held up one hand and without a word the dog shut up and took a sitting position.

"What can I do fer you folks this ev'ning?" Fleetwood asked in a very courteous voice.

"You don't seem surprised to see us. Where is Melanie Walker, Stenson

Hawk and their little PI guy?" Phoenix asked in a soft concerned voice, accented by her French intonation.

She was more attractive than the photographs of her had captured. Her blonde hair and hazel eyes seemed too feminine for the cigar burning slowly in her hand.

"It's only me and Kitty here," Fleetwood answered.

Phoenix looked around the room as she assessed its décor. She said, "Fleetwood, you should really consider an interior decorator. I can make some recommendations for you."

James held on to Gina so that one of her arms was behind her back as Phoenix moved towards them and offered her lit cigar to James. She said to him as he took the cigar, "We don't have much time."

Towering above Gina, James took his .38 revolver and pointed it to the top of her head and said in an imposing and demeaning voice, "Bitch, open your goddam mouth and stick out your fucking tongue like you're trying to toss my salad."

Gina hesitated, but complied when he pressed the gun barrel harder against the top of her head. Without hesitation James buried the lit cigar into Gina's tongue. But Gina did not move nor cry aloud.

"Stop!" yelled Phoenix.

"You asshole, I didn't want you to actually burn her you shithead!" Phoenix's anger was obvious but the French accent softened the threat.

Gina's face was tense and hardened as she looked at James because she understood she had been betrayed, but not why. Tears rolled from her anger-filled eyes but she did not feel pain. She did not feel anything. She was numb from the blunt blade of betrayal.

"You really don't want Stenson or Gina, she's sick and shouldn't be here. You really want me."

Melanie was standing in the middle of the narrow doorway that connected the small living room and the even smaller kitchen. Stenson and Mickey were at her side. As the gun was removed from Gina's head she slowly slid down the wall and assumed a fetal position. Her tears made a small puddle on the floor. The three muscular guys completed a pat down of the three as they stood in the doorway.

"Melanie, it's so good to see you. I certainly enjoyed dining with you in San Francisco," Francoise said.

"Francoise, cut the crap. Let's take care of business first."

Then Phoenix spoke, "Melanie I'm the person Francoise was representing in San Francisco, so I will give you the details of this deal."

"We know all about you, we know about Dorchel International, your father and we know about your son. We know everything about the shit with Adam and the takeover. Everything!" Melanie defiantly said.

Phoenix looked at Francoise with disdain.

"I didn't tell her, I swear," Francoise sounded fearful of Phoenix.

"Very well, I'm glad you understand my mission. Please sit down." Phoenix said as she motioned Melanie towards the worn sofa across from her.

Melanie moved cautiously eyeing the revolver in James' hand as she tried to appear relaxed by positioning herself in a casual, legs-crossed posture. Phoenix pulled up a chair to sit right in front of her.

"Melanie, I've heard good things about you. I understand from Francoise that we had a deal but you're getting cold feet."

"Look, I know you have issues with Adam but I don't. So you can undo everything that's been done including Stenson's fellowship spot and we can call it even. If I had known all that occurred in your relationship with Adam Wellington I would not have agreed to any of this," said Melanie.

"Adam also knows that you are here in Coldwater so I'm your only protection. You know the success of this takeover is very personal to me. It's important that you make the public disclosure; you have the credibility and will not appear to have a personal vendetta. The company value will fall; I will buy CORE and do to Adam what he attempted to do to my father, except for putting a gun to his head. Hopefully, it will so devastate him that he will hang himself as did my son." Phoenix said as she explained to and implored Melanie.

But Melanie said "I can't."

"James," Phoenix said as she beckoned to him.

He then walked over to Gina who was still slumped in a fetal position against the wall and placed the gun to the top of her head.

"As you may know, your friend Gina is already considered missing.

Her dead body will show up with a self-inflicted gunshot wound to the head, a suicide. Are you going to call Adam?" James asked.

James was still holding the gun to Gina's head. He looked at Melanie and Stenson, he then looked down at Gina and said in a very upbeat, matter of fact tone, "Gina baby, I do love you but I love money more. So please understand that under different circumstances I wouldn't shoot you."

Gina said to Melanie, "I'm already dead so let him shoot me."

"Gina please don't say that!" pleaded Stenson.

"James, you think I roughed up your boys in New Orleans, but wait until I get my foot in your ass," Mickey angrily promised.

"Sorry, this may be your last assignment, you won't get that chance," James responded.

"Okay boys, enough of the rough talk. Now Melanie, back to you my dear. Here's Adam's cell phone number, call him. Tell him that tomorrow morning you will have a local press conference expressing your concerns about the true value of CORE Healthcare and its illegal drug import business. Also let him know that you have a copy of the CD with him and the Senator. I know he had something to do with the death of my father, and I know what he did to my son," said Phoenix, her voice trembling.

She could hear the sound of the trigger being pulled back, James moved the gun barrel from the top of Gina's head to the inside of her ear. So Melanie said, "Okay, okay, move the gun away and I'll call Adam."

James complied.

Melanie dialed the number and Adam answered on the first ring. She delivered the script as directed.

"Melanie I know where you are and I know who's behind this but I'm sorry, there is no deal. This public offering will bring hundreds of millions of dollars when we enter the New York Stock Exchange in the morning. Thank you for all the work you've done but, I promise you this: everyone in that house, including you, will be dead within the next five minutes." The line went silent.

Looking at Stenson as she spoke, Melanie told them what Adam said and immediately Fleetwood noticed that a small red dot appeared on James' temple. Fleetwood knew that an intruder had gone undetected. He had not had an opportunity to reactivate the exterior security after the arrival of Phoenix and her entourage.

James said, "Yeah, right. That motherfucker's time will be up when this thing goes public tomorrow and when I turn in my shares, thanks to Phoenix, I'll never work again."

Before James could start the next sentence the small red dot exploded, exposing his entire brain which splattered the wall behind him as he fell forward landing at Mickey's feet. The room was suddenly riddled with bullets before anyone could react.

"Move!" Fleetwood screamed, and Stenson grabbed Gina by the arm pulling her towards the doorway to the basement. The three wise guys reached for their guns but they weren't quick enough as red dots exploded on their heads. Francoise tried to shield Phoenix but his chest exploded into a bright red mist.

"Move, move, move!" Fleetwood yelled as he and Kitty headed towards the basement door. Phoenix and Melanie were both pinned down by gunfire, while Mickey stopped at the top of the basement stairway. Stenson yelled as he lay flat on the floor with his arms extended to Melanie and Phoenix, "Take my hands, come on, take hold of my hands!"

The bullets reeled over his head while Melanie and Phoenix grabbed Stenson's hands. Mickey, with both hands around Stenson's legs, pulled all three of them through the basement door. They all tumbled down the stairs to the bottom landing.

"Come on!" Fleetwood rushed everyone through the metal door of his war room. The monitors were viewing the interior of the house where a small group of men was placing plastic explosives.

"They're going to kill us!" Melanie said as if resolved that this was their fate. A bright flash showed on the monitors followed by a deafening blast. Then Fleetwood said, "We'll be here for a few hours so let's plan our next move."

forty-two

It was early afternoon in the conference room of CORE Healthcare in Nashville on the first day of CORE's public trading on the New York Stock Exchange.

"What's happening? Where is Senator Daniels, he was to be here an hour ago. There has got to be some reason for this." Adam's frustration was to the point of violence. He was watching CNN Financial News in the conference room with other CORE executives and some of its board members. A panel of financial experts was engaged in a round-table discussion of new publicly traded stock; they had just started their segment on CORE.

"The breaking news tells us there is a scandal brewing about the executive leadership of CORE. The emerging situation has contributed to CORE's unexpectedly low opening price." said the CNN anchor.

"But how do you explain the large number of shares purchased in the last hour by one single institution? That is generally used as an acquisition strategy," commented one of the guest panelists.

"Mr. Wellington," the female voice over the intercom was apprehensive about calling Adam.

"Did I not tell you to refrain from interrupting us, didn't I tell you that?" Adam was clearly on edge as a result of the poor opening of CORE.

"Mr. Wellington, I'm sorry to interrupt you but a package has just arrived by courier which I'm told is quite important. The courier said it'll help you understand why your day is going so very badly."

Adam walked just outside the conference room to receive the package. It was a large manila envelope with a large smiley face on the back and no return address. Hastily he ripped open the envelope and removed an unfolded letter, which said:

> *Hi Adam,*
> *You are currently being screwed out of a lot of money,*
> *which makes me very happy. Check your email, we sent*
> *something to you.*
> *Phoenix & friends.*

Adam ran down the long corridor to his office. The televison in his office was tuned to the CNN Financial Program where the panel continued its discussion of CORE. Slamming his door, he turned on the computer to bring up his email. There was an email sent from phoenixandfriends.com. The greeting said:

> *Hi Adam,*
> *Glad you could join us. Please download the attached*
> *file and then you'll understand why you've lost so*
> *much.*

Upon downloading the file, there was a group picture of Melanie Walker and five people he did not recognize. They were all smiling and waving, standing in front of what appeared to be a burned down house. A small man with large ears was wearing a baseball cap, holding a small dog in one arm and a sign in the other hand. The sign said:

> *Bomb Shelters Save Lives*
> *You Should Get One*

The woman standing next to the small man looked familiar. After closer study he recognized Chloe Rousselle, although he had not seen her for some time. Her sign read.

> *I own you now!*
> *My father and my son thank you!*

Melanie's sign read,

Please view the enclosed video
We've sent copies to everyone on the
New York Stock Exchange and to all major newspapers.
You and the Senator are stars!

The group picture ended and as the infamous video showing him kissing a young boy began to play the CNN Financial Report was interrupted for BREAKING NEWS. Adam sat in the executive chair behind his desk and used the remote control to turn up the volume on the television . The announcer had started her report: "…and yes, arrest warrants have been issued for Adam Wellington, President and CEO of CORE Healthcare Enterprises and Tennessee State Senator Colin Daniels. There are unsubstantiated reports that Senator Daniels departed Nashville's Metropolitan National Airport aboard a private jet. It is assumed that he has left the country."

"It's over. Everything is over." Adam said as he pushed the television to the floor then walked over and opened the coat closet in his office. His six-foot frame made it easy for him to reach the top shelf and retrieve the shoebox he kept for protection. He then moved near the floor-to-ceiling plate glass window where he could see the family of ducks swimming in the pond.

Adam appeared calm on the outside just as the ducks seemed to glide effortless across the water's surface. Just as their legs were rapidly moving beneath the water so were Adam's emotions very turbulent underneath his calm exterior. He opened the shoebox, removed the 38. caliber Smith & Wesson, aimed the barrel downward toward the top of his head and pulled the trigger.

forty-three

Six Months Later

"Ah, Madame Walker, welcome back to the Metropolitan Club. It has been some time since you were here, but I've followed your activities in the news on television and in the *Commercial Appeal.*"

Melanie realized she had been the topic of conversation for several months and that much of what transpired had helped her to mature and become more cautious. However, everything about Pierre appeared to be the same: his perfect teeth, well-groomed hair, impeccable dress and that gorgeous pinkie ring.

"It is so good to see you as well, Pierre. And as usual you look great!"

"Thank you," Pierre lowered his head to look directly into Melanie's eyes before saying, "Would you like the number of my hair stylist, she can work miracles."

"I would like that very much, Pierre," she wondered if he was trying to be helpful or suggesting her hair needed a makeover.

"Has Madame Chloe Rousselle arrived?" Melanie inquired.

"Why yes, Madame Walker. She arrived just a few minutes ago and is seated in the dining room. Please follow me."

They moved through the lunch crowd and stopped at a small table in the center of the dining room. Phoenix stood with her arms outstretched to greet Melanie and said, "Bonjour my dear Melanie, comment vas-tu? You look wonderful! I thank you so very much for taking the time to meet with me."

"Chloe, tres bien, merci, et vous?"

Phoenix replied, "I am equally well."

Melanie extended her arms and they embraced, each planted a soft kiss on the other's cheek. They had communicated often during the past several months.

After they were seated, Pierre asked, "Would you like to hear about our luncheon specials?"

"My plane leaves for Zurich shortly, so I do not have much time. I must chair a meeting at our international corporate summit which begins tomorrow."

"Since we're both pressed for time Pierre, please serve us your famous warm spinach salad topped with roasted duck and a bottle of Merlot," said Melanie.

"A Napa Valley?"

"Yes please, Frog's Leap."

"Coming right up," said Pierre as he flashed a broad smile, turned and sashayed away.

"Well my dear, how does it feel to be a multi-millionaire?" asked Phoenix.

"Now that the Securities and Exchange Commission has completed its investigation and your company has acquired CORE, I feel quite satisfied," Melanie responded with a slight smile.

"I do regret the circumstances surrounding your resignation from McKenzie, Ward and Lawrence," said Phoenix.

"That was no problem, in fact it was the least of my concerns. You see, I anticipated a severance from that company at the onset of my agreement with Francoise. Furthermore, my association with a few of my colleagues, especially Jim Little, had become strained at best. I also needed some time to sort things out and focus on my future."

"Well Melanie my dear, that is precisely why I'm here."

A waiter served an assortment of breads, iced lemon water, the salads, poured a glass of wine for each of them then quietly walked away.

Phoenix continued, "My responsibilities at Dorchel International have been extremely demanding since the death of Francoise. I need to employ a President of the North American Division of my company. In fact, my purpose for this meeting is to offer you the position."

"Phoenix, I am extremely flattered. Your offer would certainly complete and fulfill all my professional ambitions. You've already done so much for me with the support and advice you've given me over the past six months. Presently, I have some real promising job offers on the table."

"I would like very much for you to accept my job offer so I can make the announcement at the summit meeting in Zurich."

"I really need to know more about the position before I can even consider it. What are the responsibilities of the position?"

Phoenix took an envelope from her purse and handed it to Melanie. She then said, "Enclosed is a contract which describes the duties and responsibilities of the position, the salary, bonuses, vacations and benefits."

"But this is a great leap from my previous position, and I'm not certain if I'm ready for the challenge."

"I don't have to explain what this opportunity can mean for your career and I will not coerce you. Just think about it."

Phoenix reached into her purse again, this time to retrieve a pen and a business card upon which she jotted something and said, as she handed it to Melanie, "This is my sky number where you'll be able to reach me. Think about my offer over the next several hours and discuss it with Stenson. I'd like to report at the summit that you have accepted the position. Now tell me, how is Stenson?"

"He's fine. We've worked through most of our issues."

"Has he yet accepted a fellowship spot?"

"I'm meeting him after our lunch to learn the big news. He wouldn't tell my over the telephone, but I'm resigned to the fact that he's leaving and it's unlikely that we'll be in the same city," her voice tapered off to silence.

"Well my dear," Phoenix continued in an upbeat tone, "I will rendezvous with a wonderfully intelligent man in Zurich who will spend the week with me."

"How interesting! Do I know this man?" Melanie asked with curious pleasure. She suspected Phoenix had not been involved in a significant love interest during the time they had been acquainted.

"I cannot say at this time, but I will share my secret with you after you get your surprise from Stenson. Telephone me with your decision. We'd love to have you in San Francisco."

"That's right! your North American Division is in San Francisco. I've always wanted to visit 'Frisco with Stenson."

"Melanie, I have always been aware of your strong ambition and I know this position could give you everything you could possibly ask for."

"Yeah Phoenix, I know. And I'll call you before you reach Zurich and tell you my decision."

e p i l o g u e

One year later:

"Melanie, you have Chloe Rouselle on Line One."

"Oh, thank you Kathy, please put her through." Then she said, "Bonjour Chloe!"

"Bonjour! And how is the President of our American Division of Dorchel International?"

"Chloe, I am well and the transition is proceeding quite smoothly."

"Are you and your team settled yet in San Francisco?"

"San Francisco is wonderful and everyone is making the adjustment. In fact my Executive Assistant Kathy is dating like crazy and Gina is under the medical supervision of one of America's most noted Oncologists who is based here at the University of California at San Francisco."

"Wonderful, and how are Stenson's parents? I saw his dad on Larry King Live a few nights ago."

"Well, since he won the Senate race in Alabama he's made national news. As a matter of fact he and Stenson's Mom are flying in today and so is Mick."

"Mickey?" The surprise in her voice was obvious.

"Yes, Mick."

"Is Mickey still working for Stenson's Dad?"

"Take a seat for this."

"Okay, I'm ready," said Phoenix who was accustomed to bad news as a frequent companion, so she braced herself for more of the same. But she hoped this would be different.

"Mickey's not a Private Investigator anymore."

"Why not?"

There was a long pause until Phoenix broke the silence.

"Come on Melanie and tell me what he's up to. Is there a problem or trouble of some kind?"

"Well, because things are so crazy these days the State of Alabama is providing their U.S. Senators and Congressmen their own security staff."

"So Mickey is providing security for Senator Abraham Hawk?"

"You got it."

"That is marvelous news, I thought trouble had raised its ugly head again."

"I know. I just had to create a little suspense for you."

"And how is that handsome fiance' of yours?" Phoenix asked in a warm and personal voice.

"Stenson is doing so good and he loves the surgical training program here, I don't think I've seen him happier."

"You sound in love."

"Phoenix, I'm so hopelessly in love with this man and he feels so right with me. He's good for me and so good to me."

"I am extremely happy for you both."

"Now tell me how things are with you." Melanie changed the phone to her other ear as she leaned forward to lower the volume of the CD player on her desk, "are you still into computer experts with small dogs?"

Phoenix reached over to light a cigar and looked at the tanned man lying next to her. The French doors were open to allow the cool Caribbean breeze to circulate the cigar aroma.

"But of course," said Phoenix.

"Where is he?"

"Asleep, lying next to me," she said in a whisper.

"Well, give him our regards and we look forward to seeing you guys in St. Martin next week."

"Great! Give Stenson my love."

They both said "au revoir."

Fleetwood turned towards Phoenix and found her staring at him.

"Are you alright?" he asked.

"I couldn't be better," she replied.